The Many Lives of Avery Snow

Past Lives Series

Book 1

Written by Christy Sloat

Published by Anchor Group
Edited by Melissa Ringsted

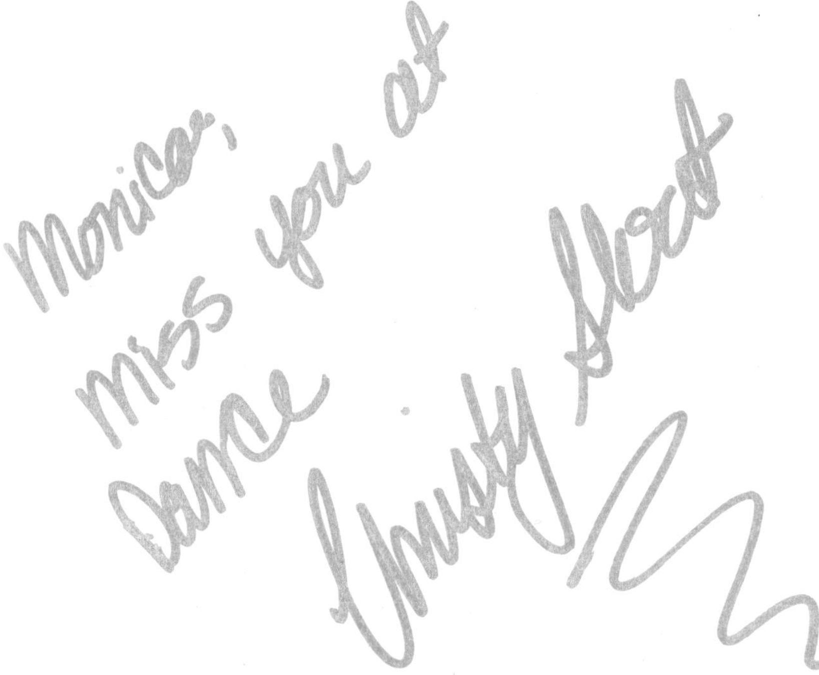

Published by Anchor Group
Edited by Melissa Ringsted

Dedication

I dedicate this book to my grandmother, Theda Arlotti. You believed in me from the very beginning, that I could become an author. You wanted to publish my first book when I was only twelve. Grandma, I thank you from the depths of my heart for your undying love and dedication. I will forever miss our talks on the front porch while we drank coffee. Till we meet again my sweet grandma.

Acknowledgements

This book would not be possible if my husband didn't ask me one day, "What do you want to do with your life?" Joe, thank you for always believing that I can do great things. You are my support system and without you I would be lost. To my little girls, Kendyl and Kyleigh, you're my sunshine's on gray days and my little angels.

Thanks to my parents Sue and Ernie for letting me just be me. I couldn't have asked for better parents.

To my awesome big sis, Desiree, for all the nights out and for the great sister talks. To my little bro, Torey, thanks for the support and for telling all your college friends to buy my books.

Thank you to Anchor Group, cheers to new beginnings!

Eye Candy & Randy Polillo thank you for my beautiful book cover! You made my vision come true.

To my friends Jennifer, Kate, Angie, Kathy, and Debbie you girls have been there for me at the very start of this book. I appreciate all the long discussions and the great advice.

Finally to the fans, I hope you will continue to follow my journey and read my books. I hope they inspire you!

Chapter 1

Lucy O'Shea

The moon shone down through my living room window and I could hear the loons on the bay. I was sure this was the night I would sleep, I hoped the loons would put me to sleep with their eerie call. It had been three months since I slept through the night. I had resorted to sleeping on my couch, where I thought it would be more comforting. Sadly, it didn't matter where I was, nothing would get me to that dream land that I so longed for. I started thinking about everyone in my apartment building, jealous that they were all sleeping and dreaming and I was not.

Nothing worked, and trust me I had tried everything: chamomile tea, warm milk, and even prescription drugs that my doctor was sure would get me at least seven hours sleep. Well doc, no luck. I was lucky to get at least three hours. When I woke up I would be drenched in sweat and I feel like I never slept at all. I would always wake with the feeling that I left something behind in a dream I couldn't even remember. The feeling would stay with me all day long. I can never shake it. It lingers in my mind like a bad memory or a feeling of overwhelming sadness.

Maybe my Aunt Paulina is right I need professional help again. I swore I would never see another shrink. I've seen several doctors in the past. The first time was when I was five. Yes, five. My father left us. Well, he was never ours to begin with.

Richard Snow was a lawyer in Laguna Beach, California. My mother, Bridgette, started working for his firm in 1982. She had never worked as a secretary before but she thought, "How hard could it be?" At the time good old Richard was married to his first wife Mary Lynn. A sweet, innocent lady who had no clue that Richard and Bridgette were starting a love affair behind her back. My mom said that they were drawn to each other, that there was nothing either of them could do to stop it, they were meant to be with each other. A year later she was pregnant with me. Richard left poor Mary Lynn and started a family with mom and I. We moved to Monterey to start our little family. They didn't marry but mom said she didn't need a piece of paper to tell her that they were to be together forever. Richard got a job at a smaller firm so he could be home by dinner and mom started teaching at the local college. I remember he was a good father when he was around. He would read to me every night, Good Night Moon was my favorite book. I would ask him to read it over and over and he would each time I asked.

When I was four that's when the arguing started. Mom and Richard fought over his sudden late hours at work. She suspected he was seeing his new secretary, Rachel. Of course my mother was right. He packed his stuff one day and told mom he was moving back to Laguna Beach to be with Rachel.

"Someday you will understand why I left. But right now it's hard for you to comprehend. I love you kid. Be good for your mom," he told me when he said goodbye, and he kissed me coldly on the forehead.

Not too long after that I started to sleep walk. I stopped eating and I went into a state of depression. Mom was very concerned for me so that's when I started seeing my first shrink, Dr. Pasao. He was very helpful to me. I saw him until I was six or seven. Soon after that I didn't really think of Richard again. Mom told me he married Rachel and they were having a baby. I didn't really know what to think about that news. I know mom was very upset because she cried that night. That's when I started to refer to him as Richard instead of Father.

The second psychiatrist was Dr. Adams. I saw him after my mom died. I had just moved to my Aunt Paulina's home and I was in a state of shock. Aunt Paul thought it was best for me to talk to a professional about my feelings. She felt she was not able to help me on her own.

Unfortunately this isn't working trying it my way, thinking that this will pass and any day now I will be back to normal and sleeping like a baby again. It's way more than I can control. On top of that, these feelings of despair after I do sleep are way too strong. They must have meaning, but I just don't know what it is.

This all started when one of the residents at work, Lucy O'Shea, died in my arms. She was a sweet old lady and a dear friend to me. I really enjoyed reading to her and talking about her life. Her stories always fascinated me, the places she had been and things she and her late husband had seen in their lifetime. I hoped to do as much as they had by eighty-seven. I hope to live that long as well.

She was in good shape for her age. Always dancing or going for walks with the other residents. Our program always stressed the importance of keeping fit, so we have dancing lessons for our seniors along with many other activities. I always took her calls when she had problems in her apartment. When I would arrive she would keep me there for quite some time talking. I think she was happy when I would show up because her face always lit up when she opened the door. That particular evening she called the main office and sounded like someone I did not recognize. Her happy, cheerful voice was muted and I could barely understand her.

"Avery, I have been pushed, I fell hard. I need your help." She said it so quietly I could tell she was in pain.

"Lucy, I'll be right there," I said as I ran out the office door. My office was not too far from her apartment but I still needed the golf cart to reach her in time just in case it was a bad fall. Kerri, my best friend and manager at the residence, was doing her nightly rounds when I called out to her from the courtyard.

"Kerri its Mrs. O'Shea. She fell, call 911."

Kerri ran in my direction and I reached Lucy's door only seconds later. It was unlocked and I rushed in finding her slumped in her kitchen against the refrigerator. She looked bad, her face was covered in blood and there was a large gash on her head. Her arm was definitely broken and possibly her hip. I could see the contorted way she laid there and I knew it wasn't right.

"Lucy, I'm here and you're okay. Kerri is calling 911." I grabbed a dishtowel and placed it on her head. While trying to comfort her with my other hand I put as much pressure on the gash as possible.

Just then Kerri came in and made me aware that help was on its way and the staff nurse, Ellie, was coming over. Lucy grabbed my arm tightly.

"He's coming back for you Avery. She told me to tell you that he knows where you are at all times and he is always watching you." My skin crawled, was there someone watching me at this very moment or was she delirious and she wasn't sure what she was saying?

"What? Who is this the person that you said pushed you? Who is watching me Lucy? Is that person here right now, is he watching me, did he push you?" I asked, trying to stay calm. This made no sense! I couldn't really stay calm either, I didn't like seeing her this way.

"No, she pushed me," she replied, pointing behind me. As I turned to look I saw no one there. Who did she mean? Was there someone in here besides us?

"Kerri, check the apartment. Lucy says someone is in here and they pushed her." Kerri nodded and ran through the rooms checking everything.

"There's no one else here and all the windows are locked shut, maybe she hit her head too hard and is seeing things," she suggested. Even though I felt this was a little rude of her to say it was possibly right.

"Cooper, that's what she said his name was Avery. She said he was with you always. You are meant to be..."And then she took a large breath in and her eyes glazed over. She looked so peaceful as she took her last breath. I had never wanted to see her die, especially this way.

"I think she is gone, Kerri. She's dead." I said with a large lump in my throat. Why would a fall kill her? I'm no doctor but I didn't think she lost that much blood. I was in total shock.

"What was she saying to you Avery, who pushed her?" Kerri asked.

"I don't know Kerri. She said a lot of weird things just now, I'm a little freaked out," I said as I let Ellie take over. She checked her pulse and confirmed that Lucy was gone.

Once the ambulance pulled out of the driveway Kerri came to find me in the office. I was drinking a cup of chamomile tea, trying to calm my nerves. Kerri had a pale face, which is so unlike her normal complexion. She is beautiful. She has long brown hair that is rich and full, unlike my blondish-brown dull locks. Her green eyes peer into your soul. She is very exotic looking and always gets the guy. I've never seen her without a hot guy on her arm. Not only are her looks great, she is a blast to be with and is the life of the party. She is very outgoing and talkative. In other words, she is the total opposite if me. Sometimes I wonder what she sees in me as a friend since I'm usually quiet and shy.

I have only dated one guy in my twenty-six years of life. I'm not ugly, but I don't think I am attractive. I have never been told that I'm ugly or unattractive, so my theory is because I lost my father and mother at a young age I have a complex about my looks. Kerri tells me she would die for my skin, that it's like ivory. I would die to be her some days, I would love to be as outgoing and beautiful.

We met here at work, a residence for seniors called Sunrise Estates. I was hired four years ago. I thought helping people would be a good career choice for me. I love my job, so obviously it was a good choice. Our campus, as we call it, is made up of three wings.

Wing A is the Independent Living, where seniors can pretty much take care of themselves and they don't need much help. They're just not able to live on their own outside. That is where Lucy was. Even though she was eighty-seven she did not need much help. No assistance except housekeeping and some medical overseeing.

Wing B is Assisted Living, where the seniors need help with activities of daily living. Bathing, dressing, eating and stuff like that.

Wing C is the Temporary Care. When a family needs, what I call a "baby sitter", to watch their loved ones. Their stay is usually a couple weeks while the family goes on vacation or a business trip. I mostly work in wing A. I'm a caregiver. I help out with their chores, I do the housekeeping, and I also visit and spend time with them. Like I did with Lucy.

It's a nice campus. The apartments are actually pretty nice. I hope someday someone cares enough about me to put me in here. But at the present time I have no one. Just my Aunt Paulina and Kerri.

"You okay?" Kerri asks me as she grabs my hand and tenderly rubs it. "I know you were close with her." Not only is she beautiful, she is very caring and sweet. She is taking this pretty hard herself, which explained the pale, drained face.

"I'm okay, I just get too close with all of them. It sucks, it's like losing a good friend," I said. I've lost a lot of people in my life, but I try not to think of that too often. "How did she die from a fall Kerri?"

"I think they said she might have had a heart attack and that's what caused the fall. But they were just EMT's, you know they can't make the final conclusion."

I looked out the window and saw the ambulance drive away. Later that night, before my shift ended, Kerri asked if I want to go out for drinks.

"Nah, I'm tired and I just want to sleep." Little did I know that this would be the first night of no sleep.

I usually get home around 12:30 a.m. and I stay up for about an hour trying to get myself prepared for sleep. This particular night though I started to think of all the things Lucy said. Who is Cooper and why did she say he's watching me? She must have thought I was someone else, someone in her past maybe? Although, she did say, "He loves you Avery." She did say me, that he loves me. Ha, very funny. No love here. I haven't had a boyfriend since Michael the lying cheating scumbag. That was five years ago. I was young and I fell for all his tricks. I swore never again and I kept that promise to myself. So much so that I don't talk to any guys. I have major trust issues.

Kerri is always trying to hook me up with her boyfriend's friends but I don't go for it. It's ok though, they don't seem too interested in me either. I have not really noticed any flirting on their part. There was Dave, he was friends with Kerri's last boyfriend Aaron. Aaron was my favorite of her boyfriends. He treated her so nice and he was fun to be around, unlike her current fling, Gavin. Gavin is cute and all, but looks aren't everything. He is not the most trustworthy guy I've met. I've seen him at the bookstore where he works really chatting up the customers but not in the usual customer service kind of way. I have also seen him give his number to several girls. I still have not told Kerri, I figure she will find out on her own. A little part of me thinks she already knows.

Aaron and Kerri were a good match. She said he was boring, but really he was just more of an introvert and less like outgoing Kerri. Aaron's friend Dave said he wanted to take me out for drinks. He told Kerri he liked my style and wanted to get to know me better. I didn't take the bait, no way, not interested. There was something about him that I didn't trust. And what about my style did he like? I don't think I have style. I can't dress, in a fashionable sense anyway. Kerri is always trying to take me shopping and buy me clothes. I like tee shirts and a cute pair of jeans. In my opinion, comfort is the key.

She is always telling me to cut my hair or wear make-up. She thinks it will accent my grayish-blue eyes. I have long blondish-brown hair and I like it long. That way I can hide behind it. I don't have time to mess with makeup. I'm au naturel, I just get up and go. No fuss, no muss.

There is one guy I really like, Dallas. He is a bartender at our hangout, a little Mexican food restaurant and bar right around the corner from work. It's called La Costa and it has good scenery, meaning Dallas. He is smoking hot! I mean to die for. I'm sure he doesn't feel the same for me, he goes for girls like Kerri. Even though she isn't interested in him, she says she is too good for him. She wants a man with a real job and he isn't her type. What confuses me is that all Gavin does is manage a bookstore. I think she knows I like Dallas and she won't cross that line. It's nice of her, but I don't stand a chance. Every time I try to talk to him he asks me about her. He is real nice to me, never rude, but I want him to ask about me instead.

Dallas is tall, about six feet six, not that I am measuring him or anything. He has brown hair, piercing hazel eyes and he is very athletic and fit. His tight black shirts make me sweat. And to top it all off he can make a real good drink. He always knows what my drink is for the night, every night it's something different. He can read my mood and know exactly what I want. In a perfect world he will stop going for Kerri and look at me and ask me out. Yeah right.

That night I tossed and turned, thinking about all Lucy had said. Who was it that pushed her? A ghost? Did I really believe in that sort of thing? I was glad she was so happy to go. It made it somehow better for me to cope with the loss. From that night on I could not sleep and weird things started to happen to me. Like seeing my dead mother in my bathroom. She was putting on her makeup. This could not be possible. I just pulled the covers over my head and cried.

And tonight, as I listen to the loons outside, it's just as bad as all the others before. I'm trying to lull myself to sleep on my couch, knowing it will not happen. I think back now on the past three months and I think maybe a psychiatrist is the best thing for me. Wow, who thinks that? A sane person or a crazy person?

Chapter 2
Landon

I sat on my balcony and watched the sun rise the next morning. It was sort of nice. I got no sleep last night, just like the nights before. Not one wink. Thankfully I was off of work today. Kerri had given me the day off so I could rest. It was Sunday and my Aunt Paulina and I had plans to eat breakfast together today. She comes to visit me about once every two months or so. She lives about six hours away, in Monterey. She says she doesn't mind the drive, that it's peaceful and helps her think. But I don't know how much longer she will be making the trip. I really think it's getting to be too much for her, but she insists on coming. She usually stays with me, or her friend that lives up here as well, Barbara. Just as I'm done showering and getting dressed the phone rings and I know it's my aunt.

"Hello," I answer with forced happiness.

"Ah, my favorite niece. Tell me, did you sleep last night?" She inquires.

"Yeah a little. I feel good today," I lie. I don't want her to worry anymore.

"Ok, well I'm at our restaurant and I put in our names so walk down and meet me. Are you ready?"

"Yes I'll be right there," I tell her.

The little diner is only walking distance from my apartment, so I put on my sandals and I head downstairs. I chose the stairs because it the only exercise I get, but halfway down I start to get really light headed. I had to sit down and take a minute before continuing. Must be lack of sleep really getting to my body. I know I'm not healthy.

I made it outside and started walking to the diner. All of a sudden I saw a light flash right in front of my eyes. It was bright as hell outside, where did the flash of light come from? Then I see it again, even brighter. It is moving and floating in midair. It's bright and shaped like an oval. I look around and no one else seems to notice it. It's meant for me to see. I feel that it's calling me toward it. I watch it float into the small park on my right. I start to follow it, determined to see what it is. I entered the park through the side entrance and the light leads me to a tree. The light sat right on the tree and then it faded away. I'm either seeing things at this point or I'm supposed to see something on this tree. So I start to look closer and all around it, when there it is, as plain as day. The words LC Loves AS Forever carved into the tree. What the heck is that to mean to me. My initials are AS, for Avery Snow. But who is LC? There could be tons of people with my initials. But what was that light that I saw? And who made it appear? I walked away dizzy and confused. This was just one of the many weird things that have been happening to me the past three months.

By the time I reached the diner my aunt is really upset at my tardiness. I had to apologize like a hundred times before that look of pissed off left her face.

"You look horrible Avery. When are you going to get some help for yourself and take care of this problem?" She asked me.

"Thanks Aunt Paulina," I said sarcastically. "I don't think I look bad. Never the less, last night I decided I will call this therapist that I found online. He is only down the street from work so I can go before my shift starts. I'm going to call today. So let's just enjoy breakfast and talk about other things."

She started to get tears in her eyes. "Your mom would be so mad at me if she saw you right now. I didn't take care of you like I promised I would. I told her it would be okay and that you would be strong and I would look out for you all my life. I can't help but feel that I'm losing you too."

My mother died when I was twelve of an aneurism. We were baking in the kitchen when she suddenly fell to the ground. And just like that I lost my mother. So how did my aunt tell her she would take care of me if my mom didn't know she was going to die? It's not like she fell ill and knew this was going to happen.

"What do you mean you told her you would take care of me?" I asked. Her eyes avoided my stare. She suddenly looked shocked at what she had just said. Then she started to fumble her words, as if trying to take it back.

"Well we never had that talk when she was alive, it was after she passed. I had a dream and she came to me. She told me to take care of you and I promised her I would. She said that you would need me to take care of you after you saw Landon. That it would shock you and you wouldn't understand. She said your dreams would become real. And they would prevent you from sleeping. So that's really why I'm so concerned with you." After she said this the waiter came to take our order. I just pointed to my order, scrambled eggs and toast special on the menu. All without removing my gaze at my aunt. I was in a state of shock.

"You think this is all related to this, because of some dream you had? I never met anyone named Landon, Aunt Paul. So don't get all upset. It was just a dream." I was trying to convince myself that what she just said wasn't at all strange. I never thought my aunt was like my mom was, meaning that she believed in the supernatural, ghosts or afterlife. I suppose since I was raised with it for twelve years so it was only natural to find that Aunt Paul believed too. Although when I lived with her she never spoke of such things. She always said my mom was very spiritual and open to all things possible.

She laughed a little and sighed, "You're right Avery it sounds crazy. But I just think how weird it is that you can't sleep a wink for three months straight. You look like crap and you need me. You may not think you do, but you need someone to help you. I'm not just saying a therapist. You need someone to help you sort this all out. You lost your mom at a young age. You never had a father figure in your life. I think it's all catching up with you. Furthermore, I really think your mom would want me to be here for you. I just want to help you. So I'm going to stay at Barb's house, for a little while, until you get better."

I nodded my head in approval and I took a sip of my coffee, my liquid awake. I was so confused at what just happened that I just went along with it. Now I have two men's names to think of, Landon and Cooper. Who the heck are these guys? Why am I worrying about it? It's just the dream of a dead woman and the words of a dying woman and now I've got my panties in a bunch over it. I decided I would go home and try to get some sleep. I'm so over thinking things. And that light must have been a glare from some kids messing around or something. There's no other possible explanation for it. Is there?

After we ate Aunt Paul walked me to my apartment. It was a nice, cool day and you could feel a nice breeze blowing from the bay.

"I love it here. You get the best of both worlds, the nice city and the forest only miles away. Listen kid, I'm going to go to Barbara's now to unpack. So if you need me, call me. I want you to call that therapist you found," she told me as she adjusted her purse.

"I will, and you tell Barb hi for me," I said as I looked at her newly dyed hair. It used to be a natural golden blonde, but with this new dye job it was now red. I didn't dare say anything about it. She was too sensitive about her looks.

"Hey Avery, you haven't met any guys lately have you?" She asked with a sly smile.

"No, and none named Landon," I answered with a laugh.

She hugged me and kissed the top of my head. She was always so loving and kind to me. Truth be told, I missed her a lot. She was more of a mother than my own mom was. My mom was too into her art and poetry to be loving all the time. She was a great mom, but more like a girlfriend. Aunt Paul was different, nurturing and kind.

After I said my goodbye I went upstairs and jumped into bed. It was noon by this time. It felt so nice to lie down. I closed my eyes and took a deep breath.

I asked aloud, "Landon and Cooper who are you?"

I woke up at 2:00 p.m. Ah yes, I got two hours of sleep. I

actually felt pretty good, except for that feeling that I have been waking with. Like I left someone or something behind. As I got up I realized I was drenched in sweat from head to toe. This wasn't uncommon lately. Every time I wake, even after my not so unusual two to three hours of sleep, I wake up soaking wet. I felt my face. I had tears streaming down it. My eyes were red and blurry. I guess I was crying in my dream. Come to think of it, I remember a little something about that dream. I was following a bright light, much like the one from this morning, except I was in an old Victorian style home. And this light was in a long hallway. It led me to a door, a beautiful oak door. That's all I remember. Why was I crying? I felt a little silly.
After I got myself together and showered again I called the shrinky dinks office. I set an appointment for this coming Wednesday at 7:00 a.m. The receptionist asked me if this would be too early. I laughed and told her I get up with the sun. It was no lie. I see pretty much every sunset and sunrise.

Monday morning I watched the early morning news with my cup of liquid awake. Today was going to be long because after my little catnap I didn't sleep anymore. I've been awake since 2:00 yesterday afternoon and never went back to sleep. I left the house in my work uniform, a black polo shirt and a pair of tan pants. Driving was a little more difficult now since I haven't been sleeping. It was hard to keep my eyes on the road and focus. I turned the corner, and was on the street where work was, when I saw a man standing on the side of the road with a broken down car. I felt bad for him. He suddenly started to wave me down. I decided to pull over, which is so unlike me. I didn't even get scared that he might be a mass murderer who could abduct me, or worse. When I got out of my car I walked over to him. He was very good looking. His hair was longer and slightly wavy. It had shades of brown and blonde throughout it. And his eyes were gorgeous bright blue and green. He was wearing dark blue jeans and a white shirt with a brown leather coat that I noticed had some grease on it. What a shame. His hands were covered in grease as well.

"You need help I assume?" I asked with a slight nervous tone.

"What was your first clue?" He asked me laughing. He had a great smile and his eyes sparkled in the sunlight. "I actually just need a cell phone, my battery is dead. And this piece of junk car just won't cooperate with me this morning."

I did notice that his car was old and had many dents in it. I have not ever seen a car like this on the road. It looked like an old station wagon. Not what I expected a guy like this to be driving. I handed him my phone and for a second my hand touched his. When this happened I saw a field with blue flowers and him standing in the field in a old fashioned suit. His hair was shorter and I was holding his hand, standing next to him. I was wearing a white cotton dress with lace on it. Much like a wedding dress. As soon as his hand took the phone the vision was gone.

"Wow," I said aloud. And my face got hot and bright red.

"Excuse me?" He asked quietly. "Wow what?"

"Um, wow you need a car charger. I mean how can you not have one. Especially now a days." I hoped this covered for my sudden outburst. I knew an old car like that didn't have a place to put a car charger. I must be losing it fast, between the light and last week thinking I saw my mother standing in my bathroom. I need that therapist right away. I needed sleep. I walked to the passenger side of my car to give him his privacy. After he called whoever he called he handed back my phone and I noticed the time.

"Oh crap I'm going to be late for work," I said "Good luck with your car."

"Thank you for your kindness Avery," he said his eyes twinkling at me.

Wait, how did this guy know my name? There was no introduction of names. I gave him a puzzled look and he smiled again, which sent chills down my spine. He was so gorgeous that it actually made me shiver.

"It was on the front of your phone," he said, pointing to my name in bejeweled shiny stickers that Kerri had attached to my phone, in an attempt to style it. I laughed.

"Yeah real pretty huh? My friend did it. Well, see ya," I said maybe a bit too loud.

He smiled and waved. As I got into my car I looked back at this gorgeous man and I hoped I would see him around again. But what would a guy like that see in me? I was calling Kerri to tell her I would be late and a piece of small paper fell out of my flip phone as I opened it. It had a phone number and a name on it. The name was Landon.

When I got to work Kerri was standing in her office looking over some paper work. She smiled when she saw me.

"Hey, sorry I'm late. I tried calling but your line just went to voicemail," I explained. "I met a guy, I mean I helped a guy. He needed to use my phone. His car was broke down." I could feel my cheeks burning from embarrassment.

"Don't worry its cool. So, was he cute?" She teased.

"Yeah kind of but I was doing my duty of helping out someone in need." I didn't want to tell her how cute he was and how he gave me his number. Or, more importantly, how his name was Landon. The same name my dead mother told my aunt in her dream. A dream she had fourteen years ago.

The fact that he was interested in me was baffling. A plain girl like me. Even though he was driving the biggest dump for a car. I know guys like that don't date girls like me. They date Kerri. As much as I didn't believe all this after-life stuff, like my mom visiting my aunt. It seemed a little too coincidental to me. My mom, like I said, was very into ghosts and the afterlife. A little too much. She would tell me she saw ghosts and she tried to help them. It really used to scare me. She was very eclectic and out there. A real hippie. She read tarot cards and would try to make money off it, but it didn't do too much to help support us. Her main job was teaching art at the local college. She was really good at painting. Her paintings were very elegant and that was her real talent.

"Well Avery we have a new resident, John Grey. He moved into Mrs. O'Shea's old apartment. So I need you to go introduce yourself and see if he needs anything," she told me.

At times I liked having her as a boss and other times I felt like it strained our friendship. She could be playful one minute and really strict the next. The other people that work here always say she favors me. Even though it can be true I don't like it because I work hard. I have earned what I have. They don't like that I get to pick my shifts and that Kerri and I always work together. They're just jealous, especially Rachel. She has been here a little over a year and she really hates me. I mean she gives me the evil eye every time she sees me.

As I walked over to meet John Grey I ran into Rachel. I always act overly nice to her, just to bug her. It's not my fault Kerri doesn't care for her. She says that Rachel is lazy and can be rude to some of the residents. Really, to be honest, I don't know why Rachel is still here.

"Hi Rachel, you look so pretty today. Did you do something to your hair?" I asked her. She just looked at me with that evil eye and walked away.

I laughed as I walked to the apartment and knocked on the door. The same door that, up until recently, used to be Lucy's door. I started to think of the last night I saw her and how bizarre it was. How she told me all those crazy things. I couldn't believe she had been gone for three months. I got a chill when I thought of it. I will never understand it I guess.

"Hello young lady," he said as he opened the door. He was a tall man with grey hair and piercing blue eyes. He looked tired or maybe sad.

"I'm Avery Snow. I will be your residential aide and caregiver should you need any help with anything," I announced in my very professional voice.

"What kind of things will I need you to do?" He asked curiously.

"Well, I can help you cook should you not want to eat at the community kitchen. I can keep you company, many of the residents like me to read to them or just talk. I can also help you with your medicines. You name it, I can usually do it," I answered. "Just call my cell. My number is on speed dial on your phone. Number five," I said pointing to it.

"That sounds good, but I think I will be eating at the kitchen a lot. I don't like to cook. My wife did all the cooking. And I'm not much of a talker. I don't like to read. I like movies though."

"Well we have a movie room as well as a library of most of the titles you might like. And in the community center we have movie night every Tuesday. Tomorrow we are showing Pearl Harbor. Have you seen it?" I asked.

"No, can't say that I have. Is it good? Sounds like a war movie and I like war movies," he said.

"It's good, it has war, love and drama all in one," I told him. "One of my favorites. We encourage all the residents to attend, all that can at least. "

He nodded. I could tell he was still in shock that he was here. A lot of the residents go through this shy stage at first. Some also get angry. Once they see all that Sunrise Estates has to offer I think they settle in nicely because we try to make it like their home. Well, a second home.

I left Mr. Grey's apartment and headed to the office so I could get my list of rounds for the day. All of the people that needed my help doing something or just needed someone to talk to.

On the way across the courtyard I started thinking about this Landon guy and the horrible coincidence of my mothers dream and this guy that I just met. How she was sort of right in her dream, telling my aunt that I wouldn't understand. I don't understand why he gave me his number. I don't understand a lot of things, like for instance why I don't sleep anymore. I couldn't wait until my appointment Wednesday with my new doctor. I hoped that he could help me sort things out. I was grasping at any hope possible. Maybe I was starting to become delusional. Seeing things was the first sign of that.

And that's when it hit me. The light I saw took me to a tree and on that tree were the initials LC and AS. Landon was this guys name and Cooper was the name that Lucy said, so that equaled LC, and I'm AS. It didn't make too much sense, just another coincidence. I took the little piece of paper that Landon gave me with his number on it. I walked into the staff room where I was alone. So I pulled out my cell phone and I nervously dialed the number. It went to voicemail. Oh yeah, he said his phone battery was dead. The automated voice said, "You have reached the phone for Landon Cooper please leave a message at the tone."

"Oh my God, Landon Cooper," I said out loud, almost dropping my phone, and then I heard the beep.

What would I say, should I say anything? It was all making sense with the names. But the biggest questions were, how did my mom and Lucy know his name and is he really watching me, and why did Lucy say Cooper? Maybe she didn't know his first name. Maybe he was some kind of stalker and my mom's psychic abilities could know this was going to happen. She said I would see him again though, and be shocked. I just met this guy.

I did have that strange vision of him after we touched. It had seemed so familiar to see that vision.

So finally, after a long pause, I just said, "Um hi Avery here, you gave me your number, I don't know why. Ok, my number is 503-2147. Ok? Um bye."

I just sounded like a total dork. He really won't call now. But I needed him to. I need answers badly.

Dallas

It was now Tuesday night. I was leaving work when Kerri pulled me aside in the staff room and said she was going to our hangout and wanted to have a couple of margaritas with me. Oh, this sounded so nice! So I agreed that it was a great idea, I needed to take my mind off of my morning appointment with my new shrink and who Landon Cooper really was. So I grabbed my coat and said, "You are buying the first round." She laughed and followed me out to my car.

We headed down the road to La Costa bar and restaurant. I hoped that Dallas was working and I could flirt with him a little, even if he would ask me about Kerri all night long. At least he talked to me.

Sure enough he was there when we walked in. He smiled at us as we walked in. His dimples made me tingle all over. I just wished that he would be interested for one second, hell for just one night. If only he could put his feelings for Kerri aside and want to be with me instead. The last time any guy was interested was when Kerri and I went to Vegas for my twenty-second birthday. She didn't want me to spend it alone. That's when I knew she would be a true friend, taking someone she barely knew to Vegas. I mean, we had just met and she and I grew to be fast friends. I remember the night very well.

It was the first time I had ever had that much fun. We went to a club the night we arrived. She had me all dressed up and did a makeover on my face. I looked pretty good, I could never redo what she did, I'm not that talented. This guy even started talking to me. So, I put my shyness aside to talk back. His name was Randall and he was easy to talk to. I was so lonely and I had just recently moved to Northern California from Southern California. I knew no one except for Kerri, so it was nice to meet new people. I learned that he too had just moved, from Texas to Nevada. He was at the club with his new friend Jack. We just were two lonely people who needed company. We spent the night together at the Bellagio club drinking and talking. His friend talked and danced with Kerri.

He was so sweet, a true gentlemen. All night he told me how pretty I was. I blushed each time he said it. That night was so much fun. We didn't exchange numbers because we knew it would not go anywhere. And that was okay, I just enjoyed flirting and talking to him. Nothing like that, or even close, has happened since. Even though I swore off men, I would not mind being with Dallas or even Landon Cooper. Just to think like that is so unlike me. I really need a strong margarita.

We sat at our spot at the bar and Dallas started to make my regular drink, a Malibu and coke, when I said, "Not tonight Dallas, we are having Margaritas. Strawberry."

"What ever you want princess Avery." Princess! I laughed. Yeah, I really look like one tonight. My hair was in a ponytail, I had no makeup on, and I was in my work uniform. Really royal.

"Here you go girls. Are we celebrating anything tonight?" He asked as he set our pink, cold drinks down.

"Yeah Avery met a guy," Kerri said. "She helped him, he was broke down on the side of the road. She thinks he's cute." Kerri laughed in a proud way. I could tell she was happy that I finally said someone was cute. I usually don't comment on guys around her. I think she was starting to worry about me. So I didn't really comment on this. I let her think whatever she wanted to. Even though she has no idea what really happened on the side of the road between Landon and I. I wouldn't tell her, she would think I was crazy. I looked at Dallas and smiled. He did not smile back. Instead he walked away and went to serve another couple of girls at the other end of the bar.

"What's his problem?" I asked Kerri.

"I don't know, its like he's mad or something. So whatever, tell me about this guy. What did he look like? Did he seem interested? Did you talk?" She asked me.

"Wow, one question at a time Kerri. I need more of my drink before I start answering all these questions," I replied.

"Well, just answer one, what did he look like, what happened? Oh, sorry that's two," she joked.

"Well, I was coming to work and I saw this piece of crap car, like an old surfer car. I think they call them Woody's, but this one was really beat up. Like it has been in several accidents or one really big one. Then, something just told me to help this guy. So I pulled over and helped him. He used my phone to call for a ride."

"That's not all, I know your hiding more details. Go on, tell me Avery." She's my best friend I should tell her what was going on, but not yet. Not until I meet with the doctor tomorrow.

"Well he was really cute and kind of flirting I guess. His name is Landon. And that's all I know. Maybe I will see him around or maybe not." I left it at that.

"Yeah, well if he was cute then you should have given him your number. Or you know what? He used your phone, you could see who he called and get his information." She suggested.

"Yeah that's a little desperate don't you think? Besides he probably just called a tow truck or like AAA. I just want to drink and relax. No more talk about Landon. How is Gavin?" Although I could tell they were fighting again, because usually she would be at the bar with him after work, I asked anyways. She looked at me and I could see the tears starting to well up in her eyes. The fight must have been pretty bad.

"Well you know Bethany, the girl he works with at the bookstore?" I nodded. I knew her only from Gavin introducing us once when I went to the store to purchase a couple of books. She was really pretty. Bleach blonde, hot body. I had a feeling they were either having an affair or going to be soon enough. Kerri didn't have to even continue talking. I just knew where this was going.

"Well I went to go pick him up last night after his shift, but I got there early. I walked into the back door, like I usually do, and I caught her and him kissing, right by the cash register. Bastard. I just flipped out. I started throwing books at them. I'm pretty sure I hit him right in the eye with a pretty big novel, cause when he showed up at my house this morning he had a black eye." She said laughing. I laughed too. That was hilarious! Not the cheating part of course.

"What did you say to him when he showed up?' I asked.

"I just told him to leave and that I was done. I think he has done it before, I just had a feeling though. But this time I really caught him. Avery, why can't I just find a nice guy? Someone like Dallas."

"Well, Dallas is single," I said. After I said it I could just kick myself. I knew he was so into her. Now I would have to sit here and see them together and wish it were me instead. I was glad that she broke up with that loser, but I don't want her to be with my crush. Even though I don't have the nerve to ask him out. Four margarita's later Kerri and I started to loosen up and joke about everything. Mostly how Gavin was a big jerk and she is so much better off with out him. Then I decided it was time for me to get going. Especially when I saw her flirting with Dallas. He surprisingly didn't seem too interested in her tonight, I wasn't sure why. Every time we come here he does nothing but talk about her. She was single now and wanting to obviously be with him, he would be a fool to pass this moment up.

"Oh Avery its our song. Lets dance!" she yelled when our song was on the jukebox. AC/DC was the band we listened to on the way to Vegas for my birthday. I was feeling no shame, no pain. So I stood up, let my hair down and headed out to the small dance floor with Kerri. We danced to our song. I just closed my eyes held her hand and sang along to the words. It felt good to be this carefree and have fun. For that little bit I forgot all the craziness going on in my life right now.

We danced to three songs after ours was done playing. Then a slow song came on. That was our cue to exit the dance floor. When I looked up Dallas was walking towards us. He was coming over to dance with Kerri, I just knew it.

When he grabbed my hand he twirled me around I said, "Very

funny Dallas. Now you have your turn to get your girl, the girl of your dreams." I whispered to him as I tried to let go of his hand and lead him to Kerri.

"No offense Kerri, but may I dance with Avery?" He asked her.

"Um, sure whatever. It's getting late anyway." she replied. She walked to the bar and grabbed her purse and stormed out of the bar.

"Oh Kerri, come on, you're next." But it was too late, she had left. She was really pissed, but I knew he was just being nice to me.

He took me tightly by the hips with his hands and stared deeply into my eyes. I didn't know what was going on. He ran his fingers through my hair as we danced slowly across the dance floor. It felt so good. His hands were so strong and gentle at the same time. It gave me chills.

"You're really dumb Dallas, you just let the girl you want walk right out of the bar. Hey, don't you have customers to serve?' I slurred. I had way too much to drink. I could barely talk.

"You're the dumb one. Can't you see you're the girl I want? I don't know how obvious I have to be. I talk to you, and only you, every time you come in here, I know all your drinks that each mood represents. How much more do I have to do to make you see?" He asked as he looked intently into my eyes. I was in a state of total disbelief. I was never the girl of anyone's dreams.

"But you're always asking about Kerri and who she is dating. I just thought you were into her. I'm a little confused," I told him shyly. My face was now beat red.

"Just let me take you home. You drank a lot tonight and I want to make sure you get home safely." He suggested as our song ended. I was disappointed that it was over so quickly and he let go of me.

I nodded and agreed that it was not safe for me to drive home. I waited for him to close the bar up. It was about an hour later that he was done serving the last drink, cleaning up, and shutting everything down. I was much more sober now and I started to think about Kerri. She seemed really hurt that he danced with me and not her. I didn't know whether to be mad at her or feel bad. I hadn't done anything wrong. And why did he choose me and not my beautiful friend? He must be a fool.

"Ready to go?' He asked as he handed me his motorcycle helmet. Even though I wanted it I felt like I was doing something wrong. That usual feeling of despair came back, I just felt horrible. The same feeling I have right after I wake up from my sleep.

"Dallas I just can't let you take me home. I feel fine now. I can drive myself. I have to go. Thank you for the offer, but I can take it from here. And I enjoyed dancing with you," I said with a fake smile, trying to cover up this guilty feeling I had. He just looked at me with his dark eyes. He looked sad. Now my guilt feeling was accompanied by hurting his feelings.

"Avery I just don't get it. Why are you pushing me away? Don't you like me? Don't you feel the same way about me?" He asked.

"Oh Dallas you have no idea how much I like you. I always have. It's just that I can't let you take me home. You worked all night. You have got to be tired. And I live all the way across town. And you live the opposite way up the freeway. It wouldn't be right to ask you to do that," I lied. I thought that if I told him that instead of how I was really feeling it wouldn't make me look crazy. Like if I said,

"Oh Dallas I feel sick, like I did something wrong even though I didn't do anything with you. I feel a feeling of despair all day and all night, except for now it's even stronger and I can't control the feeling to cry right now." Yeah I don't think that would go over very well. So I said nothing.

"Well you can say what you want, but I'm not letting you drive yourself home. If you get stopped you will go to jail. You may feel ok but I made those drinks with a lot of tequila. So put on the damn helmet and let's go," he demanded.

"But what about my car? I need to get to work tomorrow and I have an early appointment before work." Oh crap I forgot about my appointment. Now I really felt sick. I'm going to show up there smelling of tequila. A really great first impression.

"Ok I will pick you up and take you to your car. What time is your appointment?" He asked. Maybe he was hoping I would let him sleep over. Maybe I should let him sleepover. But I didn't want to ruin what I thought might be possible between us.

"It's at seven," I said quietly.

"Really seven, huh? That's really early. That's like in five hours. We better go. I can sleep all day but you may only get a few hours," he said as he led me out to the parking lot. Little did he know I never sleep. This was way better than staring out my window at the moon or watching the sunrise. At least I was not alone. We got onto his motorcycle and drove off toward my apartment building. Even yelling directions to him over the loud sounds of the bike surprisingly did not ruin the ride for me.

He got us there in fifteen minutes. He did high speeds the whole way. He was worried about me getting stopped? He was even riding without a helmet, I had his on my head. What a gentlemen, I thought to myself. He pulled up to the front of my building and I got off the bike handing him his helmet.

"Thank you Dallas. Please drive safe home, no need to go as fast as you did just now," I said sternly.

"Avery I meant everything I said to you tonight," he started saying as he held my hand in his. "I have had it bad for you since you started coming into the bar. I have just been waiting for the right time to tell you. You may not know this but I'm shy, I don't date a lot. I just work, sleep, eat and workout. I really want to do this right. I want to take you out for dinner or lunch sometime. Would you want to do that?"

How could I say no to him? He is so true and honest. The nicest guy I've ever met. I've never seen him talk to any of the girls at the bar besides me. Why didn't I ever know that he liked me, why didn't I see this before?

"Dallas I would love to go out with you. It's what I have wanted too, for the same amount of time. I always thought you liked Kerri, kind of like all the other guys. It's just that I'm going through some weird stuff in my life right now. And it may be a while before I can go out with you. I mean I want to get this straightened out first." I wanted to be honest with him. I really didn't think it was a good idea to start a relationship with someone when I'm clearly losing my mind. I hoped that a few appointments with this new doctor and I would be okay. A very naive thought.

"I'm not going anywhere Avery. I will wait until you're ready. Can I kiss you goodnight or is that too forward?"

"It's not too forward," I answered expectantly. He got off his bike and ran his fingers through my hair, all while looking deeply into my eyes. And kissed me very sweetly on the lips.

I danced up the stairs to my apartment. I was wasted drunk on that kiss and I felt so good. Dallas really liked me! I couldn't believe it. His kiss was so great, as were his lips. I unlocked my door and walked into my living room. All the lights were on in my apartment. That was so unlike me, I try to shut everything off. Oh well, maybe I just forgot this time. I shrugged it off and tried to pretend that it didn't seem super weird to me. So I started to shut every light off.

I reached the kitchen and took a big drink of water hoping somehow that I would not have a hangover in four hours when I needed to be at my appointment. This was the strangest day ever. Two guys are interested in me and they are both really cute with great potential. But being completely honest, I know nothing about Landon or Dallas really. Mostly Landon. At least I have spoken to Dallas. Landon is a stranger who gave me his number. Hey, he never called me back. He must have not charged his phone yet. Or maybe he realized giving me his number was just a nice gesture and he found someone more his type. I set down my glass of water and walked into my room.

When I opened the door my knees felt weak. The feeling of fear paralyzed me, because what I saw before me was not possible. I was so scared I could not scream nor talk. I only could stare at her.

Ianni

She was magnificent and so beautiful, yet so scary to have her sitting on my bed. She had huge silver wings, yes wings. They were so tall they almost touched the ceiling. And her hair was a bright red. So bright it almost hurt my eyes. She was wearing a white dress that was very fitted on top and long and flowing on the bottom. It was sort of sexy looking. I tried to talk but I still couldn't. It was as if there was something holding my lips closed. I swallowed and the lump in my throat seemed to grow larger. She started to stand up and her wings fluttered and flapped.

It sent a flood of feathers all around my room. They started to fly around and made quite a mess. She had a very serious look on her face at first then it turned into a smile. She took a deep breath and then spoke.

"Hello Avery. I am here to speak with you about a very interesting turn of events that is occurring in this lifetime of yours. It has happened in all your lifetimes before and seems that we cannot stop it from happening again. You are just uncontrollable. You may not recognize me, but I have been with you since you started all your paths. Since the 19th century. My name is Ianni and I am your Angel or you can call me your Spirit Guide." As she spoke I noticed the fear in me started to grow less and less severe and the lump in my throat disappeared. I felt a calm come over me and I knew I could listen to her without completely freaking out.

"You have no reason to fear me. I am here to help you. Seeing that doctor tomorrow will not help you. You know this as well as I do. It will not do any good, but you will go anyway because that is what makes you comfortable. You like to know that someone is listening and you like to receive advice. Which is okay Avery. You may return a different person, but your soul has always been the same. I know you very well. I'm talking about reincarnation just so you know. I don't want to confuse you. So I'm here because I know you saw him again. The one they call Landon now. It seems you two are really linked forever. And I mean forever in every life you have lived. But I am here to help you sort it all out and you seem to be having some trouble with this life. You can ask me questions but you have to realize I cannot answer for your future, only the past and present."

I stood there in total disbelief for a few moments. This is really happening. This Spirit Guide is in my room and talking to me. I walked toward her and reached up to touch her face when I realized that this might be rude or it may frighten her. But she did not move like she would be afraid and she did not seem to mind. So I touched her arm and she felt real, then she laughed at me as if I were a curious child. I touched her right wing and it felt like silk, not like feathers at all. There were still several feathers floating all around us. It seemed like a dream but very real, too real to be a dream. I didn't know what to ask her or where to start. There were so many questions I had. So I decided to start with who Landon was and why my mother was so worried I would see him again. Why we seemed to be linked. Then she suddenly started to answer the question before I even asked it.

"Your mother was very wise and very in touch with your past lives. She was a very good psychic on earth. Should I continue?" She asked me. I nodded. "Landon was your very first husband in 1824. You were married in London and your name then was Claire and his was Henry. He was an heir to a very wealthy estate. You both were upper high class and it was said that you two should marry, even when you were children. He was a gentleman and was a good provider to you and your three children, Annabelle, Anastasia, and Henry Jr. Henry was very in love with you. He treated you like a princess. This was pretty uncommon then. Women were not treated very well, they were meant to stay home and take care of the children and the men would pretty much live separate lives. Would you like to see what you, Henry and your children looked like?"

I answered yes, not knowing what would happen. She put her hands together and started to swirl them in circles. A picture started to appear in front of her, sort of like a very large see through picture. Her hands continued to swirl. The picture grew larger until it was the same height as her.

The woman in the picture was wearing a beautiful Victorian dress that was tight fitting on her small waistline. It had long sleeves that were adorned with lace. Her hair was up in tight curls on her head and she was wearing some sort of hat with lace as well. Her jewelry was gold with, what looked like, rubies and emeralds as the stones. She looked prudish or snobby, but maybe that was because she was not smiling. The man next to her, Henry was tall and handsome. His hair was brown and curly and he had sideburns. He was wearing a black double-breasted coat and gray trousers. The children were very similarly dressed. They were truly adorable and so sweet looking. I only had a few seconds of seeing this picture until it vanished and Ianni sat exhausted on my bed,

"It takes a great deal of effort for me to do that. I may not be able to produce another picture for a while. I'm just going to sit here and let you soak it all in."

"They were a nice looking family," I said. "Were we happy in that life?"

"Oh yes. He was very good to you. I knew you and your family well, like I said. You did not know I was there but I was always watching you. You were very lucky to be high class then. They were hard times for many women and men during that time. Cholera is what took your life in 1850. You were forty-nine and he was fifty-two. He died in 1851. He could not live without you. We know about that because you both kept meeting up in your future lives. He was really in love with you, so much that he chose to find you in the afterlife and stay with you until you were ready to move on."

"Move on? What does that mean?" I asked

"You know, come back here, start a new life. And he did so too. He loved you so much that he forced himself to not forget you in his new life. We call that reviving memories." I gave her a look, like I was totally confused. "Ok it's when you have lived your past life and you go home, to Heaven that is, and you choose to do a new life, you reincarnate. Well every time Landon reincarnates he forces himself to revive memories of you and him in your past lives. He could be five or ten years old and he starts to remember his past lives. It's pretty common to remember some things. You see something that looks familiar and you shrug it off as crazy but really it's your soul remembering. But Landon had perfected his reviving skills very well. So then he desperately looks for you. No matter what his new life involves. He always finds you and you both fall in love and are together again."

"And that's bad?" I asked. It sounded really romantic to me. Not like he was breaking any rules. If I was going to end up with Landon I was not mad about that.

"Yes it's bad!" She said in a sarcastic tone. The serious side of her was starting to dwindle and I could see a little attitude come alive in her. "You're not supposed to be with him in this life, he is not your destined mate this time. He was only supposed to be your husband once. And it's happened now in all three of your lives. And that's why I'm here. To help you live the life you set out to live when you started it. You see, when you die and come home you have a choice whether to stay or try again, so to speak. You look over your life that you just lived and you can make your choice from there. Well the first time when you came home after living as Claire you chose to reincarnate, you wanted to live a different life. So your soul moved on and you became Emily, then you lived a nice life, you were happy. Henry, or Landon as you know him now, he chose to reincarnate as well. He couldn't bear to be home without you. It's strange really because home is a place where there is no sadness or missing anyone, but he did terribly, so he reincarnated as well. He reincarnated as a young man named Cooper Shade. Cooper

Shade was poor and penniless. His destiny was to marry a lady named Suzanne Young. You were supposed to marry a man named Garrison Whittaker. He was a writer, and he loved you so. You were his muse. Then Cooper found you. He was a lot younger than you, but you couldn't resist him and you married him instead. Poor Garrison he was never the same after that. He took his own life. Oh what a shame. And Suzanne died alone and unmarried. Do you see? He messed with people's lives. What he does affects everything." She stopped and looked at me as if I committed some sort of crime.

"Well if I'm not supposed to be with him then who am I destined to be with?' I asked her.

"I told you, I can't tell you your future, only your past and present. So, like I was saying, I'm here to stop him. It's really a problem. He is the only one to do this so many times before. Many souls meet up again in future lives. But four times is really strange. And you're really having a hard time with seeing him again. You can't sleep, and you really look horrible."

"Gee thanks some Angel you are. Wait, I just saw him for the first time today, what does that have anything to do with me not sleeping? I mean Lucy told me a guy named Cooper was watching me right before she died and right after that night is when my sleeping stopped. But that was three months ago," I told her. I was starting to understand what she was saying, still finding it all very dreamlike as the feathers continued to fly around my room. But I was catching on to what she was telling me.

"What! What are you talking about? You don't remember the dreams?" She asked me.

"I don't know about dreams Angel girl, all I know is when I do dream I don't remember much. And I wake up sweaty and feeling sad or I'm crying after I wake up. I did have a dream I was following a light and it lead to a big oak door." I was sort of embarrassed to be telling her all of this.

"Ok, first off don't call me Angel girl. I told you my name. Second, there is a reason you wake up sweaty and sad. It's because he is visiting you in your dreams, his soul can disconnect while he sleeps and come to you in your dreams. You know when you dream that you are flying or watching something happen from a far? It's because your soul is traveling around. That is when he comes to you to visit. So you're dreaming about being with him and that's what's making you sad, because you have to leave him. The reason Lucy called him Cooper was because she didn't hear the full name she only caught the last name. I was there. I followed Landon's Spirit Guide to Lucy's apartment. His Spirit Guide was Lucy's Guide too. We don't just guide one soul, we guide several. So when it was Lucy's time to go her Guide, Lillith, was there with her when she passed and while she was guiding her soul to go home she delivered the message that he was here and he loves you and well you know the rest. So anyway the point of all this is that he found you again and he's trying to weasel his way into your arms again. He is totally going against the rules. Again. So I'm here against my rules to tell you to stay away from him. And once you do you will go back to your normal life. No more dreams of him, no more sleepless nights, worried auntie or weird sightings. Got it?"

She seemed like she was starting to get annoyed. She didn't even think to ask how I felt. This was the strangest thing to ever happen to me, even weirder than all my sightings. I seemed to understand what was going on with Landon though. He loved me and wanted to be with me again apparently. I didn't really find that to be a problem. But she said it was not my path and that I was meant to do something else. It still didn't make sense why I saw my mother in my bathroom or the carving on the tree. Just then the feathers in the room started to slow down and I noticed a few falling onto my bedroom floor instead of floating.

"Ok, listen because time is almost up for me. I don't know when I'll be able to talk to you again or let you see me because it's so not allowed. I will be watching you and I can come to you in your dreams, so stay in tune with them. Oh, and you can talk aloud and I can hear you. Remember two things. Stay away from Landon and try to follow your destined path."

Suddenly, in a flash, she was gone. My room was empty. With no feathers or crazy red headed Angels in it. I still didn't see why I had to stay away from him, why couldn't we be friends? All I knew was I was still going to see my doctor in the morning because I was going nuts. Also, I totally didn't want to be like my mother, seeing dead people or being a "psychic". I tried to convince myself that this was just a dream and it didn't really happen. It almost worked until I finally lay down to try to sleep and I found a feather on my pillow.

Chapter 5

Dr. Charlie

My alarm started buzzing loudly at 6:00 a.m. I was unsure as to how long I had slept because I didn't even know what time it was when I laid down. I sat up and felt very dizzy and sweaty again. My face was soaking wet and so was my hair. As I started to wake up I remembered the night's events as they started to flood back to me. No wonder I was dizzy! I had a crazy night and I knew I was definitely hung over.

I reached to the bedside table and shut off my alarm. I couldn't stand to hear that noise anymore, my head was throbbing. I saw the silver feather from the night before on the table and it confirmed, once again, what had happened. I stumbled to the shower and started the water. I had to hurry and get ready because I didn't want to be late to my appointment.

As I stood in the shower I started to cry uncontrollably. I sat down on the floor of the shower with the water hitting my back. I couldn't believe all that had happened. It made me so sad that all this was going on and I had no clue. I just wanted it to go away and to go back to my semi normal life. I wanted to date Dallas and really get to know him. I didn't want Landon to try to take that away from me. Who did he think he was coming into my life and taking away what was meant to be? He had some nerve to do this to me. He has succeeded three times before and this time I knew about his motive. There would be no way I was going to let him do it again. At first I felt that it was sweet that he loved me so much and I felt bad that he did all this for me, but now I'm mad that he is over taking my life.

I stood up and pulled myself together for the sake of my sanity. I washed my hair and body as fast as I could and then shut off the water. As I stepped out of the shower I heard a knock on my door. I thought I was hearing things so I started drying myself off, but then I heard it again. Who could be at my door at this time? I put on my robe and walked to the door and opened it a crack. It was Dallas holding two cups of coffee.

"Dallas what are you doing here?" I asked while pulling my robe tighter.

"I told you I would bring you your car but you failed to give me your car keys so I have my truck. I can take you to your car, is that ok?"

As he asked me he smiled, which showed off his dimples. I totally forgot about my car. I guess I would have remembered when I went to go to my parking spot and there was no car there. I let him in and told him to have a seat and wait for me to dress. I dressed in my work uniform and pulled my wet hair into a ponytail. I didn't apply any mascara today, there was no time. My face was pale and sickly looking so mascara would do no good. I walked up behind Dallas, who was now on my couch asleep still holding the coffee in his hands. I coughed quietly to wake him so that I didn't startle him. I didn't want him to wake up and spill hot coffee all over himself. He sat up and yawned he looked worse than me, if that was even possible. He didn't have a red head Spirit Guide with silver wings in his room last night. Well, if he did he didn't see her. Then it occurred to me Dallas has a Guide as well. I wondered what his was like and if she was here right now.

"You look like you didn't get any sleep Avery. I mean, you're beautiful as always, but you look so tired. Can't you reschedule this appointment and take a nap with me on your couch?"

It sounded so nice to snuggle with him but I did not want to blow off this appointment. I had waited too long to get some advice for my problem, even though I knew this doctor would laugh or think I was a real nut when I told him all that had happened. I didn't care. I had to tell someone and it sure can't be my friends.

"Sounds really nice and inviting, trust me, but I can't cancel. I need to go to this appointment. And then I have work at 10:00, but I have to say I will be daydreaming of cuddling with you all day long. So give me my coffee and let's hit it."

He laughed, handed me my liquid awake, and we walked down to the parking lot. I never knew Dallas drove a truck, I only thought he had a motorcycle. He opened the door for me and helped me in. His truck was lifted much higher than the usual trucks I've seen. It was very nice and clean, inside and out. I was very impressed with him. It's always nice to see that a guy who takes care of his things.

He hopped into the driver's side and started it up. The rumble of the engine was very loud, making my already sore head worse. I knew this truck was pretty fast and it made me even more attracted to him.

The drive to the La Costa was not too long and we were very quiet all the way there. I think it was a good, comfortable silence. We felt good enough around each other to know that words were not needed. We reached my car and I dreaded getting out. I sighed because I didn't want to say goodbye to him. It was nice to feel that way about someone again, and I didn't want anyone coming in between that. This was real and not forced attraction. I was very excited about the possibilities of starting a relationship with him. He was everything I thought I wanted in a man and he wanted me. That was the incredible thing about this whole scenario. For the first time in my life I was wanted by two men. Well, the first time in this life anyway.

"Well even though I want to steal you away for the day I have to let you out. So drive careful and call me when you get a break. Promise me." I shook my head yes as he leaned in and kissed me. Again, it was very sweet and warm and it sent chills down my spine. He smelled very good and I wanted to stay here so bad it hurt. He pulled away and stroked my cheek and then touched my wet hair.

"You should have dried your hair you could catch a cold. And I like it when your hair is down it really looks pretty like that. But you're still stunning either way. Now get out of here before you're late."

I regretfully opened the door and stepped out of the truck. I walked to my car and got in it as he pulled away. I shivered due to the fact that my car was very cold. I had to warm it up because my wet hair made me even colder. Then I noticed my phone was still in my car sitting in the cup holder. I had completely forgot that my phone was here, it was a good thing I didn't need to make a call last night. I looked at the screen and it said three missed calls. Who could have called me last night or this early in the morning? As I drove to the medical building I checked my voice messages. The first was Kerri, she sounded very tired and still a little drunk.

"Hey Av, it's me. I'm so sorry for storming out like a little baby tonight. It had nothing to do with you. I'm happy Dallas wanted to dance with you. I'm just a little mad and hurt by Gavin and our breakup, you know what I mean? I just wanted to call and tell you that I love you girl. And I'm sorry. Talk to you at work tomorrow. Bye."

She sounded very sincere and I knew she wasn't really mad at me. I knew she was having a rough day yesterday and drinking did not make things any better. The next message was a hang up. Probably Kerri again and she didn't want to leave another message. The last message had a long pause before anyone spoke.

"Hi Avery it's the guy you helped on the side of the road, Landon Cooper. I got your message today and I'm sorry I didn't call you sooner but I just got my phone charged. I gave you my number because I want to take you out some time. It was incredibly nice of you to help me and I want to repay you. I'm new in town so I need someone to show me around. I hope that you can be my tour guide for the day. If you're interested call me back. Take care, bye."

At first I was furious that he called me. How dare he call me and lie to me? He had no idea that I knew why he just moved here. He wasn't tricking anyone especially not me.

Then as I pulled into the parking lot of the building I started to feel bad for him. He did move here for me. I could just be friend's with him. I could tell him I knew everything and I could tell him that I wanted him to move on and meet another soul. I wasn't the only soul out there. I'm not the one he is meant to be with in this life. He would understand, he had to if he really loved me. That settled it, that is what I would do.

I walked an office that smelled like jasmine, which was really odd to me. The receptionist was very pleasant looking and that made me feel comfortable. I signed in and she asked me to fill out some paperwork. I was very nervous and I think it showed because the receptionist kept smiling at me as if to calm me down and make me feel comfortable. I glanced at the wall and saw a picture of a woman in a business suit. She looked very nice and she was gorgeous. Underneath the picture was the name of my shrink, Charlie Beamer. My shrink was a girl and she had a guy's name. I was a little thrown off by this but not upset. A female doctor was just as good as a man.

At that moment my name was called and it was time to finally meet this Dr. Beamer and tell her all of my secrets. I walked into her fabulous office and sat down in a very comfy leather chair. Her office was decorated with various candles, all of which were burning, and the lavender color was very calming. I'm sure this was an intentional decorating tactic to calm her patients. The smell of jasmine was very strong in here and it sort of bothered my nose. She came into the room through a side door and then sat in front of me. She was very pretty and her golden blonde hair was pulled up halfway while the rest just grazed her shoulders. She was dressed professionally, yet not too business-like. She held out her hand for me to shake as she introduced herself as Dr. Beamer. I took her hand and nodded without saying anything back. She took out a black folder and started writing in it right away.

"Well Avery tell me a little about yourself so I can get to know you. Then we can talk about why you are here to see me. So go ahead and I will sit here and listen."

"Well I'm twenty-six and single, for now. I work at an assisted living residence and I love my job. I love helping people and I feel like I'm doing well by working there. My mother died when I was twelve years old of a brain aneurism. I then moved in with my Aunt Paulina and stayed with her until I was nineteen. After that, I got a job at a restaurant in town and I moved into my own place. Then I decided to move here about four years ago from southern California and start fresh. I love it here and I wouldn't move back for anything." I stopped and wondered to myself if I had left anything out in my introduction stage. She kept writing and then looked up at me.

"Okay and why are you here to see me now?"

"Well you're not the first psychologist that I have seen. I've needed to see a couple before, for different things. But much different than why I need to see you now. I have not been sleeping for about three months. I have seen my general physician for my problem and I have tried all his advice. Nothing seems to work. My aunt suggested that I see a shrink. Oh, sorry, you probably hate that term." I felt bad for offending her.

"No don't worry Avery you're not the first to call me that," she said with a laugh. I could tell that it did not offend her in any way, that she actually found it funny.

"Keep going your doing well. I want to hear more."

"Ok, well some crazy things have been going on in my life lately. Things that are unexplainable and sound really nuts so please just keep and open mind," I said.

Then I continued to tell Dr. Beamer about all the things I have heard and seen in the past three months. As I spoke she kept a very serious face all the while writing in her black folder. Never once looking at me as if I were making it all up or going crazy, which helped me talk and open up. I told her all about Landon and Ianni and about my past lives. I told her about my dead mother in my bathroom and about the mysterious light that I followed into the park. About Dallas and Kerri, how much they meant to me, how they were worried about me and wanted me to get better.

After my exhausting confession I felt so relieved that I just sat there and smiled. She finally stopped writing and looked in a book that sat at her side table and flipped to a page. She then wrote something down on a piece of paper and handed it to me.

"Avery, this is a number to a man named Justin White. He is a specialist with these things you are experiencing. I really think he can help you to see why these things are going on. He is really good at past lives." I took the paper and tried to hide my puzzled expression.

"He is a psychic, isn't he?" I asked, trying not to sound rude. I didn't really want to see a psychic. If I had wanted to I wouldn't have come here.

"Well, yes and he specializes in what you are going through. Avery, it is not uncommon for people to remember their past life or see an Angel. I hear it a lot from my patients. I did not learn this in college, but I believe in it. If I hadn't gone through this myself I would have you committed for reasons of insanity, but Justin helped me and he is excellent. I know he can help you. I still want to see you and try to help you through this. I think both Justin and I can help you solve this problem, or at least deal with it. You are not alone and you are not crazy."

When she said I wasn't crazy it helped immensely and I felt better. At least for right now, at this moment. I did think it was odd for a professional like herself to go this route but I liked that she had an open mind about it. Also, like she said, she went through this herself. But then I began to wonder what her experience was like. Even more, was I the only one that didn't know about past lives being a real thing? I mean, most people believe that you only have one try, but according to Dr. Beamer it's a common thing in her practice.

"Now about your mother, you said she was a psychic?" She asked me.

"Yes, or at least she thought she was. Ianni confirmed this. I guess I never believed my mom. I just thought she was making it all up. It's hard for a kid to believe in that I guess. I just wanted her to be normal like my friends mom's. I did love her very much and she took good care of me as a child. She was all I had and she worked very hard to play the role of mom and dad."

I started to cry and I didn't know why. I hadn't cried about mom in several years, but for some reason I felt very sad and I missed her. I wanted her to be here with me right now and help me sort things out. Dr. Beamer handed me a tissue and she closed her folder.

"Well Avery, our time has ended for today but I want you to follow up with Justin. Once you do I want to see you back here. I want to talk more about your father and have you tell me more about your mom and your past, okay? So if you need anything call the office. Oh, and I almost forgot, here is a sample herb to help you sleep its called Yulu." She handed me a small package with a small purple mesh bag inside. I took the package and studied it carefully. "You make a tea with it, don't eat it, ok?'

She stood up and shook my hand again. As she shook my hand I noticed a red feather floating in the room. I shrugged it off as nothing major and left her office. I walked to the reception area and her receptionist told me to call in two weeks for my next appointment. As I left I felt a little better. It felt refreshing to tell someone my secrets and have them understand. I had to admit it was a little odd for a doctor to open up about the things she did, but it was definitely an experience to remember.

The cool air was so clean as I walked outside and I still had two hours before I had to go to work. I pulled out my phone and called Aunt Paulina to tell her about my appointment. She was very happy to hear my voice and she wanted to see me so I told her to meet me in front of the library so we could chat. It only took her fifteen minutes to get there and she looked very pleased to see me. The one thing about my aunt was she always was happy to see me and always made me feel special. She sat next to me on the bench in front of the library.

"So, did it go well?"

"Yes and I will go back in a couple weeks. It's just such a nice day and I have some time before work, I wondered if you want to walk the trail in the park?" The park trail was only across the street from the library and it was a good trail with lots of trees and foliage. It always helped me see the beauty in nature. She grabbed my hand and lifted me off the bench.

"Let's do it. And while we walk you can talk about your doctor. Only if you want to of course."

“I’d rather we just walk and talk about something else Aunt Paul. I just want to enjoy my visit with you instead.”

I didn’t want to tell her about what was going on. She would not understand any of it and she would be more worried about me than she already was. I just wanted her to think positive thoughts. She seemed to not mind too much that I wanted to keep mum. As we walked she told me about how she is really enjoying her visit with Barb and how she spent too much money shopping the other day. I felt like I was bursting at the seams and I had to tell her about Dallas.

“I met someone, well I have known him awhile we just told each other how much we really like each other. I think there’s something real there. I can trust him and I like him a lot. His name is Dallas.” I was so happy to tell her that I almost shouted it out. She looked at me, smiled and did a little jump.

“Oh honey I’m so happy for you. I hope this will be the answer you are looking for. I know it has been hard for you in your life. You know, dealing with your mom’s loss has been difficult for both of us and I think that’s why you distance yourself with men. You are afraid of losing someone close to you again.”

She was so right! I guess I never saw it that way before, but it was true, I don’t want to lose anyone else. I lost my dad and my mom and I didn’t want to lose a boyfriend or potential husband. I didn’t want to lose Aunt Paul either.

As we walked the trail it was so peaceful and serene I found myself relaxing. The forest here was amazing and I just loved to walk when the weather was brisk and cool. We walked for a little while before we decided it was time to go back. It was now 9:30 and I had to leave for work. I didn’t want to say goodbye to her but I had to. She hugged me and told me to keep in touch and let her know how my progress was with the shrink. And Dallas. I promised her that I would take her to dinner the following week and we would talk about it more. I got into my car and headed to work dreadfully. On the way there I called Dallas to let him know I was ok. When he answered it sounded like he was sleeping, I felt so bad.

“Hi, it’s Avery. I hope I didn’t wake you.” I knew I did but I wanted him to know I felt bad.

"Oh, it's ok. I kind of figured that sleep is not going to happen for me today. It all was worth it because I got to see you last night and today, a total bonus. When can I see you again? You're all I can think about."

It was so nice to hear this come from him after I just woke him up. It was clear to me that he was a patient man if he could go through the torture I have put him through and still be happy. I felt the same about him though I could not wait to see him again.

"Well I get off at ten so I can stop by your work tonight and see you."

"Sounds great, but I do want to take you out for a real date. So when is your next day off?"

"I'm off on Friday. Are you available?"

"I'm off in the day but I have to go in at night. So how about a day trip somewhere? I was thinking a picnic at the Humboldt botanical garden. Would that be okay?"

Just the fact that he already thought about our date was incredibly romantic. I agreed that his plans sounded awesome, terrific and fabulous, without saying all that of course. When we hung up I felt like I could accomplish anything and I felt for the first time like a weight had been lifted. I couldn't wait to see him tonight and get to know more about him. Learning about him was really intriguing since I didn't know too many details. Then my thoughts turned to Landon and whether I was going to call him today to talk to him. I decided I would make him wait and I would call him tomorrow.

I got to work and went straight into Kerri's office. Instantly she asked me what happened with Dallas the night before. I told her all about it and she sat and listened like a teenage girl who was excited for her best friend. I also told her that I had, in fact, called Landon and he returned my call. I just felt it best to leave out the details of the relationship and Ianni's little visit last night. She told me how happy she was for me and that she only wanted to see me happy. I knew that she would be happy for me and she felt bad for the night before.

"So that is why Dallas got mad last night when I mentioned that you met a guy," she said. I totally forgot about that incident and I wondered if Dallas was worried that I would pursue the "other guy".

"I guess," was all I could say to her. I was pretty certain that was why he got mad and I remember not liking that side of him. He seemed really mad and jealous of Landon and he didn't even know the details. What would he do if he knew he was my soul mate in three past lives and he was here to be with me again? I tried to shake the thought out of my head and I left her office to do my daily rounds. It seemed like Mr. Grey was adjusting alright. He was sitting in the courtyard talking with a couple of the other residents, Mr. Lucas and Mrs. Oberman. It was nice to see him talking since he was such a shy man. He waved to me and I waved back hoping he was having a nice conversation. At that moment I saw a huge gust of blue feathers blow through the courtyard. I looked to see where they were coming from and I saw a shadowy figure walk into Mr. Grey's apartment.

Lillith

I slowly walked into his apartment, looking around to see if anyone had noticed the flood of feathers flying around. It seemed as though I was the only one. When I entered the apartment at first I saw nothing but then I saw the shadow go into his bedroom. I followed it down the hall and into the room. There she stood with the feathers flying around the room, just like they had when Ianni was in my room. She was not as pretty as Ianni but still pretty in her own way. She was taller and her hair was very black. Her blue wings were flapping wildly and it made me step back. She looked mean and scary, like an Angel that was not very heavenly.

"Do you know who I am Avery?" She asked me. Her voice was deep and scratchy like she smoked or did a lot of yelling.

"No, but I know you're a Spirit Guide. Are you Mr. Grey's?" That was all I could think of. Why else would she be in his apartment? Then her wings stopped flapping and the scary look faded and she smiled. She looked a lot prettier when she smiled and I was less intimidated. Yet my hands still shook and I felt my heart beat faster.

"No my sweet I am not his Guide. My name is Lillith, I belong to Landon. I just wanted to visit you and tell you how important it is that you two reunite again. He longs to be with you and he is sick without you. He has searched long and far for you. He found you, indeed with my help, and the help of his cousin who knows you. I searched for you and found you here with Lucy. She was mine as well, but you know this don't you? You were visited by Ianni, she means well but she can't stop the love that you two have. She hasn't ever stopped it before. Poor thing, she broke the rules to visit you and now she bears silver wings. Ah, those white pure wings will be missed."

"What are you talking about? What are white pure wings?'

"Well, we are given white wings when we are made. It is a sign of purity and we have rules to abide by. One being to not meddle in the lives of our spirit's that we follow. We are only allowed to show you signs. If we don't follow the rules our wings change colors and we are not "pure" any longer. Well, for years she has never spoken to you she just gave you signs and visited your dreams. Needless to say you didn't follow those signs because you love Landon and you always followed your heart. Ianni felt it in her best interest to break the rules and now her wings are silver. I think they are charming don't you?"

I found the way she talked about Ianni to be condescending and rude and I did not like her tone. She seamed phony and I don't like phony people nor do I like phony Angels.

"Why are your wings blue then? And shouldn't one of the rules be to let me be with who I am destined to be with?' I was now as mad as she was. She was trying to pressure me to be with him. My tone was just as sharp as hers.

"Well I have blue wings because I break the rules a lot. For Landon and the others. I feel like they don't get my signs. So I don't see the harm in helping out. My wings have been many colors; you name it they've been it. I like blue the best but they will change after I go see Landon tonight. He will want to hear how you are doing and if you have been seeing anyone else. He is only trying to be with you, he means no harm. If you choose that you don't want to be with him he will understand. He just wants you to give him a chance again. As for your destined mate you are to be with your destined mate, but who is to say he is not your destined mate? Ianni? Me? God? No one knows, just your heart. If you meet with Landon and your heart tells you he is the one, well then so be it, but that's up to you. Ok? I must go, there is someone coming. Think about what I said ok?" She walked to the window and flew out, turning into a blue bird. When I turned around Mr. Grey was standing behind me. He looked unhappy that I was in his house.

"Mr. Grey you startled me. I was just um..."

"I saw what you were doing in here and I'm not too happy about it." I hoped he wasn't going to tell anyone. It was not something you wanted to come out to everyone. My heart stopped and I swallowed hard.

"A bird in my apartment is not acceptable. They could carry viruses and they make messes. See all the feathers in this room? I hope you will clean them up for me."

I was so happy he hadn't seen what that bird really was that I laughed out loud. He gave me a dirty look and walked out of the room. I knelt down and started to pick up the feathers on the ground and I thought about the decision that it seemed I had to make. To be with Landon, a guy that has loved me for years and I obviously loved in return, or to see what happens with Dallas. I thought I had this all worked out but Lillith's little visit did nothing other than make me more confused. I decided that I would call Landon and meet with him. Maybe Lillith was right about my heart knowing what it wants. The only way to choose was to meet with him and see how I felt in his presence. The only thing I didn't know was do I pretend I don't know about him? Or do I tell him I know all about what was going on? I also wondered who his cousin was. They were the key to Landon finding me in this whole world. I could have lived anywhere and he found me here due to a cousin who knows me. It was so bizarre.

Once my shift was over I felt so tired. More tired than I had in a long time. So tired I felt like I could sleep for at least four hours. I had so much going on in my head that it exhausted me to the point of pure agony. A few months ago and I was just a normal girl, living a normal life and now I have weird dreams, frequent Angel visits, and two men who want to be with me. I walked to my car and sunk into the driver's seat. I didn't even say goodbye to Kerri tonight. I was way too tired to talk about anything and she would go on forever about her day or God knows what else. I drove to my apartment and pulled into my parking space. As I shut off the car I looked at my phone I realized that if I was going to call Landon it would be right now because once I got upstairs I was not calling anyone. So I dialed his number and within two rings he answered.

His voice sounded so perfect. He also looked perfect if what I remember was correct. It occurred to me that our chance encounter could have been a set up. I was pretty darn sure that he knew everything about me in this life and all the ones past.

"Hi, this is Avery." I hoped then that I would not be so tired that I would sound uninterested in setting up a date. So I perked up my voice so he wouldn't notice.

"I was calling to tell you that I would love to show you around town sometime."

"Really? That sounds terrific. I was beginning to think you thought I was some crazy stalker." He laughed and even that sounded perfect.

"Oh no, I don't think you're a stalker, I just think you want to get to know me. And you want to see the town. Which is fine by me." To spend the day with my soul mate was pretty intimidating and I wasn't sure what I would show him on our date.

"Ok well when is a good day for you? I own my own business so I pretty much have an open schedule being the boss and all."

"Must be nice being your own boss. I wish I was that lucky." Then I remembered my date with Dallas. Oh no! I told him I would stop by the bar tonight. I totally forgot I had to end this call soon and call Dallas and tell him I was too tired to make it. I didn't want to be a no show and no call. I didn't want him to think I was standing him up. I knew he would understand how tired I was and that the bar was the last place I wanted to be right now.

"Um, how about next Wednesday? I have the day off and it is supposed to be a nice day. I could take you to the historic part of town if you want to. It has a lot of shops and antique stores. And there are a couple of museums if you like that kind of thing. It will give you and idea of the history of the town."

He didn't say anything for a few seconds making me kind of

nervous. I wondered if he thought my idea was not good enough for him. It was hard talking to him because all I could think of was Ianni telling me to stay away from him like he was bad or evil. I was so torn as to whether this was right or wrong.

"Are you still there?" I asked him.

"Oh yeah, I was just looking at something on my computer, I am so sorry for being rude. Your idea sounds terrific I would love to go to some of the shops and museums. It's a date. Well, not a date but you know what I mean." He laughed nervously. What did he have to be nervous about? He had found me in this town after looking all over the United States for me. He got his way and apparently he always did.

"Ok well do you want to meet me at Old Town Coffee and Chocolates? We can have some coffee then figure out what we want to do from there."

"Avery you really seem like you are pretty organized. It's a good thing because I really don't know the town very well. So how is noon on Wednesday?"

"Sounds good to me. I have to get going, I need to try to get some sleep. I have been lacking sleep and my bed is calling me. So see you then." I felt bad for ending the conversation but I really was tired and wasn't really feeling talkative.

"Ok well have a good weekend Avery. Goodnight and sweet dreams," he said.

"Goodnight to you too." I hung up the phone and laughed to myself. I was excited and giddy, too giddy. I needed to get a grip I couldn't get excited about this. I had two dates now with two totally different guys. I had gone from spinster to harlot.

Chapter 7
Dreamland

I walked to my apartment and as I turned the key I prayed that I would not see any Angels or dead people. All was good when I walked in and I felt relief. I remembered the Yulu that Dr. Charlie had given me so I went to the kitchen and made it. It smelled so sweet I didn't even add sugar. When I tasted it, it reminded me of oranges. I undressed and laid on my couch in my comfy jammies. With tea in hand I got my phone and dialed Dallas' number. When he did not answer I figured he was busy, so I left a short message saying I was too tired to make it but I would see him Friday. After the call I started to feel sleepy from the tea. So I closed my eyes and took a deep breath. I felt so sure that I would sleep tonight and sure enough I fell into a deep sleep.

The dream began with me walking down a hall and coming to a big door. The same door that I had dreamed of previously except for this time it opened and I walked through it. I saw him sitting on a bed with his hands crossed looking very handsome and calm. When he saw me his expression changed and he smiled widely showing his perfect teeth. He stood to meet me and he hesitated for a second before embracing me. I didn't push him away because something told me not to, that I knew this man. His smell was even familiar but I could not place it.

He was much taller than me so he rested his chin on my head. He smelled my hair and ran his fingers through it, sending shock waves through my body. I stood there frozen not knowing what I was supposed to do. I noticed that he was dressed very strange and it didn't go with my time period. He was dressed as if we were in the 1900's. His hair was dark and parted down the middle and his eyes were a dark autumn brown.

"Claire I have missed you so much. It's been too long since our last meeting and I have been dying to see you. Did you miss me as well?" Claire! He called me by another name but I knew this name. I looked at him confused and helpless hoping he would explain to me what was going on.

"Oh, you don't remember do you? Is it like it was the last time?" He asked me with a sad look on his face. "It's okay darling I will explain again. You're Claire and I am your husband Henry. Well, I was your husband I'm not now though." Now I knew what was going on. I knew this was in a dream and since he said he missed me since we met last we must have met here in my dreams before and talked or visited at least. I felt that this was all too familiar. He reached out to take my hand but I pulled away.

"Don't touch me I don't know you anymore. Even though you once were my husband or whatever you were I am not that woman anymore. I don't remember you. You are a stranger to me. So don't touch me," I told him

"I can help you remember Claire. I have before in other meetings that we have had. I just need you to take my hand and trust me," he said.

How could I trust him, I didn't even know him? For some reason I gave him my hand and he took it and held it to his heart. Then he closed his eyes and I did the same. After only a few seconds had gone by I felt a rush of memories flood back to me, memories that I didn't even know existed. Times before this life I live now.

I remembered the first time I met Henry and how he kissed my hand so gently. I remembered our courtship and how I fell in love with him after only a few meetings, he made it so easy to do because he was so kind and loving to me. He told me he would love me forever and never let me go. Our wedding was the talk of the town, everyone was in attendance and I felt like a queen. Our marriage was perfect, like the ones you only read about, but ours was a reality. He was a hard working provider while I stayed at home. He always greeted me with yellow roses when he returned home from his long day at work. I could smell the roses as if they were in front of my face. I could feel his touch on my face and his kiss on my lips, but it was only a memory. My heart started to race at the thought of him kissing me. I remembered our first child Annabelle and how I didn't think I could love anyone anymore than I loved her. Then came Anastasia and Henry Jr. and I did love them just the same. There was room in my heart for all my children and Henry as well. I remembered how snobby and rude I was to others around me. I did not trust anyone except my family. I hated the poor and I despised the needy. I was a true, genuine bitch. In return for how horrible I was to others, my death was a horrible, painful experience. I could not wait for the pain to leave my body! I begged for Henry to let me go and let me go to God. And I did. I went home to God and as I entered I felt at peace. The pain was finally over.

I met with my Spirit Guide, Ianni, who's wings were pure white and breathtaking. She led me to my house where I would wait for my family. It was a remarkable resemblance to my home on earth with all the same furniture, pictures, clothes and all that I felt was important on Earth. All except my family and my husband. I knew I would see them soon so I waited with great patience and peace and soon enough they all joined me.

I decided that I wanted to try again on earth. I wanted to be a better person than I was as Claire. I wanted to do it right and be a kinder person so I met with the council of Angels and they granted me a new life. They helped me set my path and journey in my next life. I said goodbye to my children and they happily wished me luck but Henry begged me to stay. He said he could not lose me again. I found this odd because I didn't feel sad for leaving him. I knew I would see him here again. There was no sadness at Home only joy.

I left anyway and was reborn as Emily Laurent. I was born to a wonderful family who gave me all they could and I was thankful for it every day. I was the woman I wanted to be. I became engaged to a writer Garrison Whitaker. He was loving and kind and treated me like gold. I had no reason to look elsewhere for love. I had all I needed in Garrison's arms, until I met Cooper Shade. Cooper was a nice man, who was much younger than I was, that was hired by Garrison to help around his home. Garrison's work would sometimes lead him to take many trips away from home. On those trips Cooper was very persistent about him and I being together.

At first it was small attempts. Then as time went his advances toward me became stronger and stronger until I started sneaking around to see him and I fell in love with him. I could not help it I was drawn to him like a fly to honey. Soon I broke off my engagement to Garrison, breaking his heart into a million pieces and soon after he took his life. Both Cooper and I were heart broken. Our love had driven him to kill himself but we felt in our hearts that this relationship was the right thing. My family did not agree and they told me that they were not going to accept my choice, so I ran off with my new husband.

When I returned Home at the age of 70 I learned that my dear Cooper was in fact Henry. I learned from Ianni that he could not bear to be without me so he found me somehow and took me away from Garrison. I came Home years before he did. So I decided to leave again and be reborn. This time I set out to live my own life and not get married to Henry. I wanted to try again and start a new family without Henry. As most people do they fall in love with other souls. I did still love him but I felt it fair to love someone else this time, my intended mate in this new life.

I was now a woman named Elsie Hodge. I owned my own bakery, which soon turned into three bakeries, one in New York City and two in New Jersey. I was strong and goal oriented when all of a sudden I was struck ill. I had cancer and it was making me so sick. I was very weak and could no longer run my bakeries so I was forced to sell them. I took my money and moved to Vermont to live closer to my family. Just when I was feeling better Henry started to haunt my dreams, which made me sick again. I tried to not sleep so that I would not have to face him. I was almost afraid of seeing him because I wanted to live a different life, to be on my own and see what happened without him for once.

Even though I tried otherwise, once again Henry won my heart and soul when he came to me in Vermont as Adam Lawrence. Adam owned a dress shop in town. He and I would talk as I would take my morning walks. I was still weak but I needed my fresh air and after my walk I would feel a very strong need to walk into a dress shop. Not that I needed dresses, or not that my life would be long enough for me to go out anywhere fancy, but at our first meeting we stared at each other for a very long time. And that was it. We lived my remaining few years together in Vermont. We never married, there just was not enough time.

I returned Home once again before him. And then again when I talked to Ianni I learned Adam was Henry's soul. He had done it again. He had somehow found me and made me fall for him.

After all these memories came flooding back to me I became angry at him for not letting me live my own life. Ever! He has stalked my every move and my dreams for decades. It was not fair for either of us to not live different lives. It was our destinies were, to live other lives, but he could not give me up. I looked at him and he gently let my hand go. His expression changed from happy to see me to nervous and waiting for me to explode.

"You look very unhappy Claire, please let me explain." He had no idea just how unhappy I was.

"You're a soul stalker Henry, or whoever you are. I remember it all. I remember living my life with you and being very happy with you. I loved you very much it is almost unexplainable how I adored you. But you never let me live any other life or love anyone else and that's why I left Home to live and love again. It is what I was supposed to do and you kept me from it. And poor Garrison, how you did that to him. All he did was love me, want to please me and he would have done anything to make me happy. You tricked me! I don't want you to bother me anymore, just leave me alone. You know you're making me sick, I can't sleep and that's affecting my health. I don't want you here go away."

He looked at me as if my words had stabbed him in the heart. The pain he felt I felt as well. I did love this man, I felt it and I remembered it, and telling him to leave me was very hard to do. I just knew it was not in my life path to be with him. I knew it in my soul. I knew he had a path that he had to follow as well.

"How can you say that? After all you just saw. We spent three happy lives together and I made you happy in each one. I never cheated, lied or hurt you in any way. All I ever wanted was to be with you. You don't understand! We are meant to be together, you are my soul mate and I can't be with anyone but you. If we are not meant to be then how do you explain why I always remember you? In every life I have led I start to revive memories. I was ten the first time I remembered you in my second life. That's not normal for a child that young. The feelings get stronger and then I'm drawn to you like a magnet. I try to forget but I can't. I can't love anyone else. "

He sounded so sad. He was right, he did love me and he never hurt me, ever. He was my best friend and lover in every life. He never lied to me, he was always honest and he gave me five beautiful children altogether. This raised a good question for me to ask him.

"How come you haven't tracked the children down like you have me, huh?" He looked almost guilty.

"Well, I check on them from time to time. Some are here and some are at Home. My memories of them don't come to me as fast. They take a little longer. After we are together I can teach you how to look for them if you would like."

"No! I want them to live and not be bothered. I will see them in Heaven when we are reunited. I want to hear about their lives and share stories. That is what I want because I love them so much. I want them to be happy. Don't you just want me to be happy?"

"Please don't ask me that, you know I do, but I can't just stand aside and let you be with someone who is not good for you. Especially when I know I can do better." I had had enough with this. He was acting like a selfish child. I had to get out of here and I didn't know how.

"I want to leave! How do I wake up? I can't talk about this right now. I don't want to anymore. You sound crazy and you're starting to scare me." I wasn't scared but I somehow knew that if

I said that he would leave me alone. Just as I said it he kissed my hand and was gone. I stood in the room all alone. I had a lot going on in my brain. My head started to hurt and I started to cry.

"Don't cry," said a sweet voice.

I looked up and saw Ianni standing in front of me. This time she had ruby red wings. I remembered seeing the same color feather in Dr. Charlie's office and I wondered if she was there checking in on me. She looked so serene and beautiful, as she had at our first meeting. Her dress this time was blue, it was the exact same fit, tight on top and flowing on the body. I felt much better knowing she was there and I knew I could trust her. I have known her for a very long time and she has guided me through so many things. I walked to her and she opened her arms. She covered me with a hug and her wings surrounded my whole body. I felt so warm and safe.

"Avery, you remember it all now don't you?" She asked me.

I nodded and sniffed. I felt drained. My brain had been through too much in this dream.

"Well then you know that he would do anything to be with you. He showed you how much he cares for your soul but you are a different personality this time. You, as Avery, you don't trust anyone. That is due to your father. Lovely man that he was. Landon won't hurt you, you can trust him, his intentions are good, but you can trust Dallas too. I know this for a fact. You need to make a decision, one you make with your heart and soul. Make sure it's the right one for you this time. Now that you have all your information from your past you can go from there. I also still want you to go see Justin and see what he has to say. He is very open with the spirits so you can talk to your mother and this may help you."

I pulled out from her hold and looked into her porcelain face. I had thought she wanted me to stay away from him. But maybe she just wanted me to make my own decision.

"Wait, see Justin? I knew it! You were there in the office. I saw your feather floating in the room. Your feathers changed colors because you were visiting me again. Why did you spy on me then? Did you not trust her?"

"No, I was her. Sorry, but you were really talking to me not Dr. Beamer. I took her body for a while." She bit her lip in shame.

"What! I was not talking with a doctor? I was talking to you the whole time? I thought I had found someone who I could really talk to and she was on my side. You tricked me and lied to me."

Not only was I embarrassed now I was really mad at Ianni. I didn't like being angry with her because she was the one person who has always been there for me but I couldn't help it. My face was hot and I turned my head. I didn't understand her. I remembered her from before, her kindness and her strength, but now she seemed a bit devious. And she was tricking me too. Telling me one minute to stay away from Landon. Then saying he has good intentions.

"Don't be upset with me. I knew that if you walked in there and told her all this," she waved her hand around the room, "that she would surely send you to the nut house. I told you not to go there. I was only trying to protect you and lead you too the right person to help. Justin White. Well, you probably don't remember me telling you because it was in a dream and you don't remember your dreams do you?" I nodded. I didn't remember any dream where she told me not to go see the doctor, or to see this guy Justin.

"As far as Landon, I don't want you to be with him, because it's not what you wanted. You're going to wake up soon so listen to me very carefully. Keep drinking the tea it will help you sleep and connect with me. Go on your dates with both guys and remember Landon will not remember dreaming all this. He disconnected his soul to be here. He will have no idea that this occurred. That's all I can say because I can't tell you your future. Last, but not least, go meet Justin. I have to go and so do you. So, Avery wakeup."

Chapter 8

Trust

My alarm woke me up and I reached over sleepily to shut it off. I sat up and stretched, raising my arms to the ceiling. I felt great. I slept for a full night and I had the Yulu to thank for it. Once I got up I made my coffee and headed to take a shower. I realized that I didn't wake up feeling that horrible impending doom that always ruins my mornings. I felt great for once.

The shower felt more than great it felt terrific. Something about taking a hot shower always made me feel good. When I closed my eyes I tried to remember if I dreamt anything last night, but I couldn't seem to remember a thing which wasn't anything odd for me. I finished up in the shower as fast as I could, even though I didn't want to leave it. Today was going to be a good day. I was off from work this morning. I only had to work a short night shift from eight to midnight. The four hour shifts were courtesy of Kerri. She knew I was having problems sleeping and she wanted to help me out in anyway that she could. This did help me and I was very thankful to her. I wanted to spend the day with my best friend and show her how thankful I was and tell her how I slept like a baby last night. I also had to fill her in on juicy details of Landon and Dallas. I dialed her number and got a sleepy answer on the other end.

"Wake up it's a beautiful day and I want to get some breakfast with you. I have so much to tell you it's unbelievable." There was dead silence so I paused. "Um, Kerri you awake or did you fall back asleep?"

"Nope I'm here I just can't believe you are calling me at eight thirty. What the hell is wrong with you girl?" I did know better than to call her this early. She was notorious for sleeping in on her days off.

"Don't be lazy! Meet me for breakfast at the little café by the library. I will be there in and hour so don't be late." I hung up the phone. I knew she was mad but she would get over it. I sat outside on my balcony watching the people below me. It was nice to sit and people watch sometimes. I drank my coffee slowly because I knew it would take Kerri a while to get ready. I figured I would give her some time.

I finished my coffee, threw on some pants and a tee shirt and left my hair down for once. After all Dallas did say he liked it better down. I came across a tube of lipstick sitting on my dresser. I haven't worn lipstick in years and I had no idea where this came from. I figured it was Kerri's and she left it here. I put it on and the pink shade was actually really complementary for my face. I stared at myself in the mirror for a few seconds. I looked different today, no dark circles under my eyes. I actually looked somewhat attractive. I laughed at myself for even thinking like that.

I left the apartment and walked to the café. It was not a short distance but I needed to stretch my legs. When I got there Kerri was still not there so I put our names in with the hostess and waited outside for her. She was always late but it didn't upset me today. Nothing would ruin my day today.

I felt my leg start to vibrate and I realized that it was my phone going off in my pocket. It was Dallas calling, I got really excited like a little schoolgirl and I took a deep breath before answering.

"Hi," I answered hoping that I didn't sound too excited. I wanted to remain cool and calm.

"Well good morning beautiful. You sound like you're in a good mood today. What are you doing today?"

"Well I'm waiting for Kerri right now, were going to have breakfast. And I think I will go for a walk later. What are you doing awake?" I knew he worked last night and he usually sleeps late when he works.

"I just woke up and I wanted to call you back. Sorry I missed your call last night. It was a busy at work. I missed you though and I wanted to call you." It was incredibly cute how he said he missed me, because I missed him too, but there was no way I was going to tell him that. I wanted to do this the right way and I didn't want to sound too desperate.

"Thank you. Well, it's nice to hear from you." Wow, did I really say that? How dumb did that sound?

"So, you going to come in tonight and have a drink after your shift?"

"We will see. I have to work until midnight, so it all depends on how tired I feel. I will call you if I can't make it."

I saw Kerri's car pull up and I knew I had to get off the phone. I didn't want her to embarrass me while I was on the phone with him. She was notorious for that kind of behavior. I didn't want to end the call though, I wanted to talk to him more, so I decided I would try my best to see him tonight no matter how tired I was. "I have to go Dallas, Kerri just pulled up. But listen I will try to come see you tonight. We are still on for tomorrow, right?"

"Oh yeah we are I just wanted to see you earlier. Is that too much?"

The fact that he was asking me if that was too much to see him twice was a little funny to me. Here was this super attractive man who could have any girl that he wanted, and he was worried about smothering me. I laughed and told him, "No, of course not. Go back to bed Dallas, you seem sleepy. See you later."

We hung up with each other and I had this permanent smile I could not erase from my face. When Kerri walked up she looked at me funny. She probably has never seen me this happy before. I don't think anyone has ever seen me this happy. I felt as if I was dreaming and I was waiting for someone to pinch me and wake me up from this beautiful nightmare.

"Hey you look...um... really good and actually a little sexy. What is with the lipstick and the tousled hair Av?"

"I thought I would be different today so I found this tube of lipstick you left at my place and I borrowed a little. You don't mind do you?" I handed her the tube. I wanted to return it to its rightful owner.

"My lipstick? Sorry that's not mine I don't wear that shade. I only wear Pink Promise. It's all I have ever worn since I started wearing lipstick but you should wear it more often, it looks great on you. Where is your rubber band? What is going on? You need to fill me in on everything!" She grabbed my arm and entwined it with hers and we walked into the café. Our table was ready so we sat and she gave me a "you better start talking" look.

I spilled all the details of the last few days. Leaving out my appointment with the strange Dr. Charlie and her weird referral to a psychic that I have yet to call. During my spilling of my guts all she did was sit and sip her soda, with no interruptions, just focusing on my every word. It must be strange for her to hear me talk about guys when she has always been the one to talk about her boyfriends. After I told her all about Dallas and our kiss and how awesome it was, and about my upcoming date with Landon, of course leaving out the Angel visits and how we were once married, she smiled showing her white perfect teeth.

"I'm so happy for you Av, You have no idea. You totally deserve the best but..." She paused looking down at her plate and bit her lip.

"What, what is it? Kerri what are you not saying?" She was making me nervous.

"Well I was talking to Alyssa, you know the waitress from La Costa? And she said she saw Dallas with another girl last night. He spent the whole night serving her and talking to her. Then he left with her. He drove her home." I felt as if I was going to cry and my stomach turned. Suddenly I felt the pinch I was waiting for and now I was awake and my dream was gone. I pushed my plate away and tears started to well up in my eyes. I was angry and sad I knew this was too good to be true. I was just a game to him. He was trying to play me just like all guys do.

Kerri touched my hand and she gently rubbed it.

"Avery, you know guys like that, they do this all the time. Don't worry you still have that date with Landon. I say ditch Dallas and go for Landon" She was trying very hard to help me out. "You want to leave and go somewhere else?"

"I do, I want to go home." I got up from the table and I scanned the room for the waiter. He came over with the check in his hand. I took it and paid without giving Kerri a simple look or a goodbye. I just left her there sitting alone. I was mad now and I wanted answers. So I knew when I saw him tonight that I would get them.

I started my shift at work later that day and the first thing I did was apologize to Kerri. She did not deserve that from me. I explained how mad I was and she was very understanding. She told me she would be here for me no matter what. Then she proceeded to tell me about a new guy she had met.

"He is so perfect," she gushed. How many times had I heard these words describing a new prospect? Too many to count.

"Well, what's his name?" I asked, even though I didn't really feel like talking. She just met this guy.

"Justin White. He is so cute Av! I think this is it, I think he is the one."

Justin White. Could it be the psychic that the shrink wanted me to see? What was going on in my life? Everyone was linked in this weird way, how much worse could this get? She said she was having a dinner party at her place on Saturday and she wanted me to come meet him. I, of course, did not say no to her after seeing her this excited. I just smiled and told her I would be there with bells on. This made her so happy and that of course was the point, to see my best friend happy.

I did my rounds, which included seeing Mr. Grey. He was happy to see me this time and he told me his sink was clogged and he needed help with the DVD player. I helped him with it all and also sat and watched Titanic with him. He said that it was a great movie and that statement was the highlight of my night. I had almost forgotten about seeing Dallas tonight until I noticed that it was already eleven-thirty.

I left Mr. Grey's apartment. He was a bit sad to see me go, but I told him I would see him on Saturday morning. I did my reports and when I was done it was twelve. So Kerri and I headed to La

Costa to see Dallas.

It was crowded, more than usual tonight, when I saw him serving drinks. I told Kerri to get a table and she did. Dallas spotted me and he waved me over. I was mad and I know it showed on my face. He still looked happy to see me though.

"Hey princess how was work? You look like you need a rum and Coke tonight, am I right?"

"Is that what you called the girl from last night? Princess, or do you call her something else? Alyssa told Kerri everything so cut the crap. I don't want you to call me anymore. And I don't want a drink tonight because I'm here to eat not be at the bar with you." I was so mad I was shaking. And I noticed my words were shaking too. My throat was becoming dry. "As a matter of fact this is the last night I will be here at all." I was going to throw up all over him if I didn't stop yelling at him. He looked at me with serious eyes. And then he started to laugh. How could he laugh right now? What was so funny to him?

"The girl from last night, well she was my Aunt Lisa. She just moved here with her son. She was way too drunk to drive so I drove her home. You should tell Alyssa to get her facts straight before she runs her mouth. Now you want that drink still or not."

I stood there with my mouth wide open and I could feel my cheeks start to burn. I was totally and completely embarrassed. I knew better then to listen to third party stories, I just don't know what came over me. I believed my friend without talking to Dallas in a calm manner first. I nodded and he poured a glass of water instead of my drink and I slowly took sips. Soon the nauseous feeling passed, but not the embarrassed feeling.

"Sit down, I'm afraid you're going to pass out. You do believe me right?"

"Yes, I just feel so stupid. I can't believe..." He interrupted me. "Stop don't blame yourself. You didn't know who she was. I commend you on your boldness, but it wasn't needed Avery, you just need to ask me next time not yell." He was sort of laughing as he said this but I know it had to have flustered him.

"I was yelling, I'm so sorry. You probably want to cancel our date tomorrow don't you?" I searched his eyes for an answer but he was still smiling at me and laughing a little more.

"No, but I want to take you to meet my Aunt Lisa first. She is awesome and I think you would like her. She needs to make friends here. My cousin moved here too. So it would mean a lot to me if you would just have coffee with us first. Is that alright?" I didn't think having coffee would be bad, I just felt nervous about meeting the family already.

"Sure, that sounds okay, is any other family going to be there, like your parents?"

He looked down at the floor and he looked almost disappointed or sad. I noticed his eyes went dark and the light that Dallas always portrayed had disappeared.

"My parents are gone; didn't I tell you that before?"

"No I, um ... I'm sorry." We had something in common both are mothers and fathers were no longer with us. I, at least, knew I could understand what that was like.

"My mom died when I was twelve. And my dad, well, he is dead to me in a different way," I told him.

"Yeah, well I had to bury both my parents two years ago. They were killed by a drunk driver on Christmas Eve. If your father is not dead than you should try to mend it. I'm just suggesting it, I don't know the whole story, but we only get one dad."

I knew what he was trying to say but Dallas didn't know the whole story and I didn't plan on telling him about Richard. In my mind he was dead, just as dead as Dallas' parents. I thanked him for my water and apologized once more for my accusations.

"I don't want you to worry about it just be ready to go by ten, ok?" How could I say no to him? He had just witnessed my super crazy side and he didn't even care.

"You got it! See you in the morning. I better go home and try to get some sleep." I didn't expect a kiss but he jumped over the bar and put his hands on my shoulders and kissed me very sternly, as if to say that he forgave me. I could feel Kerri and Alyssa's eyes burning into my back. I knew they were really confused but not only did I believe him, I would have proof tomorrow when I met his Aunt Lisa.

Kerri walked me out to the parking lot with a puzzled look on her face.

I explained everything to her about his Aunt Lisa and how I would meet her tomorrow. She did not uncross her arms or say any kind words. I knew that she doubted his story but it was not for her to decide. He was my friend and it was our relationship that we were building here. I left my nose out of her relationship drama, so all I could do was ask her to trust me. I drove off and left her standing in the parking lot with her arms still crossed.

Once I got home I took off the lipstick ran a brush through my hair. I jumped into my pajamas and slid into bed. I forgot all about drinking my Yulu tea so I only slept three hours and when I woke up at 4:00 am I was very upset. It was too late to drink it now. That Yulu tea was very strong and I would have slept at least another eight hours. So I turned on the TV and watched some old black and white movie until it ended. What was I to do now? I closed my eyes, forcing them shut. All of a sudden, like a flash in my head, I remembered my dream from my deep slumber the night before.

I sat with my eyes still shut, seeing all the visions that I saw in that dream. I saw Henry and remembered our conversation. I saw Ianni telling me all about how she took over Dr. Charlie's body. Now I was not mad at Landon for coming to me in my dream as Henry, I felt sorry for him. I knew he loved my old souls and all he wanted was to be with me again. When I opened my eyes Ianni stood there in all her blue brilliance at the end of my bed. Now with electric blue wings and her feathers flying around my once clean room.

Chapter 9

Connected

"Why are you here now, how did you know?" I asked her nervously. Just as all my memories from my dream started flooding back to me and I could remember everything. All of my past lives laid out for me to see in my tiny brain. I hoped I could get answers from her. How could all of those lives and all of those emotions not be real? They certainly felt real to me. She had tricked me into believing that Dr. Charlie really understood me. For once in my life I had felt like someone understood me. I also think it was all a trick for her to make me dislike Landon.

"You wanted me here right? You just remembered your dream. It wasn't a dream really, it was a visit from his soul to yours." She moved towards my side of the bed. "While your body is asleep and your brain is dreaming, most times you are visiting those from the past or they are visiting you."

She sat on my bed beside me now and touched my pillow. Her feathers continued to mess up my room but they were so beautiful I didn't really care. I liked the blue feathers on her the best but I knew that it probably was not a look that she preferred. She didn't want to be a rebel, doing all the things that she was told not to do. She was a good Angel. Because of me she did not have her sign of innocence any longer. Her white wings were gone forever.

"I like pillows. They look comfortable are they?" It was the oddest question I had ever been asked.

"Are you asking me about my pillow? That's a little weird. Don't you ever sleep?"

"Don't answer a question with a question. Just tell me. And no I don't sleep. I never have and never will."

"Sorry. I don't know any different so pillows are great to me. So what do you do when I am asleep?" I figured now was the time to ask her the questions I was thinking so much about.

"You're not my only human, Avery. I have many souls that I watch over and guide. You are, though, the only one who has seen me here in person on earth. But you know that right? You know that my wings are a different color because I have been breaking the rules to help you. You talked with Lillith." I looked away and nodded. She didn't look mad she just looked concerned. I didn't really know how deep their rivalry really went but I knew they did not like each other.

"Yes she came to see me and I did really talk with her. She came to tell me about Landon. She did tell me why your wings are different colors. I am sorry that you feel that you need to break the rules. You don't need to keep coming to see me."

"Really, I don't need too? Well thank you very much. Are you dumb girl? You can't handle this on your own. You are not ready yet." I got out of my bed and put on my robe. I was mad that she resorted to calling me names now. She really didn't need to be here if this was what she considered being helpful.

"I didn't mean that, I don't know why I said it. Please sit back down let me explain." She motioned me to the bed and I sat down beside her. I felt a deep connection with Ianni even though I didn't really know her in this life. I understood that she came here to help me see through this strange time and guide me. I understood that before I came here I set out a path for this life and that that path did not include Landon. Not because I didn't love him, but because I wanted to see what the world had to offer. I wanted to fall in love with someone who didn't already know me, but wanted too.

"I don't usually call humans names or act this way. It is happening because I am not so pure anymore. Also, your human influences are starting to seep into my vocabulary. I say and do things I never did before. Like wanting to lie on your pillow. That is something I never cared to do before now. I yearn to be more like a human because I have showed myself to you. It sort of opened up a part of my soul that has never worked before. It is a lot like a punishment to feel this way. So, back to you, why didn't you drink your Yulu last night? You know you need it to sleep."

"I know. I forgot." It was the truth. I had been so preoccupied.

"I prefer talk to you in your dreams. Instead now I have to come here and have rainbow colored wings every time I do. It would be much easier on me if you just drink it. It was really bad of me to take over that doctor's body. I got into a lot of trouble doing that. Once I explained why he understood though." I didn't bother asking her who "he" was. I figured it was another Angel, maybe someone in charge.

"If you knew it was wrong then why did you do it? What was the harm of letting me talk with her? I mean, you think it's better for me to talk to Justin White some freak Psychic who is, by the way, dating my best friend?"

"If you would have told anyone but me what you talked about that day, you would have had a free trip to the insane asylum. Justin is not a freak he can help you connect with someone who you really need to talk to. Your mother." I tried to interject, but she just kept talking. "And that stunt you pulled last night with Dallas, oh my you're so lucky he is still talking to you. He suffered a deep loss and you are the first girl he is letting into his life right now. Please just proceed with caution."

I felt bad all over again for what I did last night. That was so unlike me but I've suffered too and it's hard to trust anyone besides Kerri and Aunt Paulina. Another thing Dallas and I had in common, the fact that trust was an issue. I knew we could learn together to trust and to get over our losses, together as a couple. I was suddenly excited to see him today and it didn't matter that I had to meet his aunt. I was no longer nervous. Ianni must have known what I was thinking about, I could see her looking at me with a grin on her face. I focused back on her and what she came here for. What she felt was so important to visit me for.

"Listen carefully to what I came here to tell you. You are going to meet with Landon soon so there is something you need to know. He does not know who you are in this life. He doesn't know that you were once Claire. He remembers pieces of his past life as Henry and his wife Claire. He was hit with these burdening memories once again at four years old. It was sad. He went through many tests and saw a lot of doctors because his mother acted out of fear. She didn't understand why her son talked so much about Claire. Landon didn't comprehend why he was going through this until he saw Lillith." She sighed rolling her eyes "She came to him when he was older, an adult, and she told him she would help him unravel the memories, but she can't tell him his future and she could never tell him who you are now or where you are exactly. That he had to find out himself. So he made it his mission to find you and he did what he could with the information given. She could give him clues but she is not allowed to tell him too much. Once he finds out everything she can help him revive all the memories from every life you lived together. "

"Wait, when she talked to me she told me that he knew I was here. That he moved here to be with me. And that his cousin knew me." I remembered the short conversation we had in Mr. Grey's bedroom. She told me she would tell him she saw me and how I was and whom I was dating. Ianni broke into my thoughts.

"She was bluffing. She did that to lure you in. You see, if she gets you to go to him and tell him everything, then she doesn't to do it. She thinks if she tells you how much he loves and misses you then you will run to him. You will do all the hard work just like all the times before. This way she wouldn't even have to break the promise she gave as a Guide. If she breaks that promise then she will be expelled and she does not want that. Trust me, she thrives on this kind of stuff. Once you're expelled you serve a different purpose as an Angel. Not one that she wants."

"Why can't she just leave well enough alone and stay out of it?" I asked.

"It's all a game to her. He moved here because he wanted to start a new life, but she put a picture of your town on his desk and he thought it was fate. He flew here and uprooted his whole life. He wants to move on and stop these memories that he has. He felt if he moved to a new town and surrounded himself with new people that he would forget about Claire. He wants to fall in love with someone else. Meeting you on the road, well that was the doing of real fate. Not Lillith, Landon nor I. He liked you and he wants to get to know you. He has no idea that you were Claire. So proceed with caution okay?" I nodded my head and stared at the floor. Ianni slid off my bed and stood in front of me. She lifted my chin so I was forced to be eye to eye with her.

"You must understand what you have to do. It's very important Avery. You hold the key to helping him move on. The ball is in your court. Lillith can't do a thing, her hands are tied."

"I'm just really confused and I don't get all this. Why is this happening right now? I think I'm falling for Dallas. It's what I have wanted for a long time. And now Landon wants to get to know me. That means there is potential for a relationship with someone who my soul knows, wants, and fate apparently wants too. It's a lot to take in first thing in the morning. Then there's you, I feel responsible for all your going through, what you gave up to help me."

"Go see Justin White! Don't worry about me I will be fine. Once we fix all this and help Landon it will go back to normal."

In a flash she was gone. The feathers fell to the ground and I was alone in my room. I lay back down in my bed and rested on my pillow. Never did I feel luckier to have a pillow, as funny as that sounds. I felt a little sad thinking that Ianni witnessed all of the things we see as mundane, and she sees them as things she would like to feel or experience. Being a guide must be lonely to her. She has known her souls for a long time but we don't really know her. We live our lives and never know that we are being taken care of or led through our life. The only time we see her is in our sleep. And half the dreams we have we never remember anyway. I felt special that she broke the rules to show herself to me.

I spent the rest of the morning thinking about Ianni's words and how they started to make a little sense to me. Landon didn't know me as Avery and that was reassuring. Poor Landon's life has been haunted by, well, me. He should not be remembering me he should be living his life as Landon and not Henry. I felt like it was now important for me to show him that Henry is in the past and he needs to let go of it. I understood what I needed to do but it had to wait because today was about Dallas.

I rushed out the door, throwing my little blue cardigan on as I walked down the stairs. I decided to dress nicely today since I wanted to impress not only Dallas but his family as well. I choose a blue and green dress that Kerri had bought me for my birthday. It was not my style but as I tore off the tags I felt like it was time to try something different.

The drive to Dallas' place was short and I was impressed with his neighborhood. It had a family like atmosphere that made me feel comfortable. I saw the house number but thought maybe I had turned on the wrong street because this big brown home that sat on the end of the street was too big for a lonely bachelor to call home. When I saw his truck and bike in the driveway and I knew that I was at the correct address. "How does a bartender afford such an elaborate home?" I asked aloud, to myself. When I reached the door it opened and Dallas stood on the other side wearing a big smile for me.

"And here she is, Princess Avery."

"Stop, you're going to embarrass me."

"Oh come here and stop being silly." He grabbed me and held me tight in his arms. He smelled amazing and his arms felt like they would never let me go.

"Are you ready to meet my aunt? She's on the deck outside and we just started the coffee and breakfast," he said. "Aunt Lisa is excited to meet you, so no need to be nervous."

"You can tell can't you? Well, let's do it," I said all the while trying to hold my composure. He led me through his foyer and through the dining room to the deck. The backyard had clean cut grass, bright colored flowers and a swimming pool with an attached Jacuzzi. I could never, in my wildest dreams, imagine

Dallas living here. It was not what I expected, in fact it was much more than I expected. His aunt's blonde hair was hard to miss as she sat at a glass patio table that was covered with all sorts of breakfast foods. Fresh fruit, eggs, toast, waffles, pancakes, hash browns and three kinds of juice. She looked up at me and she had kind eyes, a lot like Dallas.

She stood and greeted me, "Nice to meet you finally Avery, I'm Lisa." I shook her hand and we both sat.

"Wow look at this setting Dallas, did your aunt do all this?" I asked jokingly.

"No, I did it," he answered. "I do all the cooking. I love to cook its kind of my passion. Once I'm done with my classes I want to start my own restaurant."

It was then that I realized how much I still needed to learn about Dallas. All along I thought he was just a lonely bartender and here he was, cooking all morning and dreaming of doing it for a living. All my preconceived notions were off.

"He makes the best waffles! Try them honey," Lisa said as she started me a plate. I could see why Alyssa thought he was flirting with some beautiful girl. Lisa looked very young. She had long blonde hair and beautiful brown eyes. She could pass for at least thirty. I secretly hoped I would look just as good as she does someday.

She and I started to talk. We had a nice conversation, talking mostly about her move her to California and how much she is thankful to Dallas for giving her somewhere to stay. She was very delightful and easy to talk to. She did mention how she drank too much at La Costa the other night and how she had to be driven home. As she said it I looked at Dallas and he had a big smile on his face. He was telling the truth and I breathed a little better now. After about an hour Lisa excused herself and said she wanted to go into town and do a little shopping.

Now it was just Dallas and I enjoying the warm day and the sunshine. We sat in silence, not an awkward silence but because we were comfortable with each other.

"Well, I have to ask, how you afford this house and the vehicles. I just don't get it." I said shamefully. I felt like I was being rude by asking him about his finances.

"This was my parents' house that they bought after I left for college. When they died they left it to me, along with the motorcycle. That was my dad's toy. The truck was always mine. The house is a bit much for just me right now but I hope to fill some rooms with family someday."

I swallowed my pancake and took a sip of juice. I couldn't hide my smile. This was all very reassuring, that he really wanted a serious relationship.

"I want to learn more about you. Like what you studied in college, what you were like in high school. I don't even know your last name," I told him.

"I can answer all that for you but before I do let's put all this in the house and get going to the garden. I have a few surprises for you."

I grabbed all the plates I could and we walked into the house. Once I stepped in, I looked up and saw someone standing in the kitchen. I dropped all the plates on the floor. Food flew everywhere and so did glass. Dallas pulled me back so I didn't step on any.

"I'm sorry Dallas, I don't know why I did that," I lied. I did it because Landon was in Dallas' kitchen eating a bowl of cereal.

"Hey don't worry about it! Let me clean it up. You sit down, Landon and I got this." He led me to a barstool at the counter and he grabbed a broom and some paper towels. "Oh, I'm sorry. This is Aunt Lisa's son Landon, Landon this is Avery my um my, friend," he said with a nervous tone.

He didn't know what to call me and I didn't want him to call me his girlfriend, not to Landon. I was in a very deep predicament here. I have dates with both guys on different days and they end up being cousins. Not to mention Landon is my old husband. I wanted to run away and never show my face again. Landon smiled at me and he helped clean up the floor.

"I'm going to take this glass to the outside trash I'll be right back," Dallas said.

Landon continued to clean the floor and he never looked into my eyes.

“I didn’t know you were cousins,” I finally said.

“Yeah, it’s a small world I guess. So I guess were not on for our date. That sucks.” He looked almost sad. I didn’t know what to say, my mouth didn’t seem to work right. I watched him clean my mess and never once did he look up at me or say another word. When he walked out of the room Dallas came in.

“Okay clumsy let’s get out of here before it’s too late. Let me tell my cousin goodbye.” He led me down the hallway into Landon’s room. It was quite large with a desk, at which he sat, a bed, two dressers and a walk in closet that had hardly any clothes. I saw his leather jacket lying on the bed. The same one he wore the day we met. It had looked so nice on him. I felt completely horrible, yet I felt good. Happy to see him and view him as a harmless man rather than some crazy stalker. At the same time I seemed like a player to him and that was not my intention.

“Landon, I will be out for a while so if you need me give me a ring okay?” Landon nodded and continued looking at his computer. Dallas walked out of the room and I followed like a lost puppy. When I looked back Landon looked up at me and smiled. I smiled back and left the room. We got into Dallas’ truck and I felt like I should have said something more to Landon. What kind of an idiot I was to say so little? He was obviously upset that we would not be going out together and I remembered what Ianni had told me about him wanting to move on with his life and start over. Even though I was whom he wanted to escape from, he didn’t know that. Now I wanted so bad to know him and see what kind of person he was this time. I was falling right back into the same trap.

Chapter 10

Stars

"Uh, I think I left my cell phone inside, I'm going to run in and get it." I didn't even wait for a response. I just left the truck and ran into the house. My heart was racing, what was I thinking? I ran into Landon's room and as I pushed open the door I started to tell him that I really still wanted to show him around the town and that there was no harm in that. But my words got lost when his lips met mine. He kissed me and wrapped my hair in his fingers. My body went warm, my head spun, and I felt weak and helpless. We kissed for several seconds before he pulled away. When he did I didn't want to open my eyes. I wanted to stay right here forever. I felt a spark of fireworks through my whole body.

"Is that okay that I just did that?" He asked me.

"Yes, I think so." I felt my face turn red. "I came back in here to tell you that I will still show you around town if you want." He laughed at me although I wasn't sure why.

"Well I couldn't help myself. I have not been able to get you out of my head since we met. This may sound weird to you but I really like you."

"Why would that be weird?" I asked. I knew it was weird I just wanted to play it cool.

"Because we only met once. How is it that I feel this way? I don't even know you. Dallas is crazy about you. It would break his heart if he knew about this," he said as he pointed from me to himself.

"Well, I don't like to keep secrets but I don't think this is something we are going to share." And just as I said that he kissed me again. All the same fireworks went off and I had to push him away. "Dallas is waiting for me I have to go. I will see you Wednesday." I ran back outside hopped into the truck. I pulled my phone out of my pocket pretending that I had found it, when really it was there all this time. I didn't feel guilty at first, I was feeling the high still from our kiss and I didn't want that to end.

We arrived at the botanical garden and that's when the guilt hit me like a ton of bricks, all at once. I felt like I could not breath, but I knew I had to get through it and enjoy the time I had left with Dallas. Because once he found out, I would never see him again. What I had done was unforgivable! He stopped the truck at the entrance and got out to open my door. Once he left the cab of the truck I sucked in as much air as I could, suffocating in my own guilt, making me feel sick. When he opened my door I let all the air out and decided to push Landon to the back of my mind.

We walked around the gardens and I tried to let the beauty embrace me. He seemed to know a lot about plants and flowers because he told me more about every species. I learned all about how the botanical garden was started and how he had donated several thousand dollars to it when his parents died. He was proving to be much more responsible than I even imagined. Once he touched on the subject of his parent's death he sat down at a stone bench that was surrounded by magnolias.

"These were my mother's favorite flowers. She was the kindest woman I have ever met. She taught me that everyone makes mistakes and it takes a kind heart to forgive. It took me years to learn how to be so strong."

I gulped at the word forgive. I wondered if she were alive what she would think of me and what I had done.

"So you want to know more about me? Here are the facts, born here and went to school here. Left for college, went to USC and studied business management. I didn't graduate though." As he said this he looked down at his feet like he was ashamed. His cheeks seemed to burn a deep red.

"Hey, I didn't even go to college. I'm just lucky to have graduated high school. So at least you were able to experience it." I hoped my failure helped him in some way.

"Business management was not for me, at least back then. I was too busy with the party scene." I could see a younger Dallas drinking from a keg and partying like a young college kid does. It sort of made me laugh picturing him like that.

"But now I would love to go back, to learn it all over again. What I did learn will help me in the long run if I open up my own place. Cooking school is done this June and Landon is going to help me start up the business. He owns his own business and he is really smart. He lived in New York and he bought and sold a lot of property. He has the experience, let me tell you." When he said his name I felt the guilt come back and I wanted to talk about anything else but I didn't want to be rude.

"Well, you will do just fine I know it." I smiled reassuringly.

He held my hand and looked into my eyes. I did feel so comfortable with Dallas but I still had the feeling of Landon's kiss lingering on my lips.

"Cooper is my last name, by the way. You said you wanted to know it. I know yours is Snow, right? Like Snow White." I just laughed and nodded. Cooper was a name that haunted my head and dreams, Lucy's voice speaking it. It made my skin cold. Why did his last name have to be Cooper? Why not Johnson or Jones?

We had our picnic shortly after even though I was still full from breakfast. I did not want to hurt his feelings so I ate a small tuna sandwich and some fruit. Our conversation mostly stuck to our pasts and Dallas' mom and dad. It seemed to me like he needed someone to talk to about them so I was more than happy to listen.

But once he was done talking he looked at me and he asked me the worst possible question.

"So, how would you feel about being exclusive, you know seriously serious about each other? I don't want to see anyone but you. What do you think?"

I didn't speak at first, which made his face turn from excited to confused. What was I to say? I did want to be with him but that was before today and my encounter with Landon. Once I kissed him I wanted nothing more than to stay with him and never leave his side. His pull was strong and I could feel it even from here. I had done a complete turnaround with my feelings and I felt sick to my stomach. I had to tell him something.

"You know I feel the same about you, I just have a hard time with trust."

"I know it took you forever to start talking to me when I first met you. Once you told me about your dad being dead to you, I put it all together. You have a large wall around you but I will try to push it over for as long as it takes. I don't know what your dad did, but I am not him." He rubbed my back and we sat in silence watching the birds and the chipmunks in the garden.

When I got home I threw myself on my couch, but as soon as I did I felt a rush of cold air blow past me. I stood up expecting to see either Ianni or Lillith but no one was there. I went into my kitchen and the coast was clear. I was exhausted so I made my tea, just to make sure I got enough sleep. As I sipped it I watched the TV and found nothing interesting on. That was okay because I felt myself drifting off. All I had the strength to do was to shut off the TV and it was goodnight to me.

My day had been so strange and I just wanted to escape the guilt that I was feeling. I hated myself for what I did to Dallas. He could possibly be the most perfect guy for me and I was throwing it all away for someone I really didn't know. I did have a wall up, Dallas was right, but for some reason Landon didn't even have to earn my trust or try to break through the wall. I just let it down for him like it was nothing. But for Dallas I was making him jump hurdle after hurdle for my love. I felt so sick I just closed my eyes and tried to fall asleep as fast as I could.

I was now in that dreamland, same as before. The bedroom was the same and the big door was wide open. He stood there gazing out the window into a blank sky. I stood watching him for what seemed like forever before he noticed I was there. He turned around and smiled at me, showing his gleaming white teeth. This time he was Landon. I glanced at my reflection in the mirror and I was Emily, the woman who I was in my second life. He took my hand and kissed it and stared into my eyes with such remorse. He looked sad and teary eyed.

"I'm so sorry my love but I have met another. Please do not hate me, but I am feeling something between us that I cannot deny. I have looked for you for so long but I think that it is best that we stay apart. My heart aches and I cannot go through this anymore. This girl, she is special. Complicated, but special."

I could sense the torment that he was going through. He had searched for me for a long time and he felt he could not do it anymore. He just wanted to do what was best for himself and his life. I just nodded my head, acknowledging that I understood him, but I could tell this was not enough for him. He wanted to hear that it was okay for him to pursue someone who he thought was someone else. How could I not tell him that the girl he wanted was his beloved Emily? I would be leading him straight to me and he would now pursue me even harder. I had to tell him to stay away from me, Avery. And I knew just what to say.

"Landon, you must do what you have to do to be happy. But something tells me that this woman is not yours is she?"

My idea had to work, I had to let Landon know that Claire or Emily or whoever I used to be wanted him to move on but not with his cousin's girlfriend. I knew he would listen to me as Emily.

"No, she is not. That's what I meant by complicated. She is with someone else, but I don't think she is happy with him. She kissed me and that led me to believe she wants to be with me too."

"No Landon, it was a kiss, a stupid kiss. She regrets it because she doesn't want to hurt her boyfriend. She didn't mean to kiss you but you just looked so gorgeous and she felt that she should kiss you. Maybe to see if there was something there? But there wasn't. It was a mistake. Please remember what you did to Garrison. Because of you and I falling in love because of a simple kiss he took his own life. We did that to him."

I saw visions of Garrison in my head, of his face when I told him I fell in love with someone else. Garrison was such a sweet and caring man who would have moved earth to fight for me but I ended it there and told him to not follow me. He took his own life shortly after. I know that Landon could see these visions too. He felt simply horrible that Garrison had done that and that we were the reasons why he did. I could see the pain in his blue eyes. He was holding back the tears and biting his lip. He turned and wiped his eyes thinking that I could not see this.

"No, you don't understand. She felt a spark because I felt it too. I know your mad my love, I'm so sorry. I will see you again someday but this is the last time I will visit you here. I just can't do this anymore. Do you know what it's like to be like this? Searching for you. People think I'm crazy, yeah my whole family. I have not one friend. I don't have time to settle down and make them." He had turned back to face me, his hair falling into his eyes. He was so gorgeous it made me crazy.

"All I do is look for you and it's exhausting. Lillith can only tell me so much. It's not enough to find you this time. I'm sorry. Lillith is being punished too much for what she is telling me. I have to go, please forgive me."

His voice was shaky and he walked toward me and kissed my cheek. I knew now that it was a hard life for him to search for me all these lifetimes and he was doing it all thinking that I wanted him to find me. When this time I didn't want him too. Unfortunately, now that he has found me I want him so bad it hurts my soul.

"I understand Landon. I'm so sorry that you have felt that you need to find me. You don't need to anymore. You do need to think about your family though and how much they care about you. Don't do anything that would break that."

He turned and left. I hoped that he understood what I was trying to tell him. I was left there in this room that was now turning dark and cold. I was now outside under a full night of stars. It felt so real and so peaceful. I wondered why I would dream this when all I had to do was walk outside. Nonetheless I watched the stars and saw a few of them fall. Watching the stars was the simplest thing I could be doing in a dream and it was better than seeing old lives unfold before me. I sighed and felt so light, like I could just fly. I started to float and it felt so real. I could touch the stars and they felt like air. It was starting to get chilly so I reached for my covers and pulled them onto my sleeping body. My dream self was now nice, warm, peaceful and thinking of only one person. Landon.

Chapter 11

Letting it Go

Only thirty minutes until I had to meet with Landon and I was still not dressed. Filing through my closet and tossing clothes around my room. Every shirt I pulled out was stained or just plain ugly. Finally I came across a purple polo that I thought might be okay. I pulled it over my head and it was way too loose and baggy. I had lost so much weight recently, mostly due to stress and insomnia. I tossed the shirt into the "No" pile and I sat on the floor in my underwear.

As I bit my thumbnail down to nothing I could not figure out what the hell to wear. When my head turned I saw a dress hanging in the back of the closet that I must have missed. It was a black short-sleeved dress with a sweetheart neckline. There was nothing like a little black dress to fix the problem. I slipped it on and it was more than perfect, simple yet sexy. I ran down the stairs and fumbled for my keys to unlock the car. I drove to the coffee store and I saw him pulling up in his old woody car. I laughed when I saw it, shocked that it was still running. When I got out of the car I felt sick to my stomach. It was probably the guilt taking over my body, but today I felt like it was the day for me to get to know Landon for who he is now.

As for Dallas, well I would have to deal with that later. I never exactly told him yes about being exclusive and this was just coffee and chocolate, not anything too serious. Dallas did say that Landon is lonely and doesn't have any friends. That's what I was, a friend. A friend who kissed him passionately and was married to him several times, but I was going to put and end to that today.

He stood there with his hands in his jean pockets wearing a simple red t-shirt, jeans that hugged every inch of his legs and Adidas sneakers. He looked at me and he smiled shyly, rocking his feet back and forth until I came closer. Then he hugged me with one arm and kissed the top of my head. He kept his arm around me and opened the door with the other. He led me in and pulled a chair out for me. I felt so special and I could not wipe the smile off my face. I could see the stares from a group of girls in a corner with their coffee. They were practically drooling at the sight of him. He was breathtakingly beautiful, but totally oblivious to it.

His blue eyes peered into mine as he leaned into my face. I held my breath afraid of the kiss that I felt was coming. How could I resist? I wanted it just as bad as I did the other day.

Thankfully he did not lean in to kiss me, he just wanted to know what kind of coffee I wanted. I laughed thinking how dumb I was acting and how this all looked on the outside.

"I will have a mocha latte please. That's all."

"What, no chocolate? This is coffee and chocolate," he teased. "How about I pick the chocolate and I will be right back?" I nodded and smiled.

While he ordered our coffees and sweets I looked out the window at the people walking by. Just watching people was calming sometimes and I needed to do something calm. My nerves were on edge. I was so afraid of someone seeing us here and telling Dallas. I was guilt ridden. Dallas was in my thoughts, he was so special to me. I just couldn't tell Landon no. But I was here today to clear it all up. I had to do it, it was up to me to tell Landon the truth. From what I had learned from my last dream about him was he did not have any clue that I was his past wife. The same wife he told that he could not be with because he wanted his life back. I did not like knowing all of this. I wished I could go back to the old days where I knew nothing. No Spirit Guides, no past lover, no dreams and goodness knows what else is coming my way. I had been a bad friend to Kerri these last couple of months. She deserved better. An honest explanation as to why I was so distant and I knew I had to tell her everything.

He came back to the table with two hot latte's and a box with several mixed chocolates. I had to put all of my thoughts away and focus on our conversation for now.

"Dig in," he suggested, pushing the box towards me.

There was something about Landon that was still so serious and strange to me. He was not like Dallas; he wore his heart on his sleeve and was not afraid to do so. Even though his sleeve was covered with all sorts of tattoos.

Landon was shy and mysterious. You could say the bad boy type, although he was not a bad boy at all. His eyes were kind and truthful and I knew his soul very well. It was the best soul ever. So good, in fact, that I fell for it in every life.

"Well we need to talk about the other night," he said as he held my hand from across the table. As soon as he touched me I saw a vision.

Emily and Cooper Shade swinging from a porch swing watching the sun set on a mountain in the distance. He was gently rubbing my hand with his. Keeping his eyes fixed on the setting sun. Then he started to sing, "You are my sunshine, my only sunshine. You make me happy when skies are gray. You'll never know dear how much I love you please don't take my sunshine away." We watched our two children play tag in the field in front of us. My heart sank and felt as if it filled with lead. I couldn't possibly feel anymore love than I did at that moment. A feeling of being complete and satisfied with life and all of its many ups and downs. I looked my husband in the eyes and smiled. He seemed to know what I was going to say when he said, "I love you too my sweet."

Landon let go of my hands abruptly and almost threw them across the table. He had a twisted look on his face. He saw what I saw or he could have seen something different, but I know he saw something. He shook his head as to remove it from his brain.

"What is it, headache?" I asked.

I figured the best thing was to act as if I knew nothing. Not sure if that was the best thing to do or not. If I told him the truth he would never move on and forget about me.

"Um, yeah I think it's the latte getting to me. Caffeine overload. Any how we have a predicament. Dallas is my cousin and I do not want to hurt him. He has done so much to help me, you have no idea." Actually I did I knew everything but I kept mum and just listened. Nodding my head and drinking my latte. "He is head over heels in love with you Avery. And you and I barely know each other. To be fair we were wrong in what we did and it can't happen again. I can't hurt my cousin, my blood like that."

I felt shocked that he actually said the words. I thought it was me who would have to be the one to say this but no it was him. He must have changed his mind since our last dream together. Even though he was absolutely right I still felt hurt. I had to say goodbye to him. For good. Could I resist the strong temptation, the urge to be with him? It was like a magnet was pulling me toward him. I was being told to stay away from him by Ianni and to be honest it was making me more curious, and now he is telling me we can't be together.

"You're right. Dallas is very special to me. I'm in love with him too." Wow I actually said it and meant it. It was a strange feeling to be in love with two people. One person I was getting to know and trust and he felt the same for me. The other I knew so deep in past lives and not even a little in this life. His touch so familiar yet distant but I could say I was in love with this man. So in love it touched my soul.

"Then why are you here with me? Why did you kiss me?" He seemed mad. Led on was he? Well so was I. Now I was pissed. He was starting to accuse me of being the main kisser. No way was he the one who pursued me and he kissed me first.

"You kissed me too, let's not forget. I don't know why I kissed you. I guess I was attracted to you, I felt drawn to you and we had been talking on the phone for a while," I paused took a deep breath and continued my speech. "I wanted to kiss you the day I met you, like I want to kiss you now. It's an urge I feel inside me. I came here today to tell you that I can't see you again. I know now what I want and it's Dallas. Like I said, I love him. We were wrong."

I tried to act calmly as to not draw too much attention to us. Here we were arguing about a kiss. One stupid, terrific kiss. I guess that's all it can take to change someone.

His expression changed from mad to sad. His hard face looked sorrowful. My heart hurt. I wanted him to love me and I wanted to love him for all my life but I knew that this was the wrong feeling and I had to let him go. For Dallas and for myself. Dallas was the man I was in love with in this life and I would not ruin that. Not for lust and not for my past. The past had to die. Dallas deserved someone to be with who was true to him. I was going to be that woman. I had to shut this feeling for Landon off like a switch. I stood up stared him in the eye, looking into the soul of my past lover, friend and husband and I walked out of the coffee shop.

As I walked to my car he followed. I tried to not turn back to look at him but he grabbed my arm and turned me around to face him.

"Wait this is what we both want, right? Just let me go Landon. I can't do this to Dallas. He loves me and I love him. You know that it is the right thing to do. I see the pain in your eyes. I have to go." I yanked away from him and got into my car. I rolled down the window to say goodbye again when he said the most unexpected response.

"Are you going to pretend forever Avery that you don't feel it or remember me?"

I gulped and tried to keep a calm face as my hands now started to shake.

"Feel what Landon, an attraction? Yes I do but like you said I don't even know you." I tried to divert.

"Oh yes you do. You have known me for a long time. I know you know that. You saw it today, didn't you, when I touched you? You saw our life, our kids and you saw our love. How can I let you go when I have searched for you all my life and now here you are right in front of me? My sunshine." Our song, the song he sang to me on the porch. I remembered everything. Every moment flashed into my head. He used to call me his sunshine. He knew, he knows. What was I going to say?

"You sound very confused. You just told me you can't do this to your blood and now you want to do it. You need some real help. Just let it go, let us go. I love someone else and I can't do this again to another person. I don't want to remember anymore. I want my life to go back to normal again. I just want to be without this drama. I am a different person this time." I was practically screaming at him.

"So it is you. Wow, all this time here you are. You did see it didn't you? What about the first time we met did you see that too?" He asked me.

I thought about our first meeting and the vision I saw of me in my wedding dress. I nodded. He started to get tears in his eyes. I did as well. I didn't know this would be so hard, to say goodbye to my past life that I didn't even really know anymore. I was not those women any longer. I'm Avery Snow now and I love Dallas.

"I have to go, I have something to do. Landon you have to let go. You and I both know that is the best thing to do so that no one else gets hurt. He is your cousin and you said it yourself, he loves me. Isn't that enough to know that I will be taken care of by someone who loves me?"

He slowly, with caution, reached for my hand and he leaned in my window to brush my hair away from my ear and whisper, "I will follow you to the end of forever. I love you more than anyone or anything. I will never lose hope and I will always remember our vows but I will let you go for now."

Chills ran over my body. I rolled my window up and drove to work. I had to talk to my best friend and I had to talk to her boyfriend.

I arrived at Sunrise Estates and my eyes were burning with tears. I felt like I would never stop crying. The vision of Landon with tears in his eyes made me want to turn around and say I was sorry for hurting him but I knew I had to be the bad guy this time and just stay away. I had to talk to Kerri about it all. Even though she would think this all is not true and that I was truly crazy. Just then my phone rang and it was Aunt Paulina. Oh how I didn't want to answer this phone right now.

"Hi Aunt Paul what's up?"

"Just getting ready to go to lunch, I have a date." She sounded elated.

"Wow, good for you. I can't talk right now. I want to hear details, but later though, okay? Will you call me later?"

"Sure will! Love you Avery." She hung up. I felt bad for being so mean just now but I really didn't want to talk about things like that at this moment. I needed my friend.

There she sat at her desk looking as beautiful as ever. My best friend who I had been treating like a simple stranger lately and she did not deserve that. She looked up with her glasses hanging on the end of her nose. She smiled at me and I felt so much better. I walked right into her office and slumped down in the chair. I was drained of all emotion and I felt so exhausted.

"Why on earth are you here on your day off?" She asked with eyebrows arched.

"What can I say? I missed you."

"No Avery, really what's up? You look nice by the way. Did you and Dallas have a date this morning?" Oh boy did I have a lot to tell her. Where would I start? How do I explain all the unbelievable details? She was my best friend and I knew she would stand by me but whether or not she would believe me that I do not know. Just as I opened my mouth to try to explain her cell phone rang. The ring tone was the sound of a rainforest. It was very relaxing. She put her finger up at me as a sign to hold my thought.

"Hello stranger...." Her voice went very sultry. That was my sign to exit the office. I didn't want to hear her conversation with Justin or whoever it was on the other line. So I walked over to see Mr. Grey. He was out in the corridor watching the birds on the ground as he threw small bits of bread for them to eat.

"Hi," I said as I sat next to him. He always made me feel a little better. He was like an escape to normality, a fresh perspective of life and a view of my possible future. Alone.

"Oh, its you. I thought you had the day off my dear. Why are you here, surely not to visit me?"

"No, just here to visit with Miss. Louse." I always referred to Kerri by her last name. I felt it was more professional. "Feeding the birds huh, that's awfully nice of you."

"Yeah I suppose. I was in a being nice kind of mood today," he said. He turned back to his birds and continued to give them bread. One thing about Mr. Grey was that he was quiet and talking was not necessary in his world. I sat with him for a while in silence. I closed my eyes and leaned back into the bench. It was peaceful.

"Avery, I'm done with my call. I can talk to you know," Kerri said from the main office door. So much for the peaceful silence. I told Mr. Grey goodbye and went back into the office with Kerri.

"Wow Av, I have so much to tell you. Justin is so perfect. He is the one, I just know. I can see it, you know, I just know." Her grin was bigger than any I had ever seen on her face. I knew it was her time right now to tell me all about her last few weeks and my news, if I would call it that, would have to wait.

I let Kerri talk all about Justin and his romantic ways, sending flowers, cards, and fruit baskets every day. His sweet text messages and how he professed his feelings for her just this morning when she left his house. She didn't care that he was a psychic and she actually felt that it helped her to feel more trusting with him, since he bared his secret to her. I started to feel like maybe Justin White was not as bad as I thought. If he made Kerri feel this happy, then I was all for it. She carried on for at least an hour and I was just a happy listener. My duty as a best friend. After she was done spilling all her news she asked me how Dallas was.

"Great, um, he really likes me and I think I feel the same. So it's all good right?" She smiled. I smiled back, hiding the sadness that now dwelled in my soul for Landon. Would this feeling go away? Boy I hoped so. Knowing that Kerri's party was only two days away, I told her I couldn't wait to get to know Justin better and that Dallas would be there with me, even though I knew he would be working on a Saturday night.

"Wow Avery, we're finally happy like we deserve. I think Dallas and Justin will get along, don't you?"

"Oh most definitely. Listen Kerri, I hate to leave but I got to go, so see you tomorrow for my shift." We hugged and then I left.

Now I knew for sure that she was not mad at me for being distant and she was being taken care of I felt better. I had to see Dallas and tell him how I felt. He had been waiting long enough for an answer.

I pulled up to the house and I saw his truck and bike in the driveway but I did not see Landon's old car. I sighed with relief and I walked to the door. I knocked and there was no answer for a while. After several knocks Lisa came to the door.

"Oh, Avery. Hi honey come on in. We are in the backyard and didn't hear the door. Boy, don't you look pretty today." I blushed and tried not to feel too embarrassed. I entered the house and I saw boxes lining the entryway.

"Unpacking?" I asked

"No, unfortunately not. Packing up is more like it."

"You're leaving?" I felt sad, I barely knew her but yet I didn't want to see her go.

"No, not me Landon. He is moving out into his own place. I told him Dallas has the room and there is no need to go but you know how boys can be. He found a great two bedroom apartment right on the bay. It's really beautiful. Nice view. I think Dallas said it was near your apartments."

So he was moving out and closer to me. Great, now I had to constantly be seeing him. I hoped not. I could not stand to see his broken soul any longer. Maybe his apartment would be on the other side of the bay and nowhere near mine.

"Really, huh. What is the name of the building?" I tried not to sound so forceful but I'm sure it came out that way.

"Well you know I can't really remember exactly, but I think it was Green something or other."

"Bayside Green Apartments?"

"Oh yeah that's it. How did you know?" She laughed and led me into the kitchen through to the backyard, not knowing that Bayside Green Apartments is where I live. He had to have known that I lived there. I remembered his last words to me that he would follow me to the end of forever.

Chapter 12

Dedrick

Dallas was swimming in his pool when he looked up and saw me standing on the deck. He leapt out and his body was incredible. I got to see every tattoo he had and I never knew there were so many but I giggled inside feeling like I had won some sort of prize. He was absolutely the most perfect guy. He looked like a real tough guy with all those tattoos, even though he was a big softy.

He wrapped a towel around his waist and came over to me. His dimples were showing and his smile was gleaming. He was happy to see me, that much I could tell for sure. He hugged me and got me all wet but I didn't care one bit. When I was with him I felt like there was no one else. No Angels following me, no past haunting me, it was just him and I.

"I came here to talk to you. You have a minute?"

He froze and seemed like I had just wounded him. He was expecting bad news already. He led me into the house and up the stairs into his room. It was immaculate and very preppy, a blue and white Tommy Hilfiger plaid bedspread with matching drapes. His furniture was polished and neat. There was a blue rug on the floor and his shoes were neatly lined along his bed. He sat me on his bed and coughed, I guess to clear the air.

"Well," I started. "Something happened that I think you should know. It's only fair to you and I want you to please keep an open mind and not get angry." He nodded. "I met your cousin Landon before last week. I was driving to work and he was broken down on the road so I stopped to help him. He gave me his number and we have been talking on the phone on and off. He asked me out for coffee and if I could show him the town. Then you and I started to see each other. To be fair we were not committed yet, so I agreed. Then I saw him here and I found out who he was. When I came back in to get my cell phone, we sort of kissed. It was just a kiss, and I'm sorry it happened. We met today at the coffee shop and both agreed that we do not feel anything for each other. I told him I'm in love with you, and he told me he would never hurt you." I stopped to breathe. I could not believe that I had told him all of this. I had also admitted that I was falling in love with him. He looked shocked and said nothing. I think it was all a bit overwhelming.

"I came here today to tell you the truth. I'm not a liar and I do not keep secrets. If we are to start being serious with each other I wanted to tell you first off. Without you finding out later. I really do feel love for you and I don't want to be with anyone else. You are what I have wanted for so long and it's like a dream. I came here to be honest and that is what I did. Now please think it over."

I got up to leave and he did not try to stop me. He just sat there staring at the bed. Never looking up at me as I left the room.

When I got home there were no messages on my voicemail, and no missed calls. I was so mad at myself in a way, but proud in others. I told him the truth but my heart ached and I felt so sad that he did not at least care that I was honest. Not only had I lost Dallas now because of my stupid mistake, I let Landon go as well. I was such a mess lately. Yes I was sleeping now and I was no longer a walking zombie but my so-calle-life was in shambles. My best friend couldn't know about my situation nor could my aunt. After them there was no one else to talk to about it. Except for Ianni. She was no help to me even though she knew me more than I knew myself. Ugh. All she says is go see Justin White.

I made my Yulu tea and just smelling its aroma calmed my nerves. I realized that my supply was getting low. I would need to stock up soon. I could hear rain hit my windows. A storm had hit. My lights went out. They only went out for a couple seconds but it was long enough to scare me. I ran into my room and turned on the TV while I lit a few candles, but not too many because I didn't want to burn down my apartment. The ambiance was kind of relaxing. I lay there, mindlessly watching TV yet thinking of my day. The worst day besides the day mom died. It was like my heart was ripped in two. I felt a horrible sadness today, one I haven't felt in many years. Maybe Ianni was right about speaking to mom. Maybe she could help me. Maybe she could just be there for me, as she should have been in times like this. I started to cry. I mourned my mother tonight. I thought of her touch and loving side that I missed. I didn't see it too often, but when I did it was comforting. When Richard left she became tough. Her trusting embrace fell, much like my trusting side. Who was I to put up a wall? Look what I did to Landon and Dallas, I led them on. I did just what my ex did to me. Who was I to play these games with these two incredible men? Look at me. I was no one. Just some plain Jane with a dagger ready to rip your soul in half. My tea was now cool enough to drink but one sip and it was goodnight Avery. I laid my head on my pillow and felt a tear run down my face.

The room was different this time. Cold and gray instead of welcoming. Landon was not here and neither was Ianni. I sat on the bed and dust flew around me. I coughed feeling it in my lungs. I looked out into the night and there were no stars this time. A cold chill ran across my neck. I turned and found no one behind me. I wondered if this room was in my old home with Landon.

"Ianni please come. I need you tonight. Where are you?" I called out. Silence. Then I heard a sound. It was piercing. What is it? I wondered and the fear took over my body. I started to run. It was like I was running in mud. My legs felt weak instantly. And then I saw feathers. This time they were black, ebony black. I touched one and he appeared in front of me, a large Angel with dark eyes. Black eyes. He stood in front of wings at full span.

They must have been twelve feet wide from side to side. His dark black hair hung around his cold pale face. He looked like death. I screamed yet no sound came out of my mouth. He laughed, it was roaring and thundering. I could not move, scream or do anything else at this point. All he did was laugh and stand in front of me.

Finally I realized this was my dream and I controlled it. He was in my head, in my world and I wanted him out. I had enough creepy Angels surrounding me. Enough drama in my life now. I closed my eyes and I called for Ianni. Pleaded for her to come and help me.

Ianni you are my spirit guide and I need you. Please come, there is a horrid angel here and I don't know what to do. Please Ianni help me!

I opened my eyes and looked around and she was not there. He was still there. Yet he was not laughing. He had drawn in his wings.

"What do you want from me?" I yelled, finally my voice was working. "I never have seen you before. Who are you?"

"Did you know that the soul is most vulnerable in dreams? So it is my perfect time to talk to you. You needed me here, you may not see that now but you will. My name is Dedrick and I hold all the answers."

"I don't recall asking any questions that needed you to answer them. Why do I need you here? I have a Spirit Guide."

He reached out and slightly touched my face. I shuddered at his touch. His hands were cold and clammy. He was beautiful and hideous at the same time. I had never seen anything like him. He was not like Ianni or Lillith. They had intimidating features sure, but they were not terrifying. They were Angels and this was no Angel. He may have had wings but I could tell he was not from Heaven.

"You feel so scared. Please don't be. I'm not here to hurt you Avery. I'm here to help you. I have an offer for you. One everyone receives in times of need. Guides like me always reach out to the souls like you. We always visit dreams and try to help. You are in a time of need. Your life on earth is a living hell." Then he started to laugh again. "Oh, sorry, I was just thinking about that stint you pulled on Dallas. Poor guy. You are a real bitch. I mean who kisses someone's cousin and then tells them all about it? Talk about dragging him through the mud. Poor guy, oh well." I stepped back looking around still for Ianni. She should be here. I needed her.

"Stop it! I have Ianni and if you don't go now I will call for her." It was all that I could think to say. I hoped that it would work but I knew it wouldn't. If she was going to come she would have been here already.

"Oh no! Not your spirit guide. Oh lets call her together shall we? Ianni, Ianni, Ianni! Come out, come out wherever you are!" He was mocking me. He was pretending to be scared of her. I knew then that if this type of Guide wasn't afraid of Heaven Angels I was in trouble.

"She isn't coming Avery, she knows better. She and I don't mix. You see her powers can't stop me. She is just a life coach, not a powerful Angel. You see there are several jobs in Heaven and hers is the minor leagues, its minimum wage." He was taunting her and it was making me even more mad and fearful.

"Stop it! You don't know anything, you're not an Angel. You're an impostor,"
I spat.

"You know so much do you? Well let me tell you something little girl, I was an Angel. I sat at the highest seat in the council. My job was very important."

He was now shouting and his voice was booming through the room. My head was hurting from the sound. I had to wake up, that is what I had to do, but it wouldn't work. I had drank the Yulu tea and I knew I would be asleep for a while. It was worthless. I tried to run again and my legs were still stuck.

"You can't go anywhere. You're here with me for a while babe, so just sit back and relax." He waved a chair underneath me and my knees gave way and I was forced to sit.

"So if you were so important then what happened? You said you were an Angel. What the hell are you now?" I was trying to act as if I was not scared to death but I don't think it was working.

"Please wait and hold all questions. I will get to it in time. Just shut up and let me talk. You see I sat in the council. I was part of the ReLife council. We made the decision on whether or not humans would go back and reincarnate. I was on the highest seat, meaning I was the one who ultimately made the decision, but that job became so very tedious after the thousands of years I did it. I wanted to be with the human's. I envied the Angels, like your Ianni. I wanted to guide the spirit and help them on their path. There was something so magical about seeing your human spirit born into the world and watching them grow, helping them along. I was so sure that my human's would be great. I knew that not all of them would go on the right path. There is always that chance that they would go bad. You know, turn out to be murderers or drug addicts and really mess up their life. Once they came home we would send them to the Receivers and from there they would be kept under strict surveillance and they would be rehabilitated. Once that happened it was up to the ReLife Council to decide on whether to send them again. Most do not go back. Most of them stay Home and live there."

I was so confused I had always thought the bad guys go to Hell. Was I to believe this lunatic?

"Oh yeah the bad seeds go to Heaven. Everyone does. Jesus died for our sins Avery. Even the worst come Home. Hell is for those who sign their souls over to Lucifer. Most soul's can be saved. The ones that can't don't go back to Earth. They stay Home and learn to live again. It is so beautiful there. Rolling hills, trees, statues, monuments even oceans. It's a lot like Earth except there is no pollution from cars, no anger, no killing, no death, its absolute freedom and beauty. And it is torture." He screamed the word *torture* like he was in pain.

I jumped out of my chair and he threw me back in it.

"You know sadness, don't you? Your mother died, your father didn't want you, no boyfriends because you can't trust anyone. And your best friend is so wrapped up in her boy toys that she doesn't have time for you."

"Stop it you don't even know me. You're not going to invade

my dream and try to scare me." My hands were starting to tremble. I kept telling myself that it was just a dream and that I would wake up soon enough.

"I am not here to scare you. I am here to help you, I already told you that. Now let me finish my story," he yelled, spit flying from his twisted mouth. I was stuck here with him and there was nothing to do but listen.

"I pleaded with my superior to change my job. I wanted to be a Guide or even a Watcher. Either one, it didn't matter. I wanted to help the soul's on Earth. I knew it was meant for me but I was turned down countless times. So I stopped working altogether. I just didn't want to do it anymore. Now that was odd. Here I was in the most beautiful and peaceful place in this universe and I wasn't happy. Gee, maybe being told how to do things for all that time made me a little angry."

His face darkened and he turned away from me to look around. My dream this time was in the old house but it had a scary tragic look to it. Like it had been in a fire. The walls were charcoal gray, tapestries hung with holes and the floor was filled with ash.

"I choose to leave and become human. It was the only option that I could find that would benefit me. So I was sent to earth. I had no family, no friends, no guides. I was alone. I was what you call homeless. Sent here as a man, not a baby. Not born like you human's are. Being sent here as a man was not easy. I had no home or job. I lived on the streets for several years. And then I met him. He was so full of life. He was once like me. Lived in Heaven and was cast out because he was not happy. He was sent here as a man too. So he started looking for help. For another way of life."

"The Devil?" I interrupted.

"No silly girl, his name was Benjamin. He was once an Angel but he sold his angelic soul and being for eternal happiness. Oh what a life he and I lived, for centuries. We can now live forever. No death. Just life."

"Then if you're not an Angel why do you have wings?" I pointed to his deep, black wings. They were quite beautiful and gothic. He unfolded them and they began to flap hard. Feathers flew everywhere and the dark gray room started to come back to life. Colors were now alive. His darkness turned everything to light. I put my hand in front of my face to shield it from the feathers.

"I'm a guide of a different sort. I am an Angel, just not a heavenly Angel. I work for someone else. The wings are so cool aren't they? I guide the lost, the broken, the damaged and the needy souls here on earth. The one's who do not find the answers that they so long for. Like you Avery. You need help don't you? You have no one. You're all alone, a meek and mild girl, with beauty that no one can see. You had a few chances at love and well you blew that. Landon will try to get you again, and you just might let him, but really is that the life you set out for this time? Dallas, he will not forgive you for what you did. You cheated. He hates cheaters. Your mom is gone, your dad is gone. Aunt Paulina well she is getting closer to death every day. Yep she will leave too. Just like Kerri will. She will get married have kids all while you stand by alone and watch her. You can have more. I can help you. I will be your new Spirit Guide. I can guide you into a life that you want. Anything you want."

He was now starting to dance around me as I sat in the chair. He was acting like a crazy person. I knew not to listen to his lies. I kept calling Ianni in my head, hoping for a sign from her. I was so terrified of what he was going to do to me. It was the scariest nightmare I had ever had.

"If you want Dallas, I can give him to you. A life with a love like that. It would be remarkable. Do you want beauty; I can give you that too. Do you want Landon? Sure you can have him. I will erase his memories and he will never know about your past lives. That would be nice, right? Everyone gets the choice in their life. The Angels like me visit all souls who are lost. We turn them into movie stars, rock gods, business executives, billionaires. We help them be whatever they want. You don't think that these people actually have talent, did you? Nope, we give them all they need. Hollywood is our creation. They live forever. No death. The city of Los Angeles. Better known as lost Angels." He didn't even pause to take a breath probably because he was dead inside.

"They were once lost soul's who came down from Heaven. Like

you, they chose their path and life took over. Their Guides forsake them time and time again. Then they end up lost. That's where I come in. I help them cut the ties of their so-called Spirit Guides. What is it you want Avery?"

I took a breath. A deep, painful breath. I don't even think I took a breath the whole time he was talking to me. So what he was saying is that all the actors, actresses, models, famous people all over were from his creation? They sold their souls and became whatever they wanted. He also said they did not die. I have seen many famous people die. How could he explain that? He was telling me that he could give me whatever I wanted? What was the price I would have to pay? There had to be a catch, there always was. Look at some of the famous people, they don't have it all. Harassed by photographers, no privacy in their lives. Some of them get hooked on drugs and alcohol. Hollywood was a dark place. I knew that without talking to him. But then again, some were not like that. Some were kind and giving. There was no way he was telling the truth right?

"What do they do after their very public deaths?" I nervously asked him.

"Reincarnation my dear. What did you think? Your kind was the only to relive your lives?" He laughed again, that terribly haunting laugh.

Suddenly the bedroom door flew open and Landon was standing there with his arms open to me. He looked scared to death as he stared up at Dedrick but he still acted brave. He motioned to me to run to him. I was unsure what to do at this moment. I knew in the fibers of my soul that Dedrick was bad news. Yet I was a lost and lonely soul. I had lived a life of grief, had no friends left. It was true about Kerri. She was falling in love and even I knew he was going to be her future not me. I ruined my relationship with Dallas and Landon. Landon, when I think back to our past lives, he is familiar and loving to my soul, but this life, I didn't even know who he was anymore. And I was told to stay away from him. My chair edged closer to Dedrick without even realizing it. My mind was pushing me closer to him. His offer for some odd reason was sounding good to me. I was going mad. How could I think this is real?

"What the hell are you doing Avery? Get away from him. Come to me. He is selling you a bad deal. Please." He begged and pleaded for me to come to him. I wanted to go but my legs were stuck. It was impossible to move.

"She is weighing her options Landon. Let her make up her own mind will you. You know she doesn't need you! She is a grown woman." Dedrick was taunting him now.

"Shut up," I yelled. Just then I was able to stand up for myself. My legs started to work and I got out of the chair.

"Keep going Avery. Tell him to go away and leave us alone. He has no choice but to leave if you tell him. Don't believe his lies, he can't promise you anything."

I looked to Dedrick and a smile came across his face. He just stared into Landon's eyes. He was terrible, I knew it, but I also knew my life was terribly messy.

"Go away leave my dream. You are not welcome here. I live for me and no one else. I will go to Heaven when I die." I could barely talk, fear was muting my voice, but at least it seemed to work.

"As you wish, but I will come back if you need me." He winked at me and he was gone. I fell into Landon's arms, just collapsed, and then I woke up.

Chapter 13

All the Answers

My eyes burned once I opened them. My breathing was heavy and I was sweaty and cold. I jumped out of my bed, turning on every single light in my apartment. I was totally consumed with fear beyond any fear I had ever felt. A dark demon of a man was just begging for my soul. Trying to end my soul forever so I could have a better "life" on earth. I wanted to say yes to him. The whole time I felt a need to say yes. Like it was being pulled from my mouth. All the while hating him and myself for wanting a new start. A new life with no more pain. Just pain and sorrow in the afterworld. Dedrick did not say so but I knew that's what I would be signing my soul over to. To spend my afterlife in Hell. He didn't have to say a thing. I felt Hell spew from his mouth.

Suddenly a knock on the door made me jump and scream. Was he here for me again? He was probably mad that I told him no and he was here to hold me captive until I said yes to him. Could he sense that I wanted to say yes? I slowly walked to the door.

"Who is it?" I asked when I had my hand on the door handle. It was 2:00 in the morning. Who could be here now? It had to be the evil Dark Guide.

"Avery, it's me Dallas." His voice sounded tired and strained. What was he doing at my apartment? This was not a good time to talk. Not for me, not after what I just went through. Would I tell him what just happened? He would know something was wrong with me. I opened the door and tried to hide my fear behind a crooked smile.

"Wow it's really late, or early, what are you doing here?"

"Avery, what's wrong? You're shivering." He touched my face. His hands felt so comforting on my skin. "You're soaking wet. Are you sick?"

He came in and practically pushed me onto the couch. He turned on my ceiling fan and gave me a blanket that hung on my chair. It felt good for him to be here with me. I felt a lot better, just seeing him had made me feel instantly better.

"Dallas, did you just get off work?" I asked.

"Yeah, I did. It was the worst night. I couldn't think about anything else but you. I'm sorry that I didn't say anything to you before you left my house. I was just in shock, I didn't know what to say." He looked down at the floor. "I admire you for your honesty, I really do. I didn't know what to say then and I still don't. I just know that without you I feel sort of lost. Before you came into my life..."

I had to stop him before he said anymore. I stood up the blanket falling onto the floor.

"No, please don't I can't do this right now. I can't hear you end this right now. I just went through something really traumatic and I can't be broken up with too."

"Would you just sit down and shut up? I am not breaking up with you." He paused. "Oh, sorry for telling you to shut up. That was wrong."

I just laughed. I didn't take offense, I needed it. Someone to wake me up out of my delirium. He was so cute. Sitting on my couch with his brown eyes looking glassy and tearful. He was crying and he didn't even try to hide it. Only a real man could cry in front of a girl.

"I don't think that what you did was very nice, but you are right. We were not technically in a relationship. I wanted to be, but I knew you and I were just dating. Basically I do feel a bit confused as to why the two of you kissed, but I did what you asked, I thought about it. And I love you. I forgive you." He leaned into me and kissed me. It was soft and comforting exactly what I needed. He loved me, and he forgave my mistake. I was so happy right? This is what I wanted right? I thought of Landon and how he just risked his life to save me.

He came into my dream to help me because he loved me too. He would follow me and help me forever. I knew he would always be there for me. I kissed Dallas harder this time. More passionately showing him my love for him was real. Like I had to prove it to him. He picked me up and carried me into my room. He laid me into the bed and shut off all the lights that I had previously turned on. When he returned he had two aspirins and water. I took them hoping that my weird fever would dissipate. I asked him if he would go with me to Kerri's party and he said yes. He would have to call out of work but he said it was worth it.

He took off his shirt and climbed into the bed with me, kissing me and caressing my hair. He knew I did not feel well. He nuzzled into my neck and he fell asleep. I did not. I was too scared to see Dedrick again. I knew I felt safer with Dallas here in my bed but I knew he could not help me in my dream world.

I left the house for work at 8:00 and left Dallas asleep in my bed. I was as quiet as I possibly could be, practically tip-toeing around to get ready. I left him a little note saying, "Thank you for forgiving me. XOXO."

The drive to work was very calm and I just listened to the sounds of the wind through my open windows. No music today. I felt so much better in the daylight. I knew for some reason that I was safe and Dedrick could not get to me. When I pulled into to the parking lot I saw a small black BMW in my parking spot. So I pulled into the one next to it. It was Kerri and Justin. I got out hoping to avoid having to talk to them. I didn't want to talk to Justin until tonight. I knew I had to talk to him at their party, I just didn't want to now, but I was too late. They caught me.

"Hey girl," she called. "Come check out my new purchase." The car was hers. I looked at my car, then back at hers. Yep, I was jealous. "What do you think, isn't it really pretty? Justin said it was just perfect for me."

She was really excited. Justin smiled and waved at me. He got into the driver's side and she kissed him goodbye and ran to catch up with me. I didn't think Justin noticed that I did not wave back. The two little lovebirds were in their own world. I was more than happy to have her taken care of. But really, why a psychic? Couldn't he be a musician or a writer? I mean if she was looking for someone totally different than the types she usually went for how could she say that Dallas' job wasn't a real job, look at Justin? I did get a good look at him and he was very normal looking. Nice clean cut hair. Nice clothes. He was very good looking.

"I think your new car is really pretty and you deserve it." She beamed and seemed to glow once I approved. We walked into the office and went our separate ways. She to her office and I to do my rounds. I read the little notes on our residents and one was a little disturbing to me. Mr. Grey has been very hostile and bitter lately. I was sad to read this. I knew that I hadn't really spent much time with him. He was delicate, he needed companionship. Gordon, the other caretaker, wrote that Mr. Grey told him he hated him and only wanted me to help him. Oh, that was harsh. I felt sad for Gordon, who was a pretty nice guy, but then at the same time he was not attentive like me. Gordon's residents usually like to talk. And he does not. Mr. Grey needed a companion so he would be my first stop today. I knocked on his door and it took him a while before he finally answered.

"Oh, well look who it is. Where have you been? You call yourself a caretaker? Hmm you don't take very good care of me. You're never here. And when you are its only for a couple hours. Why?" He said in the grumpiest of tones.

"Well good morning to you too." I walked into the apartment. It smelled of rotten food. I almost threw up all over his filthy carpet.

"What is going on in here? Your carpet is a mess and it smells like something died in here."

"I asked my questions first. I will answer you after you answer me. Well, go ahead." He stood there with his arms crossed trying to be intimidating. I wasn't going to fall for his antics. He didn't scare me

"I have only been working four hours a shift because I have been having some personal issues." I made sure to make personal sound more pronounced. "And I do take care of you. You're my favorite resident. If you don't try to get along with the others you are going to be miserable. So, now it's your turn." I covered my nose from the awful smell.

"Well I don't like the others so I told them I don't need their help. Really, I need help, but just your help though. You're the only pleasant one here. I hate the others." He walked away and sat on the sofa.

I laughed without him seeing me. Actually it was kind of flattering that he liked me best but his place definitely needed some attention. Even though he said he didn't need help, the other caretakers need to help anyway. I put on my rubber gloves and started cleaning. His trash was full to the brim and the carpet just needed a good vacuum. After thirty minutes of cleaning I told him I had other residents to help but I wanted him to go to movie night tonight. He nodded and I left so that I could do my other rounds. I had to clean for Mrs. Stonefield and Mr. Carson. It was now noon and I saw Mr. Grey feeding the birds in the courtyard. I sat with him again. It was like a little getaway to be with him. He was quiet and I needed that. I leaned on the bench and closed my eyes. I could tell that Mr. Grey liked my company. He just sat there still and quiet even after he ran out of bread.

"Avery."

I jumped. I must have dosed off. I looked around and Mr. Grey was still sitting there saying nothing. He had dosed off as well. I was unsure of who had said it. There was no one there but the two of us.

I saw purple feathers by the ladies bathroom so I got up from the bench. Mr. Grey did not stir. I entered the room not knowing which Angel I would encounter. I looked around but I saw no one. Then there, sitting on the sink, was Ianni with purple feathers now. They were so pretty with her fiery red hair. I knew I had to tell her how mad I was that she had let me down. She didn't come when I needed her the most.

"Oh, here you are. Where were you last night? You know I really needed you." I started to cry. It was all coming back to me.

I felt so abandoned and alone. I wished that I never knew about her because I had started to rely on her a lot more than I should. She hopped down from the sink and came towards me. She looked sad and sorrowful.

"Avery, I can't even begin to explain how sorry I am. I wanted to help but I couldn't. I'm forbidden to step in and help when it comes to the Dark Guides. It's the law. Trust me, I wanted to break it. I wanted to be the one to help you but if I did there would be extreme circumstances." The pain in her face made me believe that she truly could not help me. She bit down on her lip, it made her angelic face look more human.

"Why me?" What a selfish thing for me to ask except it was all I felt at the time. Selfish, scared and naïve. I was in the dark as to what was going on with my life. I needed answers.

"You are depressed, sad, confused, everything they look for in a human. They thrive on those times in your life when you need help. They trick humans into believing that they can actually help you. You can be so weakened by their lies that you will say yes. And then they do the unthinkable." She turned away. I thought I saw tears but when she faced me once more I saw only glistening eyes.

"They kill you and take over your soul."

"Kill you? He said that actors and actresses are so famous because of him. Do they only kill who they want? I don't understand." I started to pace. Now I was even more fearful.

"Look at me Avery." She stopped me and turned my face to hers. "Those people are a shell. They kill them and steal their bodies to use for themselves. Do you ever wonder why some people, famous, rich or whatever, are nice and perfect one minute and crazy the next? It's because they use their bodies. And they don't stay in the same one all the time. They share. It's like they pass them around. One Dark Guide will be one person for a few weeks and then someone else will use that person's shell for the next week. It is the only way that they can be "human". They are trying to get you now and that's why you need to make up your mind and choose who you want. Get back to the normal you."

I nodded. She was right, I had to make a choice. Although I thought I had, and then Landon had to come save me. It made me confused all over again.

"So what happens to that person's soul?" I was scared to know the answer.

"We both know what happens to them. Their soul serves a Dark being." I swallowed because I felt terrified. I did not want to know much more than I already did.

"How do I get rid of this Dedrick? It was hard enough to say no once, I don't think I have the strength to do it again." I could feel the tears starting to well up in my eyes.

"Avery, do not feel guilty for that. Saying no to a Dark Guide is not easy. They have very strong powers that are hard to deny. Listen carefully; your mother can help you. I must go, but be careful and stay strong."

"Wait, one more question. Dedrick mentioned a Watcher. What is that?" I needed to know so desperately.

"A Watcher is sort of you Guard. He is watching you and trying to keep you safe, as much as possible, but He cannot help you all the time. The Dark Guides are strong, it will be hard for your Watcher to defeat them. That is why it will take you and all your strength. Dedrick wants to be human; it's all he ever wanted. You are all he ever wanted. He will stop at nothing. Just know that you are not alone. We are with you no matter what. We are trying to help."

It was so hard for me to believe that the dark side was so strong and heavens angels could not defeat them.

"Aren't you stronger Ianni, you are an Angel? Is my Watcher here now? I just can't see him right?" I felt like I was ambushing her with questions.

"No silly, he walks amongst the humans, he blends in but he is not going to tell you he is your Guard. Unlike me. They are not like that. You will never know him like you know me." She stopped suddenly and her eyes got wide.

"Someone is coming I have to go." As soon as she said it, she disappeared. The bathroom door swung open. It was Rachel with her sour face.

"What are you doing in here, this isn't the staff bathroom."

"I could ask you the same thing Rachel." I had taken enough of her crap. I was in a pissed off mood now and I didn't have the strength to try and be nice.

I pushed past her and went back to escort Mr. Grey to his apartment. He was already gone so I finished my rounds and before I knew it my shift was over.

Once I got home Dallas was no longer there. He had left a note telling me he went to his house to get his stuff and he would meet me back here in time for the party. I plopped myself down on the couch and was alone with my thoughts. I was not going to let Dedrick win. I would talk to Justin and see if he could actually be the key to my mother's answers. I had to do this to save myself from Dedrick. I sat and stared out my window watching the bay and all its inhabitants.

A few hours later Dallas came back. I answered the door and he looked so handsome. He was dressed in dark Jeans and a crisp navy blue polo. I noticed a bag in his hand that came from a little boutique that I had passed many times. I had never shopped there because it was very pricey. He handed it to me and stepped in.

"For you, a little present," he said.

I blushed. No one had ever gotten me a gift from a place like that. I tore through the tissue paper and inside was a gorgeous vintage cocktail dress wrapped so nicely I didn't want to open it. It was sleeveless and made of silk chiffon and lace overlay. It was an off white color with a beaded waistline. I lifted it up to get a better look. It was perfect for tonight. Not at all what I would pick out for myself, but that was because I had no style. What a nice thought to get me something. He must have known my nerves were on edge, and that my clothes suck.

"Go on, try it on." He ushered me into my room. I closed the door and he stood outside. I could hear him lean on the door. I slipped the dress on, being careful to not tear anything. It was a perfect fit. I stood in front of my full-length mirror and I just stared at this person. I had never, ever, thought of myself as pretty. Being with Dallas made me feel that way. I really thought about it and realized that this was the only life that I wasn't pretty. All the lives before I was more than pretty, I was model material, but this go around I was a plain and simple woman.

"So, there is something I have to tell you," Dallas said from the other side of the door.

"Bad news or good news?" I asked. Hoping it wasn't bad news.

"Well that all depends. I went to see Landon before coming here. I decided to not fight with him. He is my cousin, and he is like the brother I never had. Avery, he is a mess. He feels terrible for what happened." I leaned on the door listening. I felt terrible too.

"Well, I think he just wants to be normal. He has had a tough life. Ever since he was a child he always spoke of this woman named Claire. We all thought she was his imaginary friend but, he said she was his wife in a past life."

I just listened hoping that Landon didn't indulge in any information tonight.

He continued, "Although we totally don't know what to think, my family has always tried to help. So anyhow I invited him to come with us tonight. He can't be alone, he looks horrible. I just want to help him." I opened the door and he almost fell on top of me.

"Oops, sorry," I said as I stabilized him. He laughed and stared at me in the dress.

"Wow you look ravishing."

"I have never been called ravishing before. Now don't change the subject. What did he say? Is he going?" I wasn't mad just frustrated. I thought I could try to get over him and now he was going to be with us all night long. Now I knew that he was feeling so terrible I felt terrible. And the pain in my heart started to ache for him. I wanted him to feel better too.

"Well I think he needs to meet new people and this is one of the best ways for him to do that," he answered.

He stood staring at me with his gorgeous eyes. I felt like I could melt from his stare. He was very convincing. I nodded and put my best dress shoes on. I let my hair stay down and just brushed it out nicely. I put a bit of mascara and lipstick on and was done. We walked down the stairs to Landon's new apartment, just one floor down. Not only did he now live in my apartment building, he was right beneath me. Dallas knocked and Landon swung the door open. He stood there not trying to look at me but still I could see he was. He was so cute. I bit my lip trying my hardest to not think that way about him.

"Let's hit the road," Dallas said.

On the way to the party was the most awkward drive I had ever encountered. I sat in the passenger's seat of Dallas' truck and Landon in the back. There were not too many words said between the three of us, except about the beautiful weather we had been having. Here I was still stuck on who was right for me as I held Dallas' hand and smelled Landon's sweet scent from behind me.

We arrived at the house a little late. I knew Kerri would not care. It was like me to be late. Usually I skip all together but when I do go to parties I come late. I have a hard time getting ready and getting out of the car. I hate parties. I hate the music, the loud people and most of all the fact that I don't fit in.

This party was huge. A little get together this was not. All of the friends Kerri had, and it seemed all of Justin's too, packed the small house. Kerri's house was simple and sweet, the perfect little home for a bachelorette or for a small family just starting out. I know she would love to fill the two extra rooms with little babies. And she just might get that if Justin is her Mr. Perfect.

I saw Kerri standing with Justin and a few of our co-workers when she waved to me. She looked so cute in a new dress as well. Justin smiled and waved too. He looked cute with a pair of jeans and a nice twill blazer. I took Dallas' hand and walked over to them. Landon dispersed and started to mingle. Just like a single hot guy would do when he was lonely. I tried to shake the feelings away and put on my best smile.

"Well Dallas are you going to be doing our bartending tonight?" Kerri asked with a smile.

"Sorry kiddo I am off tonight but if you need that perfect drink you know I can help you out. By the way I'm Dallas, you must be

Justin." They both shook hands.

"You know Dallas, I do need that perfect drink. So do you mind?" Kerri whined. She had a way of whining when she wanted something. Not something that bothered me, I was used to it. "Av, you can stay and get to know Justin. I will get you a drink too."

"Um, thanks. I think," I replied. So this was it the moment of truth, the chance I had to ask him if he could reconnect me with my very dead mother. I know I will look really stupid but if she was going to help me I had to do it. I leaned in and opened my mouth to ask this strange request.

Before I could he said, "Yes I will help you. You don't even need to ask. I knew you were coming here so I have already contacted her and she is waiting."

Chills ran through me as he led me through the crowded party to one of the vacant back rooms. There sat two chairs and a small table. No magic crystal ball or tarot cards, just a plain setting. It was a little less intimidating. The room was dim and his blonde hair looked faded. He had a nice smile that was trusting. He laid his hands on the table across from me.

"Avery, take my hands. Time is short and she has all the answers."

So I did just that and I closed my eyes.

Chapter 14

Close Again

Some time went by and I waited for something to happen. All that happened, though, was me thinking about how sweaty Justin's hands were. I opened one eye and scanned his face. He really was cute. His blonde hair was spiky and messy like he had just rolled out of bed. He looked a lot older than Kerri. I wondered how much older. I shut my eyes again, still nothing.

"I am thirty-five," he blurted out, "And my hands are sweaty because it's hot as hell in here." He stood up and opened a window. A nice cool breeze blew in and it really cooled things off, although my nerves were still on edge. I should have been in shock that this man read my thoughts, but after everything, I was sort of used to it. He grabbed my hands again and we closed our eyes.

"Think of her. That is what I want you to do. Don't think about me, or how cute I am. Think of your mom." I scoffed at his little comment and I did as I was told. I pictured her and only her. I thought of how she looked, how she smiled. Her hair was a lot like mine and her eyes were the same bluish gray. I felt hot air and smelled gas from a stove. It almost sickened me. Then I smelled something sweet. Cookies. I opened my eyes and I was in my old house. The kitchen where my mom died. She was standing in her apron pulling cookies from the oven. She looked happy. She looked alive. I reached out for her. And she reached back. We touched and I cried. Harder than ever before. My mom was here. I was touching my dead mother. She hugged me and patted my back.

"You are so beautiful. Look at you." She pulled away to examine me.

"I am not beautiful it's the dress. It has that effect." I was embarrassed. She had always told me how pretty I looked but I never believed her. We embraced again. I looked around for Justin but he was not here.

"It's just us honey. You and me again baking cookies. I thought you would like this memory. Not of me dying, of course, but you so loved to bake with me. So this is what I came up with. Are you comfortable?" She asked.

How could I not be? I was with my mommy. She handed me a cookie and led me to our dining room table. It was still the same. My seat was covered in stickers from when I was a child. Any time I would get stickers I would always decorate my kitchen chair. My mom did not care. She thought of it as self-expression. We sat and I stared at her. She looked so real. I could not stop looking.

"It's really you. I don't know what to think right now." My voice was raspy. She tucked a piece of her hair behind her ear. It was still shiny and alive just like before.

"Well I have some answers for you. So let's get to it. We don't have much time." She leaned forward and looked at me so seriously.

"Are you in Heaven?" I asked.

"No, I am not able to pass on yet. I'm sort of stuck you could say. I did something that is not acceptable and you are the key to releasing me so I can move on. That is why I visit you sometimes. I visit because I haven't yet moved on. Those of us who are stuck can still visit." She looked away and then brought her eyes back to me. The bathroom putting on makeup, it was her.

"The bathroom was really you. I thought souls could only visit in dreams. Is it different for you?"

"Yes, once I pass on I can visit in dreams. You saw me in the bathroom, yes. Sorry if I startled you honey. I also placed the lipstick and the black dress in your house. You need better clothes." She smiled. I knew those things weren't there before.

She was trying to make me pretty.

"Mom I want to help you move on. I will do anything I can to help." It didn't matter what I needed to do. I wanted to help her. I needed to help her. Just as she had always helped me as a child.

"You can. Just by simply listening to me now. Landon is the one in trouble."

My head started to hurt at the sound of his name. I didn't want to talk about him. I wanted to protect myself from Dedrick but she wanted to give me answers so I would listen.

"I saw him coming before you were even born. I knew your fate. That he would stop at nothing to reunite with you. The two of you are twin souls. You are an Affinity." She ate a cookie.

"What is that?" I asked, because I had never heard of the term.

"God created you so perfectly he split you into two. One soul a man and the other a woman. You can't help but find each other. It is destiny that you two should be together, but it is very hard to be with your twin. You are so much alike that it is a struggle. It's like being with yourself twenty-four seven. I know because your father is my Affinity. That is why he left his first wife to be with me, but we struggled. We drove each other mad. Although our love was strong." She ate another cookie and then continued.

"Affinity's can be best friends, sisters, brothers, daughters, sons, husbands, wives, or nothing at all to each other. Sometimes they never find each other on earth. Only in dreams do most Affinity's find each other. It is there that they can be together with no problems. Because once you awake you are back to living your daily life. You, my daughter, had been haunted by his dreams once. Lucy told you about him. It opened up a path for him to come and see you. Landon, he dreamt of you since he was born. He is the stronger soul. That is why he can revive his memories." She paused as though to make sure I was still keeping up. I nodded and gestured for her to go on.

"With your father and I it was too hard. We will always be twin souls. Fortunately we will not have the struggle to be together at Home. Things are easier there. What I have done is why you are being visited by Dedrick. He came to me first. I had not yet met your father but I was searching for him. All our memories of all our lives haunted my every thought. I was not just clairvoyant, I was the stronger soul. So I would do anything to see him again. Dedrick knew this. So he found me in my dreams and he offered me whatever I wanted. Well I turned him down. I knew he was bad news from the start. Years later, I found your father on my own. I didn't need Dedrick's help. Then your father left me. He said he couldn't take my seriousness, or my crazy thoughts about being psychic." She now looked sad. I remembered this face. She always wore this expression.

"So he didn't remember you did he?" It made sense to me.

"No he did not. So I let him go. It was what was best for us. Even knowing that, it hurt so badly. To let him go ripped me apart. It killed me to see you fatherless. Luckily I healed, and you need to as well. Dedrick came back eventually. He wanted my soul again. I knew I couldn't leave you alone and go with him. It took all I could to pass up his strong promises. He promised me that he could give me your father back and that you would never be alone again. I knew it was all lies, that I needed to get rid of him. So I made a deal with him. I told him about Landon. I knew your future. I knew he was you other half and he would come for you." It didn't surprise me that she knew, because Aunt Paul had told me she knew.

"Once he found out about you and Landon it was like he hit the jackpot. He wanted Landon more. Landon was the stronger soul. And I knew his future. I knew he would be handsome and successful. He wanted it. All he wants is to be like Landon. The perfect soul to steal. Your souls are famous at Home, the only souls to be reunited in every lifetime since your creation. No other Affinity's have ever achieved that. So I told him who you were and he agreed to wait and take Landon instead. I am so sorry to involve you but because of what I did, making a deal with him, well that's how I got here. Turns out that is a big no-no." She hung her head.

"Wait so, he doesn't want me?" I asked.

"Nope, you were just a gateway to get to Landon. Once Landon came into your dream to help you that was all it took. Now he will take him. You have to help Landon, it will not be easy, but because of what I did if Landon is taken I will stay here for a long time. Until Landon's soul is back at Home and you have forgiven me."

"Mom, I forgive you." I put my hand on hers and squeezed. I would do anything to help my mom. Unfortunately I had no idea how to save Landon from Dedrick.

"I don't want to be famous mom; I didn't want any of this. I just want to be left alone and be with Dallas." Tears ran down my face as I stared at my beautiful mother.

"Time is running short. There are a couple things you need to know in order to help Landon. First, you need an Angel willing to break some rules, second you need a Watcher and third you need one half of an Affinity besides yourself or Landon. Someone like your father."

"What?!" My father? What did Richard have to do with this? Yes he was half of an Affinity but mom said herself he was the weaker soul.

"He is your blood. It is very rare to have two Affinity's in the family so it will make you very strong. Find him honey, I have to go. All my love sweetheart, all my love."

Just like that my eyes flew open and I was back in the room with Justin. My mom was gone and I felt sick. I lost her all over again. Justin squeezed my hand reassuring me that it would be okay. I started to cry hard and I couldn't stop. My world was upside down. I was famous in Heaven and a nothing here on earth. The man that shared half of my soul was in danger and it was up to me to save him. On top of that I needed to ask my stranger of a father for help.

"Listen Avery, I will do all I can to help you, but you have to pull yourself together. You heard your mom. The weaker you are the worse it gets."

"You're right. I need to be strong right now." I wiped the tears and sat up straight.

"I know this is a horrible time to tell you this, but I am in love with Kerri."

"I figured as much. So?" I wasn't sure why he was telling me this. He was looking very nervous. Biting his lip as he pulled out a little black box.

"I am hoping to turn this party into an engagement party." I gasped at the beautiful ring in the center of the box. Wow, my best friend would have all her dreams come true. I was suddenly so happy that whatever I was feeling was momentarily on pause.

"Really? Wow that is so perfect. You are such a great guy for helping me. Thank you. And I know that you will take care of Kerri." He smiled and closed the box. He sat up and headed toward the door.

"So I need to go out there and propose to her. I am so glad I could get you all the answers you need. I will continue to help you, but for right now let's go celebrate." I stopped and looked at him. He was kind and perfect. He knew all my thoughts. He knew I was thinking this of him, because he was not only psychic he also read minds as well. He was like the strangest person I had ever met but I was getting very used to strange lately and I just didn't care. I cared that he was in love with Kerri and I knew he would take care of her.

"Yes I will. I will never lead her into harm; I will always lead her away from it. No one would ever love her more than I will. I know her future and it looks really good." He laughed and so did I.

We walked out into the very over crowded living room and he found Kerri as I scanned the room for Dallas. I only found Landon. He was talking with a very pretty blonde. They were talking very close to each other because the music forced them together. It was very loud, but that didn't bother me. The pretty blonde bothered me. Why?

I was jealous of her. I wanted him to move on but something inside me wanted him to be leaning into me, like he was leaning into pretty blonde. He looked at me just then and our eyes locked. Pretty blonde was still talking but he was staring at me. We were twin souls and it was going to be really hard to not want him but I had to do it for the sake of our lives. I had to help him stay away from both me and Dedrick. I looked away from him and it pained me inside. My heart burned and I pulled myself away. I had to find Dallas, my boyfriend. The man I was in love with in this life. I knew that I could still have Landon in my life as a friend but I couldn't live without Dallas. Finally I found him. He was making drinks for Kerri and a few of our fellow co-workers. I hated that he was working on his day off. So I marched over and pulled the bottle of vodka out of his hand.

"No way! You not doing this. I love this song and I want to dance." I really did like the song. It was slow and romantic and I wanted to feel him against me. I also wanted to save him from Kerri and the others.

"Thank you Princess Snow. I wanted nothing more than to dance with you." He smiled and kissed my cheek. We danced to the song and he rubbed my back tenderly. He was so sweet I could be in that moment forever.

"So did he do any good for you?" He asked with a sly smile.

"What?" I stopped and looked at him. How did he know that I needed something from Justin?

"Well I had a little visit from a freaky little Angel named Ianni last night. I know it all Avery and I am not scared. I know that Landon and you used to be married in another life. And I also know you are the girl he has been searching for." His voice was a bit shaky at the Landon and you were married part, but other than that he seemed strong.

I froze. I stopped dancing and stared into his beautiful eyes. He knew and he didn't care. A tremendous weight had been lifted from me. He didn't seem to be freaked out by this news. In fact, he seemed to be okay with it. I smiled and hugged him so tightly I didn't want to let him go. He hugged me back just as tight. I had to remember to thank Ianni for what she did. Goodness knows what trouble she got into for telling Dallas all that she had.

Just then I saw Justin pulling Kerri to the front of the living room. She seemed to be totally confused. The music stopped and Justin bent down in front of her.

"Kerri, I know its fast but I want to be with you forever. I want to wake up next to you every morning and kiss you goodnight every evening. There is no doubt in my mind that we are meant to be together. Will you..."

She didn't even let him finish before she blurted out, "Yes!"

Everyone applauded as she jumped into his arms. Dallas and I said our congrats when she showed off the ring even though I had already seen it. She looked happy and he looked proud.

"Come on, let's go outside where we can talk. It's so loud in here," he said as he led me out to Kerri's deck. The night was still and silent. The stars were all out shining so bright. It was a great night and terrible night all wrapped into one. All the pressure to fight a demonic Dark Guide on one side and all this love before me, surrounding me, on the other.

"You really know and you don't care? You don't know how much that makes this a lot easier." I confessed, "I know it's crazy and unbelievable but it gets a lot more complicated trust me."

He tucked a piece of hair behind my ear. "Avery, I don't understand too much, but what she showed me is very compelling and it's hard to not understand. I have always believed in the afterlife. It also helps me be at peace with losing my parents. Knowing that they are either here on earth again, or in Heaven waiting for me." He smiled. He looked peaceful. I liked that somehow this story had helped him deal with their deaths.

"We have to save Landon. I don't know how to begin to tell you why." I paused. "My mom did help me. She also gave me a huge assignment to take on and I need all the assistance I can get." He put his hand on my mouth.

"Shh, I know Princess. I know it all. Ianni told me about Dedrick. She told me he is dangerous and it would take a lot to stop him. What I don't know is why he wants you. I will do what I can to stop him though."

"No, you don't understand, it's not me he wants, its Landon." He was misinformed because Ianni didn't know all the truth. His eyes widened. He was now understanding it a little more.

Chapter 15

Dad

We spoke outside for what seemed like hours but was probably only a few minutes. Dallas was getting even angrier that someone wanted to hurt his girlfriend and his cousin. I could see the protective side of him coming into play. His muscles were tense and he kept looking inside, watching Landon. He stroked my arms and at times looked at me with sympathetic eyes.

"We can do this. I know it. There is no doubt. We have to do whatever you're mom said. We have to see your Dad." When he said this I tensed up and shut down. Hearing this again killed me. What would I say to my absent Father?

"We have to get out of here and plan what we will do," I said. "Let me say goodnight and I will meet you by the truck."

He nodded and I went back inside. I found Kerri showing her ring to some of her old high school friends. I told her that I was tired and I wanted to get home. She hugged me and told me to call her tomorrow. I knew that I couldn't call her until I figured out this situation. I agreed anyhow. Justin found me and looked at me. He knew my lie of being tired was only a cover up.

"I will be there tomorrow to help, so expect me about noon. Okay?" He said. I was a fool to think he didn't already know our plans.

"Yes and thank you Justin," was all I could say. He kissed my cheek.

I now had to tear Landon away from pretty blonde. This would not be easy. He saw me coming and he took her through the front door. I followed them. Once we were outside pretty blonde was all over Landon. Kissing him and leading him to her car. I didn't know what to do at this point. I couldn't tell him not to go with her but it wasn't safe.

Just then a gust of wind blew through pretty blonde's hair and started to get stronger. I saw a swirl of yellow feathers surround them. Pretty blonde drew back from him and started cursing.

"What the hell?!" She said loudly.

It was Lillith causing the wind. She knew that Landon wasn't safe either and she would stop Landon from going home with this girl.

"Hey don't worry I have your number I will call you. I gotta go with my cousin. So drive safe," he said as he led her into her BMW. She said some more things as she sped off into the night. He turned to face the feathers. Lillith laughed as she appeared to us. I was shocked to see this soft side of her. Her usual harder side had faded.

"Now Landon, you know you should stay away from girls like that. Naughty boy," she teased. He laughed and then shot a look at Dallas who was watching from his truck. Suddenly he looked worried.

"It's okay. He knows everything and we have a lot to talk about so I would suggest you get into the truck before more people come outside." She looked at me, up and down. Her once nice eyes had turned mean again. "Nice dress but we have a long drive you might want to change before we hit the road."

"Hit the road? I am not going now. I figured we could leave in the morning." I was angry now at her presence. How could she know everything Dallas and I discussed? Unless she was listening to our conversation, which I knew she was. She was sneaky like that.

"If we go back to your apartment it won't be safe for you to sleep there. You have to try to trust me on this one. Let's just get you changed and we will leave. Please Avery."

Oh crap now she was being nice again. I wondered why my house wasn't safe. We jumped into the truck and stopped at my place. I grabbed a few things and changed into a very comfy shirt and jeans. Dallas changed at Landon's so it was just Lillith and I alone. I expected a long lecture but she was very silent. Her and her yellow wings just sat there. I wondered if she, like Ianni, wanted to see what it was like to be human. She seemed to stare at my things for a long time, being very curious.

"Okay I am ready," I announced.

"Good lets go. Your place is depressing." All I could do was roll my eyes at her. Whatever.

The drive was going to be very uncomfortable, yet again, but I had more to think about now. I was going to see a man who left me at four years old and started a new family. I didn't know how I was going to pull this off. My stomach ached and my head hurt. This was harder than talking to my dead mother. Dallas reached over and held my hand in his, ever so gently. Just to let me know he was here. I could feel Landon's eyes burning through me. Sure enough, when I turned to look at him, they were staring right at me.

"Landon, focus! Did you hear anything I just said?' Lillith yelled. She had been talking for the last hour about how we needed a rebellious Angel, a Watcher, and another half of an Affinity. She also spoke about how it was imperative that he start cheering up and stop sulking. The more his head was clear the easier this would be.

"So Dallas, you're not mad at me?" Landon said, completely ignoring Lillith.

"Landon, how could I be? This is not something you did on purpose. You're special, you both are, and you're magnets to each other. I can't be mad at that. I don't want to lose you guys." How Dallas could still be so positive and forgiving was the reason I was in love with him. Any other sane guy would have run for the hills.

I wondered where Ianni was. Who was she helping and guiding now when I need her? I felt like this was all up to me. How would I get my unbelieving dad to believe me?

We pulled into an all night gas station and Dallas hopped out of the truck.

"Be right back," he said as he closed the door. As soon as he did Lillith grabbed me by the shoulders and turned me around.

"Hey!" I yelled trying to pull her hands off me.

"Listen honey. This is a big deal. Once we achieve this goal of beating Dedrick, I have to shave your memories. If I don't I can't go back home." I stopped squirming and listened.

"What does that mean? Are we going to forget each other?" Landon asked. He pulled a strand of hair out of his eyes. I realized then that I really didn't know too much about him in this life. I had only been around him a few times and he doesn't talk much. He was still a stranger to me but I felt so deeply for him.

"Well, there are things "they" don't want you to remember. Like um, your past lives. And we have to do this for your safety," she answered.

"Why not before? Why not do this all the times before, huh? Why make me go through this so many times?" Landon was mad now and his face was red.

"Landon that is something we don't usually do. I mean we really have to have special permission. Gunther is allowing it now. I have tried to do this before. Trust me, I have fought for it and so has Ianni." She looked at me when she spoke Ianni's name. I wondered who Gunther was. I was sure he was on the council that Dedrick spoke of. He wanted us to forget each other. He wanted us to forget all this even happened. That posed a question. How much would we forget? Before I asked Landon asked for me.

"Well, how much are we going to forget? How much will we remember?" Lillith stared at him, her dark hair shining blue in the moonlight. She looked so punk rock. I stifled a laugh.

"I can't really say. Sometimes, because we are only shaving bits and pieces, you just forget what has occurred in those parts of your life. Like for instance Avery," she looked me in the eye. "You will forget about Ianni, Landon being who he was in the past, and you will forget seeing your mom."

I choked at the thought of forgetting to see my mom. I had to remember that. If that was taken away I would be a mess all over again and I would lose her forever, never knowing if she made it Home.

"No, I don't want to forget my mom. How will I know for sure if she makes it? What if you take too much and I forget Dallas?" Landon cursed loudly and got out of the truck. "What? What did I say?"

Lillith laughed at me. I hated her right now. If she wasn't an Angel I would love to hit her in her pretty little face.

"He loves you dummy. Can't you see that? He is hoping for you to forget Dallas. He is hoping that he will revive his memories of you again, like he always does, and that you will choose him this time."

At that moment Dallas came back into the truck. I knew this conversation was over. I had to think about all that Lillith said for the rest of the ride. I chewed on some licorice that Dallas got me and we waited for Landon to stop sulking and get back into the truck. The ride was a very quiet and I blamed Lillith and her big mouth for it. I could not help but worry for Landon. All his life, or lives, our romance consumed him and now that he has a chance at change he is not sure he wants it. I wasn't sure if I wanted it either now that I knew all about Home, my mom, and Landon. Did I really want to give that all up? At first, all of this strangeness was so confusing and scary, but now it was my life and I was used to it. Dallas was now in the know. So that made things so much easier for me.

"Okay, should be about another thirty minutes Avery. Are you ready?" Dallas asked as I stared out the window.

"Really, we are that close?" Suddenly I knew I had to face the father that abandoned me in only thirty minutes. Not only that, I had to tell him the very things he ran from. I had to convince him to help us fight a Dark Guide and try to save someone he didn't know.

Those thirty minutes went by faster than I expected. Soon we pulled in front of a beautiful white home. It even had a picket fence surrounding it. Roses all around the home were still blooming even though winter was approaching. A shiny blue SUV sat in the driveway. I thought of all the children that probably piled in that car. I thought of how many times my dad took them to dance class, or soccer practice. I felt jealous of those kids. I didn't even know them and I hated them. They got my father. They got the father I was supposed to have. The one that was stolen from me. Rachel had to come in and steal my father.

I gulped and tears were coming fast. I knew I could not stop them. So I just let them fall and buried my face in my hands and cried to myself. I felt hands on my back. Landon, Dallas even Lillith were all trying to console me. Except now that Landon was touching me I saw a vision come on. I didn't want this to happen but I couldn't help it.

Garrison and I were sitting together in a dining area. In came Cooper. I was betrothed to Garrison, but I yearned for Cooper. Garrison and I were discussing his going away to New York for a week. He was telling me that Cooper would be working on the house and doing the yard work so I would not have to worry about being alone in the house. The house was very large. I was afraid to be alone in this big house. When I looked at Cooper that fear dissipated and I was happy Garrison was leaving.

Then like a flash of lightning the vision was gone and Landon's hands were off my back. I gulped and sucked air in. I felt like I had just been suffocated and then had just come back to life but no one seemed to notice.

"Avery, you don't have to do this if you're not ready." Dallas was always trying to make me feel better but I knew I had to do this. It was now or never. I pushed the vision as far away as I possible could.

"No, I have to do this now or I will never have the guts to do it again." I glanced at the clock and it read 3:00 a.m. The lump in my scared throat seemed to pulse at the thought of seeing him. My father. He would probably slam the door in my face. Or would he try to hug me. I couldn't stand the thought of his hands on me. I wanted my mom's arms to embrace me.

I knew at this moment that it was now or never. We drove all this way and as much as I didn't want it to be true, I needed him. The other half of an Affinity. So I opened the door and jumped out of the truck. I looked at Dallas, whose eyes seemed to be misty with tears. I loved that he felt how I did. He was so patient with me, especially now. Driving us all the way out here and feeling my pain.

"Ok, so here it goes," I said as I closed the door. I walked the small path up to the door. The outside light of the house lead the way to the beautiful navy blue door. The golden door knocker was wet with dew as I touched it. I slammed it against the door hoping he would hurry up. My nerves were shot and I didn't know how long I could stand out here.

Suddenly I heard the creaks of footsteps on the floor, like someone coming down stairs. He was coming. My throat was burning now, burning with fright.

The door opened and there stood a man I didn't recognize. The strong man that once was my father was now a frail man with white hair. His blue eyes were bloodshot. Dark circles loomed under them. He wore blue pinstriped pajamas. They were very wrinkly and dirty, stained with food and God knows what else.

"Avery, is that you?" This was the first thing he said to me. In years of not hearing his voice, I knew it still. I wanted to cry seeing him like this. My father was old. He had aged in what seemed like, to me, overnight but was really twenty-one years.

"Yes, Richard I am so sorry to be bothering you so early in the morning. We drove all night to get here, and I just need you to listen to me for just a few minutes. My friends are waiting in the truck." He looked to Dallas' truck and then back at me.

I stopped. He put his hand up to stop me from talking.

"No need, I know why you are here." He replied.

"No Richard you don't. Whatever you are thinking it's the complete opposite of that," I answered. "Do you mind if I come in for a minute? I don't want to wake anyone so I will be very quiet."

He laughed an empty laugh. "There is no one here for you to wake. It's only me now. Rachel and Cora left."

"What do you mean left?" I asked, not expecting what he was going to say next.

"They left me. Almost a year ago now. Rachel took Cora to live in Italy with her family. Cora is in college there and Rachel works at some

Bistro. She is dating a man that is no older than you." Pain came across his face. "Please tell your friends to come in and I will tell you more." He turned and walked further into the house. I waved for them to come in. I knew at this point this was not going to be a quick visit.

It was midmorning when my eyes opened. I sat up, looked around, and stared at my surroundings. I was in a bed with Dallas next to me but it was not my bed. It was a guest bedroom. Somehow Richard had talked us into sleeping first before we talked. He said he just couldn't talk at 3:00 in the morning. So we took the guest bedroom upstairs. Landon slept on the couches down stairs. Lillith had managed to conceal her wings for the brief moment of being introduced to Richard. Then Richard stumbled back into his room and closed the door. We all took our places to sleep and dispersed. Lillith just said she would sit and wait until we all woke up.

I woke Dallas, which he didn't like too much, but he got up and stretched. He smiled at me, that sweet innocent smile, so I pulled him back into the bed with me. I held him and stared into his beautiful eyes. How could things not go right? I knew I had to do whatever I could to help save Landon and to ensure my future with Dallas.

"I think we are the only ones awake right now," he whispered. Chills went through my body. His breath was warm against my skin and his hands started to caress my hips.

"Yeah, I think your right. So?" I teased.

"So kiss me." He took my face in his gentle hands and kissed me. It was so tender and sweet that I melted right into the guest bed. I didn't care whose bed it was, that was the effect Dallas had on me.

Then I remembered I slept and had no dreams, or at least no dreams that I could remember anyway. So maybe being around Richard was a strong repellent for Dedrick. I didn't know and I didn't care.

Dallas continued to kiss me and things started getting heated. My shirt had been removed, and I didn't even notice. He was kissing my neck and playing with my hair. I knew that this would be the first time we would make love. Although it wasn't how I had planned it, I could not resist him. Once his pants came off I got a pretty good view of all of his tattoos. They were so beautiful, so colorful. His arms were completely covered with sayings and artwork. I ran my hands all over them trying to feel the beauty of them. He lifted me and adjusted my body so he was directly on top of me. I ran my hands over his strong back and he smiled. He was in very good shape. I suddenly thought about my body. I was thin, but not in shape. As he kissed my stomach I didn't think he minded.

He was so beautiful and so good to me. I wanted him to be with me forever and knew it at this moment. I knew I wanted to show him this. In my mind this was one way to show him how bad I wanted him, it may not have been the right way but it felt right. Everything about Dallas felt right. His muscles in his arms tensed as he slid off my pants. I shivered. It had been a very long time since I had been intimate. I was scared in a way. Scared that it would hurt and scared of getting hurt but I went with it. I wanted him so bad that I just pushed those thoughts to the back of my mind. We quietly continued to make love.

Chapter 16

Finding the Watcher

We had somehow fallen into a sleep-like state and it was now about noon. I heard voices downstairs. They were all awake and I had to go talk to Richard. I rolled off the bed, aching in places that had never ached before. Dallas grabbed my pants and handed them to me. We dressed in silence, although I'm not sure why we didn't speak. I thought maybe he had been disappointed in me. Maybe I was bad in bed? I cringed at the thought. Dallas was great, that I knew. Tender, loving and sweet. I searched his eyes for any hint as to why he was being so quiet when he spoke.

"We better get down there. Come on." As Dallas and I walked down the steps I saw all the pictures of my half-sister Cora. From birth to graduation they filled the walls. She had olive skin like her mother and she had Richard's eyes. She was beautiful. She had the looks I wished I had gotten from Richard. Instead I got my mother's pale skin and thin frame.

"She looks like you, don't you think?" Dallas asked. I laughed as I stopped at her last picture on the wall. A picture of her on a sailboat. I didn't see any resemblance between the two of us. It was like looking at a swan and I was the ugly duck.

"Are you mad at her, you know for getting the father that you didn't? Or are you sad that you didn't get to know her?" Full of questions now wasn't he. I didn't want to think too much about that but I was forced to now. I didn't want to ignore Dallas.

"No, I am glad it was her that got this life, the privileged life. Because if it were me, then I wouldn't have met you." And then I kissed him. It was very honest. I could not imagine life without Dallas. Especially now.

We walked into the kitchen and they all sat at the breakfast nook. Landon looking very sleepy. Richard with a blank stare and Lillith with her now pale orange wings stretched out for all to see. I had to do a double take. Richard had to be seeing this, but he wasn't running away.

He looked at me and smiled. A weird, shocked sort of smile. I smiled back but it was a very strange one on my behalf. He stood up to give me his chair and I sat.

"Well we can pretty much say that your dad knows about everything." Landon spoke, his face cold and hard. I knew he had to have known about Dallas and I. What we did. But how? We were so quiet. I could not meet his gaze. I felt his eyes burning into me. I suddenly felt so bad. Like a tramp. Like I cheated on him.

"Yeah they filled me in. I can't say that I didn't know this was real. I mean your mom spoke about it for years. I just chose to ignore it until today." Richard was being strong. I knew he was going through a lot. So my focus had to shift to him now. His life was in shambles and even though he left me it felt it unfair to leave him now.

"Richard, um, dad." I cleared my throat. "There is a big sacrifice in what we are doing. This is very dangerous ground and I understand if you don't want to help. But please, we need you."

"Last night I told you I knew why you were here because I had a dream about your mom. She told me you would be coming. She also told me why I had to help you and your friends. So I am willing to do whatever is necessary to help you. Avery, I have always loved you. I am a horrible man for what I did to you and your mom. So I will try to make up for that." Tears threatened my eyes but I fought them off. I would not cry right now. I had to be strong and focus on our goal.

"Ok, enough with the drama. This isn't some talk show where you all reveal how sorry you are blah, blah, blah. This is real." Lillith's annoying voice cut through me like a knife. Landon gave her a harsh look. It was rude of her to say, but in way she was kind of right. We should talk about the personal stuff later. Things were getting a bit thick at the moment.

First my father was telling me he was sorry for all he did to me and I didn't know how to respond. Second, Dallas and I had just shared something very special and he was acting a bit distant. I knew in my heart he loved me. Maybe it was the setting? This wasn't the most romantic place to make love for the first time. Third, Landon's eyes pierced my soul. I don't know how but he knew what had happened and he was sad. Just then I glanced his way. He turned away from me like I was an enemy. Then there was a knock at the door.

"Who could be here?" I asked Richard.

"I don't know. I don't have anyone." He sounded so sad and alone. He had no one. He had no friends. How desperately sad. He walked to the door and opened. There stood Justin. He had said he would be here at noon. He had to know where we were he was the Psychic. He was also proving to be a bit more than just psychic. He was a psychic-telepath extraordinaire.

"Mr. Snow, I am Justin White, a friend of Avery and Dallas. It's nice to meet you. Can I please come in?" He was always so polite. Impeccable manners. Of course Richard let him in and led him into the kitchen. He smiled at us all. Where was Kerri? Of course since I thought the question and he was a telepath, Justin answered.

"She is working. You know that girl is very dedicated. But I'm here to help in any way I can." He scanned the room and frowned at Lillith. No one seemed to like her.

"Well, what now?" Richard asked.

"I am not too sure. I mean, I know what mom asked of me, but I still need to find the Watcher and an Angel willing to break the rules." Lillith stood up, hands on hips and all. I figured she would do it, but I never really asked her if she would. I was not in any place to judge her even though she had a bad attitude. She was an Angel and she was helping Landon.

"I am, of course, willing but there will be major ramifications if I do. Let me just tell you that for now. I can't really explain what but it will be worse than the changing of my wings."

She turned red, almost as if she was embarrassed. Was it possible to make her feel that way? I didn't really know but it made me feel better that I only needed to track down the Watcher. I also wondered where Ianni was. I needed her once again and she wasn't here. Justin was quick to my side his hand on mine. I had just noticed that they were shaking. He smiled at me and it was somehow very calming.

"So, how are we going to do this? You know, find my Watcher?" I asked.

"Well, from what Lillith said before you came downstairs, you know who your Watcher is you just need to think about it," Richard answered. That was not helping at all. I need to think about it? Um, sorry people but not helping.

"No Daddio, that is not what I said." Lillith's tone with Richard was starting to bother me. "I said she needs to meditate on it. Meditation can do so much for a human. It can almost bring you to Heaven and back if you focus. Being as tired as you are Avery, I don't think you will have a hard time with it. A lot of times humans need to be sleepy to really focus. I think you should go outside and just try it. Clear your mind of all your worries and just think only of your Watcher. Hopefully it will come to you. While you do this we will try to think of something as well."

She made it sound so simple. Just meditate and focus. Okay, first of all I had never, ever meditated. So I feared that if I sat there long enough I would just fall asleep. That was the last thing I needed to do! Even though last night I slept without Dedrick's intrusions I wasn't too sure if the same could be said for now. So I went outside anyway. I felt the cool air on my skin and a chill filled my entire body. I found a chair on Richards's deck. A nice wicker chair with a yellow pillow. I sat staring out at the landscape. The pool, with its little ripples being made by the wind. The trees blowing and swaying and I closed my eyes. Focus and think about my Watcher and that is what I did. I was instantly transported to a memory.

A day very similar to this. Wind blowing, trees swaying. Garrison's eyes filled with tears as I told him that while he was away on his trip to New York I had fallen in love with Cooper. He begged me to change my mind but I didn't. I had selfishly fallen for Cooper, the man Garrison hired to help around our home. To make our home welcoming for me, the soon-to-be bride. I stared into his eyes and they seemed so familiar to me now. A beautiful brown. With the tears I couldn't be sure as to why they were so familiar. I went inside the house and grabbed my already packed bags as he sat in the foyer with his dark hair hanging in his face. My gloved hands touched his cheek. A tear soaked the tip of my index finger. Then I left. No words. I just walked away.

I met Cooper at the end of the road. We left town and never looked back.

A week later I was sitting with Cooper at morning tea reading the paper. A story of a suicide was on the second page. Famous author Garrison Whitaker had hung himself in his barn. It crushed me, and Cooper, as well. So bad in fact that we didn't speak to each other for days. Whenever we tried to speak, only sobbing came out. We had killed him with our betrayal.

My eyes popped open and Dallas stood before me.

"I am sorry to interrupt but I came to say bye." He had his keys in hand.

"Why?" That was all I could muster up to say.

"Well, I have work and I have finals tomorrow. I don't want to leave. Trust me," he said as he sat down in front of me.

"I understand. I know this is a lot to take in. A lot to deal with."

"No, it's not that. I just have to get back to my life." He put his head down. I could tell he didn't want to leave. "No, that came out all wrong..."

"Stop. I understand. This is a lot to process and you have a life. I don't fault you for that. This will all be over soon and we can get back to us. I promise." I grabbed his hand. He was so patient with me. How could I possibly be upset that he had to get back to his life? What I was going through shouldn't mess with his future.

"You're so great Princess Snow. That's what I love about you, your honesty. Don't worry, I'm only a phone call away and I will be thinking of you every moment. I spoke with Justin and he agreed to take you and Landon home." He kissed me and I melted. I wanted to go with him and forget this all. But I couldn't.

"Can I walk you out?" I asked.

"No, stay here. Focus and meditate," he teased. One last kiss and he turned to leave. Then he stopped and turned around again. "Hey, one last thing that might be strange but when we were kids Landon always called me Garrison. No big deal but I thought it might help."

I almost fell over from the shock. Just hearing that name brought up a lot of emotions. Maybe it was no big deal, but it was a huge coincidence. Then he left, this time for real.

I looked at the people left inside. Ianni was here now. She must have come in while I was outside. I wondered what she was thinking. Lillith was talking very closely to Landon, who stared at me with those burning eyes. Richard sipped coffee and stared into space. Justin was coming outside.

"Okay, so that is strange huh?" Justin said as he came out.

"What is?" I asked shyly.

"Come on Avery, you know, Garrison??"

"Oh yeah. You heard that? Well, could be coincidence, right?"

"You know better Avery. You know that in your heart it could be true. But we have more pressing matters. Come inside, we have devised a plan." He pulled me out of the chair and my legs felt like Jell-O. Could it be? How in the world could this be possible? What a twisted thing to consider. Like Justin said, I had to sort of push that aside for now. We had to find the Watcher.

After a long discussion, or rather speech, from Lillith and Ianni we devised a plan. They told me that when I entered Henry and Claire's old home in dreams my Watcher was always there. I just don't see him.

"So it is their home then?" I asked Ianni. She nodded. It didn't seem to resemble what my memories told me about the house.

"Are there other doors in the house that you can see?" Lillith asked Landon.

"Many doors but I always only enter one. Why?" He asked.

"Well the watcher could be in the other doors. This time, we are going to enter the dream with you and we are going into the other doors. While Landon is with you, Avery, in the main door. Then we will see who your Watcher is." Lillith answered. It was so matter of fact, like she thought it up all on her own.

"So you're going to chance me seeing Dedrick again?" I was now scared. Well more like terrified. What if I could not say no to him? What if this was it? Landon drew nearer to me. He took my hand. I let him because, if not for him, I felt like I could possibly fall.

"Don't fear Avery, we will be there with you. You will be safe," Ianni said, sounding very sure and convincing again. It must be a Spirit Guide thing. "So you must drink your Yulu tea tonight. We will all be with you to make sure you wake up when you need to. Richard has agreed to stay with you as well," she continued.

I looked his way and he smiled. And Landon looked at me and there were those eyes again.

"Can we talk a minute?" He asked. How in the world could I say no?

"Yes." I replied.

Chapter 17

Getting to Know You

He sat down next to me on the other chair. At first he looked away looking at the trees. Then he was staring at me intently. I had a hard time looking back at him. He almost made me nervous. His good looks didn't help with the nervousness. He was such a beautiful man. I started feeling like I had when he was Cooper. I knew why I had fallen for him back then. There was just something about him. I felt like I could be with him and there would be only calm. Like the day in the coffee shop. I was just so comfortable. A man I hardly knew anything about, but we just had coffee together like any couple would. He took his wallet out and handed it to me. I held it in my hands and gave him a puzzled look.

"Everything you need to know about me is there in that wallet." His voice was almost rugged and raw. Kind of like a person who had been crying for hours.

So I opened the wallet and inside was several pictures. The first was of a woman in her early twenties holding little blonde baby. It was Landon and his mother. She was beautiful and he was adorable. The next picture was of Landon and Dallas. They were hugging each other, probably no older than six or seven but still best of friends. There was no doubt about that. I could see how happy they made each other. I could picture them playing together. Army men or cowboys, playing tag or hide and seek. A smile appeared on my face. It truly made me happy to see this picture.

The next picture immediately took the smile off of my face. A girl in her wedding dress. It was Claire. Me. I stared at the face of a girl I had seen in my dreams, seen when Ianni showed me the visions. How insane was it that I was looking at myself from the past? I quickly turned to the next pictures. Three children sat in a small chair, our children.

"How did you find these pictures?" I asked just staring down at their little faces.

"If you do a little research it's unbelievable what you can find. I just found our old town in England. I contacted a genealogy expert and told him that I was a distant relative. He gave me tons of information. Pictures and records everything you can imagine." He was smiling now. He seemed pleased to be showing me these pictures, like he was finally telling his secrets.

"Keep looking. They are all in there. All of our lives." And he was right. Emily, Cooper, Elsie, Adam, and all of their children. All of our children.

"How….. How can you carry these things? How does it not rip out your soul to know these people are gone? All of our children are gone." It was really the first time I had referred to them as our children out loud but it felt so refreshing to not pretend. We were and we are an 'us'.

"It helps me. I don't know, I sort of feel haunted everywhere I go. Like the past is haunting me. So when I learned about us, and I mean really learned, I felt better. Like I wasn't searching anymore. I haven't always looked for you in this life. There was a long period of time when I stopped. I focused on my life and career. I felt so much better once I at least had your pictures. It was right after my trip to Europe that I decided that I would stop looking."

He took the wallet and shoved it back into his pants. Then leaned back and looked to the sky. The wind was still blowing and the trees were still swaying. He looked like he was more comfortable than I had yet to see him. Maybe just being out here talking with me was what comforted him.

"I even had a relationship. It didn't last too long. That was because of my career. It takes a lot of your time. I just don't want you to think that I am some sort of freak."

"No, well I did call you a soul stalker. I am sorry for that." I felt so ashamed now. What an awful thing to call your soul mate

"Ahh, don't worry about it. I am so used to being called names. People always thought I was a freak. When I was a kid I remembered everything. I called my mom Emily." He started laughing and so did I. It really decreased the tension.

"But they were more scared than anything else. They didn't understand why I was talking about you and why I wanted to be called Henry. I even asked them to call me Cooper for short. I thought that it would be fitting because that is my last name now. But it didn't fly." He laughed again. He continued to tell me about how his parents sent him away. I had already heard about that part of his life. It sort of angered me but I understood that maybe they didn't know what to do with him. They didn't understand and fear took over.

"So, I have a question," I said when he was done.

"Anything."

"Ok, did you really call Dallas Garrison?" He froze at my words and I sort of did too. It seemed like he didn't want to answer.

"Well only because his eyes. They looked so much like Garrison's. So it was just what I called him. I was a just a kid."

The eyes! That is why they looked so familiar to me in the vision. They were the same brown, even the same shape. Almost almond-shaped. They also had this sadness in them. It was almost like eyes were the haunting factor now. Eyes were the windows to the soul right? That's why Landon's pierce me and Dallas' look just like Garrison's.

"So how do you deal everyday with knowing who you are? How do you not go a little crazy?" I asked.

"I think I am a little crazy, don't you think so?" He admitted.

"No. I mean you did search for me in every lifetime."

"But...that is love. I mean real love. It's crazy, it's not sane and it's not mediocre. Love is fearless, ridiculous, do anything, foolish and everything in between. And that is how I feel for you every single lifetime. I can't escape you."

He took a deep breath, almost like it was a weight taken off of him to say these things to me. I, on the other hand, had stopped breathing, to the point of almost passing out. He reached for me and just as his hand almost touched mine I stood up. I could not tolerate another vision. I wasn't sure if I would have one but it seemed every time we touched something cosmic happened. I could not chance that.

"Well this has been a long morning for me," he said so matter of fact. "I just want to tell you one thing before I go inside. I will not ever come in between your relationship with Dallas. I just want to see you happy. Really, honestly, happy and if Dallas can do that for you, well then I will let it be. But I do want to be in your life. Can we be friends?"

Friends? How could we just be friends now? After all these lifetimes together I felt as if we were closer than that. I felt a draw to him, a pulling that made me want to escape this world with him and not look back. But I had to just accept that we would be in each other's lives.

"Yes, friends," was all I could say for now.

"We may be family soon if things with you and Dallas continue the way they are." His voice cracked a little. I could tell it was hard to be the friend already.

"Um...."

"Well, who are we kidding? Dallas doesn't fall in love every day. And the way he looks at you it's just like the way I looked at...." He stopped.

"Me." He nodded in and agreed. He swung his head to shake the long hair from his eyes. My heart leapt at this simple thing that I notice Landon doing almost every five minutes. At that moment he stood and walked away. And I was left there standing alone.

I tried very hard to not watch him walk away. I could feel the presence of everyone left in the kitchen. I could only guess at what they were thinking.

I slumped into the chair. My chest was aching and my head spinning. This was a horrible day for me. In so many ways it could have been a great day, now it was ruined. I closed my eyes for just a second and as I did I tried to control my breathing. What did Landon want me to say? How could he bring those pictures out here and expect me to just say, "*Oh yeah we can be just friends!*" He knew that he was making me sick with decision. Every day lately that's all it's been, making decisions. I wanted my old lonely life back. Right now! I just wanted to be quiet old lonely. No Angels, no boyfriends, no past Avery.

I stood at the opening of a barn. It was very muddy and the stench from the cows and horses stung my nose. Yuck! It was very unlike me to visit a farm. I looked inside and the barn was extremely large, unlike any I had ever seen before. It wasn't red, it was green. I took a step forward and I heard a whinnying. A horse. I never liked them.

"In here darling. Come back," a man's voice said. It was familiar, I knew it somehow. I listened and went towards the back of the barn. He was there in the back in a stall with a cream colored mare. His back was to me. He was brushing her gently with great tenderness. She whinnied again in pleasure. Whatever he was doing with the brush she seemed to like it.

"It's Adele's grooming day darling. Would you like to ride her later? I can saddle her up and you can ride her right after lunchtime." Still his back faced me as he spoke.

"Who's horse is this?" I asked.

"Don't be silly darling, Adele is your horse."

"My horse? I don't have a horse. I don't even really like horses."

"You're in a rare mood today darling. Come a little closer. She senses you're here and you know she must see you now that she knows you're here." I walked closer to the mare and the man, my feet getting stuck in the mud. It was almost difficult to walk, but it was true what the man said. The horse, Adele, she did sense me being there. As I drew closer to her she started getting more restless. So I walked faster and finally reached her stall. I reached a shaky hand out towards her. She nuzzled up to it. I felt her breathe on my fingers and it calmed me.

"See darling. I told you. Now if you don't want to ride her then why are you here?" A great question. Why was I here in this barn? Where am I? Who was he? Heck, who am I?

"Who are you?" I asked him.

"I think you know who I am Avery. You haven't been able to stop thinking about me."

"What? Why did you come to me? Am I dreaming?" It had to be a dream. It was a dream. Only it wasn't a normal dream. Not my normal kind of dream.

"Darling, I didn't come to you, you came to me." Ok now I was frustrated. He was talking to me but still facing the mare.

"Turn around and show me who you are," I demanded. "And stop calling me darling." Just then he turned around. His eyes, the brown eyes shaped like little almonds. Garrison.

"No, it can't be. How can you be here?"

"How can one person be anywhere Avery? I just am. I am here to show you what you can't see." He was calling me Avery. I looked down at myself and sure enough I was Avery. I wasn't Emily, as Garrison had once known me as.

"What can't I see?" I asked. As soon as I did he disappeared. I heard a horrible crack. I ran towards the sound, it was on the side of the barn and it wasn't in my sight. The barn was filled to the ceiling with hay. As I came around the corner another noise filled the barn. This time it was a horrible creaking noise over and over. That's when I saw him, hanging from a beam in the ceiling, Garrison had hung himself in the barn. He had hung himself after I left him for someone else. For Cooper. I screamed and he swayed side to side. That horrible creaking noise. I could try all my life but I don't think I will ever forget this sound. I put my head in my hands willing myself to wake up.

"You're not going to wake up Avery. You came for an answer and I still have to give it to you," he spoke, in a soft voice. I was too afraid to lift my head. "Look at me Avery. Look at me and open your eyes."

"I can't, I can't see what I did to you. I am so sorry. I loved you, but I loved him longer. You see, it wasn't you. It wasn't anything you could control. We have been together for centuries. We are twin souls and you didn't stand a chance. No one did." I felt that I needed to tell him all of my feelings. I did once love him. That was all true.

"You are not at fault; no one is, now look at me," he demanded.

"No, I am at fault! We both were. You wouldn't have done this if I didn't leave you. If he would have left me alone. Left us alone." It was all true. If Cooper would have only done what Landon is willing to do now for Dallas and I. Just let us be happy. If only he could have just done that then Garrison would not be hanging here in front of me now.

"Please darling, open your eyes. I promise you it's all okay now." At these words I did what he asked. I opened my eyes. Instead of seeing Garrison I saw Dallas hanging from the beam. I was too terrified to scream. My throat was suddenly wrenched with pain.

He was smiling and he switched from Dallas back to Garrison and then back again. I closed my eyes and opened them once more. Was this some trick?

"It's me. I am back and we are together again. My soul is elated! Happy and healed, to be here with you. You make me feel this way. Don't be scared my darling. You did what your soul knew best. You went with your Affinity. I don't blame you for that. But this lifetime I have you and we will be together forever."

The next thing I knew I was being shaken awake by my father. He stood over me, shaking me and yelling. I couldn't make out the words. All I could hear was the terrible sound of wood creaking, of Garrison hanging himself.

Chapter 18

Go Away

"Avery, falling asleep was reckless, and irresponsible." Ianni's voice was so loud I was sure everyone on the street could hear her. I just tried to drown it all out. I was done now. I was done with these Spirit Guides, the Dark Guides, and my father, all of them. Who was she to call me reckless? I couldn't control my sleep. I just wanted my apartment and my bed. I wanted to go to bed and forget that all this happened. I was simply giving up. Waving the white flag, hoping someone would see it. Please somebody see it. Someone in Heaven. God or my Watcher perhaps? At this very moment I felt defeated and done. Even though I had not even tried to defeat Dedrick or even tried to move on with Landon as my so-called-friend. I had felt like I had lost a battle. A battle of my past life. Learning that the man that I gave myself to completely was now a love from my past as well. I could not deal with all this news anymore.

I stood up pushed everyone away from me. It was all very slow motion. They didn't even fight me. They just let me walk past them. I stormed through house and right out the front door. I kept walking and walking until I found myself at a park. I didn't even know how I had reached this place. I didn't know my way around this town. I didn't even know my way around my own life so it was just the way things were right now.

Then I saw it. A flash of light, just like the one outside my apartment building. This light was very similar and I knew darn well that this was no reflection off of a car or kids messing around. This light was meant for me, just like the first one was.

So like before I followed it into the park. This park was very different from the one at home. It ran right alongside the main beach. The smell of the ocean filled my lungs. *Breathe, Avery, breathe.*

I kept walking into the park until I found myself on a cliff, surrounded by palm trees and a bench. The light was gone. I looked around and I didn't see it anywhere. It was as if it vanished or I had imagined it all. I sat down and then I felt a peace, a calm, come over me. Looking at the waves of this beautiful ocean. Listening to the seagulls call and the children play down on the shore below. I saw a family of four play with a soccer ball. I also saw an older couple standing together with their pants rolled up and their toes in the sand. They shrieked when the cold water ran over their feet. I laughed. Simple things in life like that seemed so far away from me. It seemed like I would not get to play in the sand or feel the ocean on my toes while holding my love's hand.

I knew who would get to. My best friend Kerri, I was happy that she would be able to enjoy life like a human should. I wanted all of this for her. For me, it seemed to escape my grasp more and more everyday. I was now living the paranormal. Living in a life of constant strange and the utter unbelievable. I closed my eyes, just focusing on my best friend and all the visions I saw for her life. Little kids, a big beautiful home filled with nice things. Justin treating her like the princess she was. She deserved it all. I no longer felt jealous of her, but just simply happy.

It was then that I felt it, a hand on my shoulder, but when I turned there was no one there. I tried to convince myself that it was just in my mind. I wasn't exactly stable at this point. When I closed my eyes again I didn't care if I fell asleep. Let Dedrick come, let him take me. Let him do what he wants. I don't care. My life this time is over and I will not return. I can't keep going through this again.

"My gosh child, stop feeling so damn sorry for yourself would you?" Now I knew that I wasn't imagining this voice. His was one you could not forget. Mr. Grey. He was sitting right next to me. He was wearing a track suit of sorts. It was god awful ugly, but he seemed to like it because he sat proudly.

"Mr. Grey, what are you...?"

"Listen, don't you start asking what am I doing here or why am I not in my place. Those are stupid questions. Come on girl, you have been dealing with the supernatural for how long now?"

"Um, a few months I guess."

"Nope, wrong answer! Try your whole life." He was being very smart assed, so true to his nature. I suppose he was right. My whole life had been surrounded by weird.

"Your mom is fighting for her place in line, do you understand that?"

"What? How do you know anything about me or my mom?"

"Honey, I'm the one you're looking for. I am your Watcher. I know everything about you. I finally had to get you alone and tell you who I was. Instead of focusing on your task, like you should be, you're too busy running away and feeling sorry for yourself."

All I could do at this moment was laugh. I knew it was the wrong thing to do, but this was so funny and exciting that laughter just blurted out of me. He looked very serious and unhappy but I couldn't help myself.

"Compose yourself Avery. We have things to discuss and a lot of work to do. Your mom is hoping for you to fulfill your duty and you have a Dark Guide on your tail."

"Yes, I'm sorry. I am just so happy. I saw this light and it led me here to you. Are you the light?" It was all making sense to me know. He was guiding the light, he had to be.

"I had to show you things or else you would walk right by them."

"What are you showing me here? You?"

"No. I brought you here so you could see beauty in life and stop feeling sorry for yourself. So things are a little complicated right now." A little complicated? Did he know my life well? "But you have a job to do so stop sulking. You have a life awaiting you. Once this is over you need to live it. You have to just be strong and fight. I know you can. I have seen you do it before."

I was still in awe that my Watcher was lonely, cranky John Grey. The words he said, they did make sense but I just wanted to jump off the cliff in front of me. I needed a good slap to get me back to my reality. So, my life was complicated, I could do this, I was strong. I thought of my Aunt Paulina. She was always telling me I could do whatever I wanted in life, she was my own personal cheerleader. It was then that I realized I needed to go home. I had to get back in touch with her and Kerri. I had a job I had to get back to. I could fight Dedrick and deal with everything else and still live my life. Right?

The next thing I knew I was standing in my living room my head dizzy. I looked around. I was alone. No one was here. It was just me and my home. I grabbed the phone and called my aunt. Of course Miss busy-all-the-time didn't answer so I left a quick message along the lines of, "I'm okay, just checking in. Call me." The next call I made was to Kerri.

"Hello, this is Kerri." She sounded so professional on the phone.

"Hi it's Avery."

"Oh my God what's up?" Not so professional now. I had to laugh.

"Listen, I can't talk long. I have to get some sort of rest, it's been crazy lately. I just wanted to check in and tell you I will be there for my shift tomorrow."

"Avery, take all the time you need. Really, it's no big deal. I have coverage. Rachel has been taking good care of Mr. Grey." Another thing to laugh at. Mr. Grey wasn't really a resident after all now was he? I wondered where he was right now. Was he there pretending or was he somewhere else? With his being my Watcher it made me ask a lot of questions.

"Hello, you still there?"

"Oh yeah sorry. I'm just tired and my mind is wondering. If you're sure about me not coming in tomorrow then I will just stay here and rest." I wondered what she thought about me being super tired and not coming in.

"Avery listen, I don't know exactly what is going on but I know that you're not well. So take some time off. I have it covered and you have not taken your vacation time this year. Take it now and go away for a little mini vacation. My parent's cabin is still open. You can go there for a few days to get away." It was just like my best friend to be so helpful. Her parent's cabin would be a perfect place for me to get away and for all of us to get our plan together. And hopefully once it's all over Dallas and I can spend the rest of the time there, just the two of us.

"That sounds so great Kerri. You know I will be better soon and I want to go dress shopping with you as soon as I get back. So don't go without me okay?"

"Did you really think I would go without you? Come on Avery, you're my maid of honor."

"I am? Really?"

"Well who did you think I would ask? Rachel?" We both started cracking up at the thought of Rachel being Kerri's maid of honor. I was more than happy to think about the upcoming wedding. Focusing on a normal future was something I had not done since Lucy died. My life was in an uproar of sorts. Maybe shaving my memory would not be so bad. I shook my head at that thought.

"Can I go up there tomorrow?" I asked.

"Avery you can go today if you want, it's all yours. Don't worry, I have an appointment for dress shopping as soon as you get back, so it's perfect timing really. Okay, I gotta go. Love ya!"

"I love you too girl."

Chapter 19

Mini Vacation

I literally started packing my bag before I hung up the phone so I was done packing in less than twenty minutes. I had everything I needed for my little mini vacation. This was going to be perfect. Now I just needed to tell everyone my plans. I didn't know how to get a hold of my father, Ianni, Lilith or Mr. Grey, but I knew who lived right downstairs from me. Whether or not he was home remained to be seen. So I put my shoes on and went to check. When I reached his door I stood there for a few moments. I wasn't too sure that I wanted to knock. It was so hard to see him and I had stormed out of my father's house like some sort of child and then disappeared without telling them.

The door swung open and Lillith grabbed me and pulled me into the apartment. It was almost completely empty. There was no furniture in the living room but there was a table with one chair. How sad. One chair. Not two or four. No one to share a meal with. No one to talk with or play cards. Now that we were friends, though, technically we could play cards and share a meal.

"What is going on with you? Do you know how worried we all have been?" Lillith's voice almost sounded as if she was really worried about me, as a human, and less worried for me as Landon's love.

"Well I had to get out. I went for a walk." I looked around and Landon was in the kitchen peeling an orange. He didn't seem worried about me. So much for friends.

"A walk? Well I hope that walk was worth it because we have

been all looking for you all day."

"All day? I just got here an hour ago, how could you be looking for me all…." My voice trailed off as I looked out the window that now showed a dark night. "Wait, what time is it?"

"It's near 8:00," Landon answered.

"But how could that be? I was just at the beach and then I met up with Mr. Grey and he sort of transported me home. I swear Lillith." I felt so confused.

"Mr. Grey who is he?" Landon asked, all of a sudden sounding like he wanted to talk instead of being anti-social.

"He is my Watcher." Then I explained how I walked down to the park and followed the light and Mr. Grey appeared to me. I also told him how I knew him from Sunrise Estates and how I got home and called Kerri and found a great place for us to go make plans for how to save Landon.

When I was done Lillith just sat there without speaking, her wings sort of fluttering, sending loose feathers onto the carpet. She apparently had nothing to say. Landon handed me an orange and I tore into it. It was so good and as soon as I was done he gave me another. Our hands touched and I felt a shock. A swirling of feathers surrounded us and another vision came, whether we wanted it or not.

I was on a bed in a beautiful apartment. In a huge bedroom, with a window that looked out to a beautiful view of the mountains of Vermont. It had snowed the night before and it blanketed the ground. I felt a pain in my arm and looked down. Once again my arm had blown up to the size of a balloon. That was when I just pulled the IV out myself. I was so tired of being tied up to machines. I just wanted to die in peace with no cords or attachments. Just Adam by my side. I tried to call to him but my voice escaped me. So I grabbed the buzzer and pressed the button. Within seconds he came in, his dark hair so disheveled and messy that I had to laugh.

"What is so funny Elsie?"

"Your hair! When is the last time you brushed it?" He tried to slick it back but it kept falling into his eyes. "Its okay, you're still handsome. Now come here and help me would you?"

Once he took one look at my arm he flipped out. He didn't like the thought that I was dying. I heard his prayers by my bedside asking God to give my cancer to him. He wanted to switch places with me. He knew it wouldn't happen but he asked every night. I, on the other hand, was ready to go. I was tired of the pain and this life. He fumbled with the IV as it leaked fluid all over my sheets.

"Iris? Iris can you come in here?" He called to the nurse. She was so sweet. A single mother who did this for a living. How sad and tragic to watch someone die.

"Oh Elsie, what did you do?" She took my arm into her warm hands and bandaged it up. Then she tried to find a vein in the other arm. It was impossible to do, my veins were gone. They had given up just as I had. They had fought as long as I had fought and when I gave up so did they.

"Iris stop. I don't want the damn IV anymore. I don't want any of this shit."

"Elsie please," Adam pleaded. He knew I was giving up.

"No! No more please Adam. I don't want to fight anymore. I have fought. I gave the greatest effort and now I want to enjoy the first snowfall without beeping machines and IV's. I want you to take me out to the snow. I want you to leave me in it until I melt away with it."

His eyes watered and Iris did as I asked. She unhooked every machine. I had a very strict plan in place and when I told her it was time she was to do as I asked. And she did.

Adam just sat and watched as my attachments came off, tears running down his cheeks, but I had a smile on my face for the first time in months. It was the first real smile.

"Adam, take me outside now. I want to feel the snow on my face."

"Okay Elsie I will take you out for a little while. If that will make you happy."

"You have made me happy Adam. Nothing else in this life. Not one second was I happy without you."

We stood there for a moment with our hands still touching. Our eyes locked onto each other's. It was the first vision of Elsie and Adam that we had shared together. I was suddenly struck with a horrible sadness. I felt so sorry for Elsie and Adam. Their time together was so short and it was stolen away from them. I remembered feeling the sadness. Feeling the pain of having to say goodbye to him. I didn't really have a really strong memory of our time together. My past lives were to me like dreams. I could remember bits and pieces but not the whole thing. It seemed so foreign and unreal.

I couldn't take it anymore so I stumbled backwards and left the apartment. No one came after me as I almost ran back to my apartment. When the door was shut I slid down it and cried. But as I looked up I saw a shadow pass over the floor. I dried my eyes so that I could see. Maybe it was just a shadow from the trees. Who was I kidding? Someone was here with me I felt it. I stood up.

"Hello?" I called out, as Ianni came out of my kitchen. I jumped almost out of my skin.

"You scared me almost to death!" I shouted at her.

"Sorry. Are you okay?" She came up to me and put her hand on my shoulder. It felt nice to have her here. I fell into her arms. She just stood there for a moment, without hugging back, but then I felt her arms wrap around me.

I woke up on the couch in a panic. Sweat beaded on my forehead and nose. My clothes stuck to me. I looked around for Ianni and she was not there. I had dreamt but it wasn't one that I remembered too well. I did remember something but I couldn't quite place what it was. I stood up and looked out my window. Still nighttime.

I walked, or dragged, myself to my room. Undressed from my dirty sweaty clothes and got into the shower. I started it cool and then increased the temperature to warm. It felt nice to be alone in my home but I did miss Dallas. And strangely I missed my father too. I needed to contact him and let him know I was okay. Something told me he knew already though.

After my shower and after I was in my comfy clothes I settled in on the couch with a bowl of ice cream. I was done with sleep for the night. I was too afraid. I didn't need to chance any encounters with Dedrick or anyone else. I turned on the TV and flipped channels until I found a good Lifetime movie. A love story of course. It wasn't hard to stay awake. I had gotten very used to it by now. Not long after I found myself watching yet another sunrise. The mornings were getting chilly. The weather was surely changing. I walked into the apartment and my phone rang. It wasn't normal to get a call so early so that had panicked me.

"Hello?" I answered.

"Hey Princess Snow," Dallas said cheerfully.

"Hi! I have so much to tell you I don't even know where to start."

"Well I can't wait to hear it all. But I want to hear it in person so open your door would ya?" I ran to my door and there he stood with two coffees' in his hand. He was a lifesaver.

I waited until he set them down before I jumped into his arms. He enveloped me into his warm and comforting arms. He smelled like stinky bar but I didn't care. At this point I didn't care if he smelled like trash, I still wanted his arms around me.

He lifted me up and carried me to my bed. We laid in it and just stared into each other's eyes. When he finally kissed me I didn't want to stop but I had to tell him all about my Watcher and of course about the cabin. I hoped he could get the time off of work. Now I was nervous to tell him. I didn't want to go if he could not be there. I don't think that I would have fallen apart at Richard's or at Landon's if he were with me. It was then that I realized that he made me feel stronger and stable. Even though he did I also couldn't think straight while I was with him. Like how I should have been focused on the fact that he was undressing me instead of thinking about my Watcher or the cabin. So I shut it all off and helped him out.

"You seemed preoccupied, are you okay?" He asked as he dressed himself. I just laid there staring at his tattoos and I regretted seeing him dress.

"I am I guess, I'm sorry. I did enjoy being with you just now." It was very true. Making love to him was beyond perfect. "But a lot had happened since you left that day at my fathers."

"Oh I'm so sorry. You did try to tell me that and I totally ignored it. I guess I just wanted your body too bad to think about anything else." I laughed but he didn't. He was serious.

"Well I wanted your body too. So I kinda decided it could wait."

"Well tell me. I want to hear about all of it." He lay next to me and played with my hair while I told him everything that he missed. Except the vision Landon and I shared. I figured he didn't need to hear about that.

"Can you take the time off? At least for a few days?" I tried to make a pouty face but I don't think it helped my case. It probably made me look stupid.

"I think I may be able to swing it. I can ask if the new guy can cover for a few days. But I have class Wednesday and it's in a restaurant so I kind of have to be there."

"Yay!" I squealed. "Okay I want to leave and be there today. Can you leave with me today? Then we can have a whole night just to ourselves."

"Oh I think I can definitely swing that. For a whole day, and night, alone with you? No doubt about it. But I have to get a few hours' sleep and a shower. Can I crash here?" I nodded and kissed his nose. He was so cute.

"Take a shower first cause you smell like a bar."

"Oh, thanks." He joked and then I got to see him undress which was just what I wanted. As he showered I packed my bags and had a little breakfast. I heard the shower shut off and then I heard a big thud as he fell into my bed. I shut the door to give him some peace. I decided I would go for a walk and then go to Landon's and tell him to come to the cabin tomorrow.

Chapter 20

A Finger's Touch

The walk was long and brisk. As the sun came out I found myself wanting to stay out longer and go do some shopping. So I walked to some of the shops along the bay near my apartment. I had wanted to check them out but never got the chance. The first store was a typical candle store filled with candles and incense. Not long after I left with a minor headache. Once I reached the outside I took several breath's of fresh air and felt better. The next store was the one I had wanted to visit the most. I was called Angel's & Air. On the outside it looked like a bookstore but as I walked in I realized I had been a bit off. It was a bookstore, but also was a coffee shop, oxygen bar and ceramic trinkets and gifts. The book section was tiny but I perused the sections on Angels. I guess I hoped to find a book on "How to Ward Off Demonic Angels" or "How to Have Normal Dreams Again Once Your Soul Mate Invades Them." But no luck. I did come across a book on past lives. The premise was really unbelievable, a boy who remembered his past lives. I decided to not buy that book for I fear that it would cause me to cry. I had been doing enough of that the past few days.

I checked out the oxygen bar and passed on that as well. What drew me closer were all the ceramic gifts. They were so beautifully done. Angels flooded the shelves. The scary thing was they all looked so much like Ianni and Lillith. So human yet, their huge wings took over their whole bodies. It was then that I saw a glass figure of a man and woman, not quiet holding hands, but their hands were very close. The man walking in one direction and the woman in the other. She stared straight ahead but he looked back at her with a face of regret and longing. It was spooky and familiar.

"Ah, I see you have found one of my favorite pieces." I looked up to see the lady from the oxygen bar. She had a kind face. She looked about forty or so but she had shockingly red hair. A lot like Ianni's hair.

"Yes, it's beautiful. What does it represent?" I dared to ask.

"Well it's my own representation of loss."

"Loss?" That was not what I saw in it.

"Well, loss of love. He lost her and she carries on in her life like she is happy. But see her hand almost touching his?"

"Yes," I answered.

"Well she is not entirely ready to lose him forever. She still has him at a fingers touch away." My body filled with chills and I gasped. Her eyes questioned my reaction but I just nodded and tried to blow it off.

"Looking for anything special?" She asked me with a franticness to her voice.

"I am not sure. Just looking for something for my boyfriend or maybe even for my friend. She just got engaged." The word boyfriend came out more choked than smooth. It was so foreign to me to say.

"Well I bet she is with her soul mate. I have a lot of soul mate items. I make all of these here." She led me to the other shelves and she wasn't kidding. There were a ton more items with a man and woman embraced and almost every one of them had an infinity symbol added to the piece.

"Infinity," I spoke.

"Yes, well really Affinity, but the symbol is the same."

"What did you say?" I could not believe my ears. I had never heard that term used before recently and now this woman had said it and I was certain she knew exactly what it meant.

"Affinity. I have books on it are you interested?"

"No I know what it is. My mother she told me." It wasn't exactly true but I couldn't tell her my Spirit Guide told me. I would look crazy.

"Your mother must be very smart if she knows Affinity's. That's very rare. I will let you keep looking. I will be over there if you need me." She pointed towards the oxygen bar and walked away. I noticed her nametag said her name was Katherine.
I continued to look for something rare to get Kerri. After a few minutes I found a beautiful wood carving of a couple at an altar. They appeared to be outdoors. There were flowers surrounding their feet and it looked so perfect for what I imagined for them. I could imagine Kerri putting it on a shelf to show off for years to come. There was an inscription on it that simply said, 'Union'. I turned to look on the other side of the wall and I noticed a burnt orange feather on the ground. When I looked up Ianni was standing in front of me. I jumped and almost dropped the sculpture. She reached out and grabbed it to secure it.

"What are you doing here?" I asked in a hushed whisper.

"You need to get out of here. This is not a safe place." She had a very worried look on her face but I couldn't understand what she meant. This place was harmless.

"You should leave, not me. Someone could see you."

"I mean it Avery! Pay for your stuff and go back home. Now! I am your Guide, it's my job to Guide you, and this place is very dangerous." She was completely serious. I didn't see the harm in a store like this.

"I don't see the problem but whatever you say." I gave her a bit of attitude. That was what you got with me lately. I had about no patience with being told what to do.

"I can't say much but the shop owner, she is meddling with the wrong kind of crowd. Oh no, here she comes." Just as she said it she disappeared, only leaving behind another feather. I did see Katherine walking my way so I decided to just take Ianni's advice and pay for my stuff.

"Oh, all set?" She asked.

"Yep, sure am, thanks." I walked to the counter and heard the doorbell ring as someone else walked into the shop.

"Oh honey you came to visit me," Katherine said. I looked up and saw a handsome man wave towards her. She looked so happy to see him. He was tall with graying hair but a very GQ face. He belonged on the cover of some magazine or on TV, not in a town like this. He smiled and every one of his teeth gleamed white. I was very impressed with Katherine's taste in men.

"Is that your husband?" I asked.

"Oh no. He is my soul mate though," she beamed. "Ben come over here, this young lady she knows of Affinity's, isn't that rare?"

I was a little struck at his name. It sounded familiar but I took a second look at him and he did not look like anyone I knew. He walked over and stuck out his hand. I took it and his grip was firm. He looked me right in the eye.

"Hi I am Benjamin, Katherine's other half. Nice to meet you."

"Hi, I am Avery." I said as we continued to shake hands.

"Avery, what a beautiful name. Very unheard of for a girl." That was rude I thought, although it was sort of true. I couldn't blame anyone for being honest.

"Avery you must come and try Katherine's oxygen bar. She has so many blends it would shock you. Have you tried any?" He asked as he tried to lead me to the counter.

"No thanks I really should get going. But, maybe next time." I pulled my hand from his grip and went back to the counter. Suddenly he turned to Katherine and he looked into her eyes very deeply and said, "Lock the shop we are closed for lunch."

"Wait...I haven't paid yet." I protested. Were they going to close up with me in here? Were they so desperate to talk to someone about Affinity's? She did as he said and ignored me completely. After she walked away he turned on me and grabbed my hair.

Chapter 21

Hold Your Breath

I screamed. It had all happened so fast I didn't expect it at all. His grip was firm like his handshake and he was not letting go. He dragged me over to the oxygen bar and slammed me into the chair.

"Sit down Avery," he said through clenched teeth. "You have caused a lot of grief to me lately and I will not have that." My head spun in half confusion and half pain.

"What? I don't know what you're talking about I just came here, I never met either of you before." Now I was sobbing. I was terrified. He laughed and it sounded so much like Dedrick's laugh I screamed again and he slapped me. I tasted a bit of blood inside my mouth. I was now in a state of shock.

This was really happening to me. Stuff you heard of on TV but never expected to happen to you. Ianni was so right to tell me to leave. I should have left right when she told me too. Now I was trapped in this store with a bunch of freaks and no one would know I was here, except Ianni. But what could she do to help me? I just prayed that she would tell someone. If she even knew at all what was happening.

"Now, like I said, Katherine has many blends of oxygen. Some are infused with a scent of strawberry or coconut. In my opinion you need this one." He pulled up a mask with his right hand while his left had most of my hair in it. "This one has Yulu infused in it. Oh it's perfect for the person who can't sleep. Can you sleep okay Avery?"

I shuddered. It had to be Dedrick! Who else would know so much about me and also be so evil? Evil! Then it came to me.

Dedrick had said that he had someone who showed him the way of the Dark Guides. His name was Benjamin.

"Putting the pieces of the puzzle together yet?" His voice sounded grainy and mean.

"Let me go you freak! I am not giving in to you and I won't fall into your traps."

"Oh come now Avery. This isn't a trap. I just happened to come by and see my soul mate and here you are. That is not a trap, that is coincidence. Don't you think?" He continued to yank on my hair. "I knew meeting Katherine would do me some good at some point. Now I can stop playing house and I can take what's mine."

"What's yours? What do you want from me?" I asked.

"Why your soul of course. You see, Dedrick may have promised dear old mommy that he would just take Landon, but she did not factor in that I would want you. I thrive on twin souls. Do you realize how strong that it makes us?"

Even though he held my hair I shook my head in disgust. What he said was true. Dedrick made a deal to not take her, or me, but that didn't mean that another Dark Guide could not take me.

"What about Katherine? Is she a Dark Guide too?" I looked at her. She looked so confused and scared as she bit her nails.

"Oh no, she is just another minion of mine. She is just a soul to use when the time comes. She is a twin too. Can you imagine how strong I will be?" I had no idea how strong he would be and I didn't care. I definitely had to get out of here somehow. Katherine started to look more scared than confused now. I think she understood what he was saying. She edged toward the counter. I watched her taking small steps back and she put her lips to her mouth making a small quiet "Shh" sound. Benjamin fumbled with the attachments of the mask to the oxygen. I was too scared to do anything.

"Now here we go," he said. "You are going to go to sleep and dream. And when you do Dedrick will come to you and guess what? Landon will come save you again. Landon is already sleeping, I am sure of it. I am sure he will be surprised when Dedrick takes him. You will be too weak to say no to any of

Dedrick's demands. With this much Yulu you will be so out of it."

I started to squirm, finally trying to fight back. Just hearing that Landon will be taken any minute from now gave me the incentive I needed. I knew if Benjamin put that mask on me that it would be all over. We would lose the battle that we hadn't even started. As I moved his grip tightened on me and he threw my head back. He put his face so close to mine and then his face shifted. The gorgeous GQ look was gone; he was now a young faced man with blonde hair in dreadlocks and eyes so black I could see my own reflection.

His wings slowly started to stretch out behind him. They were as black as his eyes but they looked aged and worn. Not as beautiful as Ianni's or Lillith's wings. I heard Katherine gasp but Benjamin paid her no attention.

"Don't move!" He screamed. "You are going to do this. I won't play games with you like I do the others. I am taking you willing or not."

"What others?" I cried. "Like Katherine?"

"Oh yes just like her. She was just a weak soul when I found her. Just a few promises and she was begging to make a deal with me. It was only a matter of time before I take her too."

"What do you mean by 'take' her?" I figured if I could stall him by asking questions then whatever Katherine was trying to do she would have a bit more time. I hoped that she had a good plan.

"Take! You know the definition don't you? I procure souls Avery. I need them, they make me stronger. I feed on them. They are my means of "food". Whereas you sloppy humans eat cheeseburgers, French fries and all that nasty crap, I eat the souls of well, you and others like you. I prefer Affinity's because they make me stronger but I will take any soul. Especially when I can't find an Affinity." He continued to yell his words in my face. "There are times when I go many years without finding them. That's when I will take just about anyone. It's not hard to find a willing soul. Some pathetic human who is so willing to sell their soul for just a bit of happiness."

He laughed like he had just told a funny joke but it wasn't

funny. I knew my mom had made a deal with Dedrick. I also knew Katherine was a victim just like my mom was. She had no idea what exactly Benjamin was. She was fooled and thought he was her soul mate.

"Now sit still and let me do this or the ramifications will be very dangerous to you and those you love." He started to fit the tubes in my nostrils and the others behind my ears. I could feel the stream of air start. I held my breath. I started to pray that someone would help me. I could not hold my breath forever.

Just as my lungs felt like they were going to explode I thought of Dallas and how much I wished we had more time. I hoped he would be strong after he learned about my death. I thought of Aunt Paul and how I hadn't seen her much. I also thought of my father and how he and I could have just been starting to get to know each other. We could have had a real relationship if time allowed it.

Lastly, and more deeply, I thought of Landon. I thought of how I had failed to save him like I wanted to. I mostly just thought of his face and his beautiful tortured eyes. It was at that exact moment that I realized that I had been falling in love with him. I closed my eyes and took a breath. I just could not hold my breath any longer. The smell was strong, I knew it was Yulu right away. I had smelled it several times from the steam of my teacup. It was sort of earthy but sweet as well. It was a good smell. Not one I disapproved of but at this moment I didn't really have a chance. I could feel myself falling asleep and I could not fight it any longer.

Chapter 22

Katherine

I was walking in the same house, going to the same door. I reached for the handle with no fear just uneasiness. Just as my hand touched it I was ripped out of the dream. I awoke and sat straight up. Screaming and punching. I was ready to fight now but there was no one to fight. There was just Katherine standing there with a glass pitcher in her hand and all the water on me. I stood and she reached her hand to help me but I did not take it. I was not sure where Benjamin was and I knew when he came back he would not be happy to see me awake. I shivered. The water was really cold.

"I am sorry Avery. I had to wake you up and I didn't know what else to use." She shrugged, seemingly unafraid of Benjamin's return.

"Where is he? I have to get out of here." I started to look for my purse. Then I decided screw the purse and started to walk toward the door.

"He is gone Avery. I got us help and he is gone. I don't know for how long or if for good but I did it." She smiled sounding very proud but I saw in her eyes that she wasn't enormously happy with it. For some reason she had fallen in love with Benjamin.

"How?" I asked. "He is so strong, how do you just get rid of him?"

"I had met my Spirit Guide a few weeks ago. In my dreams, of course, she came to me. She was beautiful, she told me so much about the path I had set out for myself and apparently I was not living it. She also told me how dangerous Benjamin was. At first I didn't believe it but she came back the next night saying things about him that I saw but chose to ignore. So I decided to listen. I started seeing things in him that my Guide had told me to look for. I believed he was made for me. I was delusional and it was because of him. He had tricked me but I made a deal with him." She sat down and took a deep breath. She was just now coming to terms with what was really happening.

"I made a deal with a Dark Guide. He came to me in my darkest hour. I was married for fifteen years. We were so happy. We were not the type of married couple that wanted kids, that was just how we were. We wanted to travel and see the country, but the country is only so big and you can only travel so long. Soon we ran out of things to discuss and do together. It wasn't long after that I wanted to move up here and start my own coffee shop. He was so willing to move here I think he just hoped that new scenery would help our marriage." I started to squeeze the water from my clothes while I listened intently.

"So we did it. We packed up our things and made the move. We found this great house right by the bay and things really were working out so much better. Until he got a new job and I was busy making plans on my shop. I was too busy to notice that he had met someone else until it was too late. He told me she saw things like he did. She wanted to travel and see the world with him. To him it was like a new pet to train and show off. He had already taken me everywhere but with her it would be a new experience because it would be with her instead." She started to tear up. She looked around her shop and sighed.

"So I did it anyway. I opened a coffee shop and gift store. The whole oxygen bar thing came later. I was happy to have my shop but I was so lonely. I had left my family and friends and I had no one. I fell into such a deep depression that even the anti-depressants didn't help. I just wanted to love again. That was all I wanted. I didn't even want my ex back. I just wanted to be with someone. So one night a dark winged man came to me in my dream and he told me he would give me anything I wanted. I could have asked for anything. Do you know what I asked for?"

"Love," I replied.

"Yes, love. I wanted to be with someone who would love me as much as I would love them. The man told me he would give it to me, for a price. The price of my soul."

"Wait, you gave up your soul for love? Why?" It seemed too tragic to be true.

"Oh he was so hard to say no to." I remembered that feeling with Dedrick. Now she looked like she understood how stupid it was to give up your soul for love. I thought then that maybe I was being a bit harsh on her. For judging her for what choices she made in her life.

"So you gave in, didn't you?"

"Yes I did and I didn't realize what a mistake I made until now. When Ben came to my store and started talking to me I had no idea he was the same man from my dreams. He certainly didn't look the same. He was more attractive and he was wingless. He looked my age and he looked lonely. Like me. So I befriended him and we began a friendship. Soon after that we fell in love. I knew that the man in my dream had followed through and I began to forget the whole dream. It just faded out of my memory. I was in love and I knew nothing of my deal that I had made. I just was living for the moment."

"Okay so this doesn't explain how you got rid of him just now." I sat down realizing that he wasn't coming back.

"Oh yes of course. My Spirit Guide helped me do that. I couldn't do that all on my own. While he held you down I contacted her the way she told me to. Just as you passed out another type of Angel, one I never seen before, he came and fought Benjamin off. Now he is gone." She hung her head and looked so sad. I felt for her but I knew that I had to get out of here. It seemed so selfish of me but I didn't want to stick around and see if Benjamin would come back.

"I am so sorry Avery to get you involved. His influences were just so strong. I usually did everything he asked of me. This was the first time I ever saw him hurt anyone and it was just like my Guide had told me. She was so right."

"So what happens now, to you I mean? You sold your soul.

What will happen?" I asked her. Obviously she had been thinking of that as well because she looked terrified.

"I don't know?" She shuddered. "I don't know who this other Angel was but he said to stay here and not to leave. I am so scared." I reached out and hugged her. I felt too bad to leave now. I just held her as she cried and I thought of Ianni and how she held me like this last night. I sort of knew how Katherine felt.

"You must leave Avery. Things are going to be happening here and you must go. You cannot be involved." I looked up from Katherine's red tangled mess of hair and saw a beautiful Spirit Guide standing in front of me. She was serene and pure looking. I let Katherine go and stepped away.

"What is going to happen to Katherine?" I asked her. She smiled at me and I felt peace flow through my body. Suddenly all my worries for her were non-existent.

"Katherine, it's now the time we spoke of. We must meet him, he is waiting," the Guide said. "Come my child, hold my hand, I will lead you to him."

Katherine took her hand and I watched her walk with the Guide to the back of the store. The Guide turned and looked at me. She smiled at me once more and then a man, no not a man, an Angel came into view. He was very built and beautiful as well, but there was darkness about him. Not darkness like with Benjamin or Dedrick but it was there. He took Katherine's hand and I backed out of the store. I found my purse on the ground and I ran out of towards the street.

Chapter 23

Making Promises

When I reached my apartment door I heard talking inside. I figured it was Dallas on the phone but when I opened it I saw Lillith, Ianni, Landon and Dallas all sitting together. I must have looked like hell because they all jumped up and gasped when they saw me. I put up my hand in front of me, I couldn't explain it all to them right now and I didn't want anyone coming near me. Ianni came anyway. She had a look of guilt on her face.

"What happened just now?" I knew she knew what just went down. I felt her question was unnecessary. She was the one who warned me but, like she had told me before, she cannot help me against the Dark Guides. There was nothing she could have done to save me. She had already done all that she could, and instead of listening to her and leaving right away I stayed. I was such a moron for not listening. It was like I was waiting for evil to come around.

"You know what Ianni? I do not feel like explaining what just went down. I think you can fill everyone in. I need a shower." I pushed past her and practically ran into my bedroom. I showered and washed away Benjamin's touch. My face ached and my head hurt. I had a slice on my lip and inside my mouth. I also had a patch of hair that was missing from him pulling my hair out. I did not cry though. I stayed strong but I refused to discuss the nature of the incident. I could hear them all talking in my living room. Now they were all quiet as I came into the room. Their eyes looked at the ground instead of me.

I went into the kitchen and started a pot of coffee, my liquid awake. I felt the pull of sleep start to take over my body. Not to mention the pain that was now starting to hurt like hell. My phone rang and it scared me almost to death. I reached over and answered.

"Hi it's me, Dad, um... Richard. How are you?" He sounded a little bit more chipper than he had when I last saw him, but still a bit shy. All I could think was why did he have to call right now?

"Better I suppose. I have a plan to discuss with you and the others. But the best place to pull this off is at my friend's parent's cabin. Do you have a pen?"

"Yep, go ahead." I mumbled off the directions to Kerri's parent's cabin. I hoped he would be able to get there okay. He was really a key player in all of this. We didn't talk too much longer. I apologized for leaving his house like I did and he accepted.

When I hung up with him Dallas was standing next to me. He just reached out and held my hand. His firm grip gave me a bit of strength that I needed. With his other hand he traced my lip and lightly touched the cut. I winced.

"Is what Ianni told us the truth? Did Benjamin really do this do you?" He looked really pissed.

"Yes he did but he is gone for now. So let's move on and let's plan our trip to the cabin." I let go of his hand and he followed me into the living room to face the others. I had one question to ask and then I wanted to forget what just happened.

"What will happen to Katherine?" I didn't ask anyone in particular but it was Lillith who answered. Her normal smart-ass tone was subdued this time. I was very thankful for that, I was in no mood for her attitude today.

"The Angel who took her was a Deliverer. She is Home now. Because of what she did, the deal she made, she will never return here or live anymore lives. She is one of the lucky ones." She answered so matter of fact and with almost no compassion. I had to remember that this was their job and they tried not to get emotionally involved. It wasn't like Lillith didn't care but Katherine was not her soul to guide. Landon was like her baby. He was the one she cared for most. I thought then that if it was

Landon who made the deal and if it was he who was taken she would not be so stone faced.

"Is a Deliverer an Angel of Death?" Landon asked. I looked at him, surprised by his question. I hadn't thought of that, but he had. He wasn't there to see what I saw, yet he knew what happened to Katherine.

"Yes. That is all I can say about them. So let's not talk too much about it. Just do not let that be any of you."

I was not going to ask any more questions about them or about Katherine. It wasn't hard to figure out what happened. She made a deal with a Dark Guide and her soul was his to take. If this Deliverer didn't come and take her Benjamin would. So it was either go Home and never return to Earth or give her soul to Benjamin and live God knows where. Katherine had saved my life by "calling" her Spirit Guide. She must have known that she was going to die. I didn't imagine her Spirit Guide would hide that information. I said a silent thank you to her, where ever she was.

Lillith and Ianni stood and spread their beautiful multi-colored wings, almost mirroring each other.

"We must leave. We have meetings with the Council but we will return at the cabin Dallas spoke of. In the meantime, please do not leave each other's side," Ianni said sternly to the three of us. Just like that they were gone.

I fell into my couch and fought to stay awake. There was so much to discuss about our plans. I was glad Dallas had told everyone about the cabin, so that was one less thing I had to talk about.

"Okay, so we are all packed and ready to go. Now what?" Landon asked looking awfully peppy and awake.

"First things first. Let's make a pact, a promise more or less," Dallas replied. "Let's promise each other that no matter what happens at the cabin we will stay together. The three of us. We will not leave or do anything stupid."

"What do you mean stay together?" I asked him. Why would we leave? That would be plain stupid.

"I mean even if something bad happens we will stay together. Like if one of us, well if one of us gets delivered." He cleared his throat. "If someone dies or gets taken by a Dark Guide the remaining people stay together."

"No way will that happen." I was trying to think positive and here was Dallas downer bringing me down.

"Avery its true, something bad could happen. It's best if we do make a promise and look at reality. You saw a woman get taken by the Angel of Death. I mean, wake up! Bad things are going to go down." Landon was practically screaming. His voice was uneven and his eyes were tearing up as he spoke.

I gave in, grabbed their hands and I looked at them both. I loved them both. There was no way I could break Dallas' heart and tell him this, but it was true. I felt a strong past love of Landon's soul and a strong present love for Dallas. I still didn't know if Dallas was Garrison and I certainly didn't want to discuss that right now.

"I promise. We will stay together. The three of us. We will fight for our souls," I said.

"I promise too," they both said at the same time. We stood there holding hands, a united threesome.

When we headed out we had everything packed in Dallas' truck and it was not as uncomfortable as it was the last road trip. This time we were all on the same page instead of holding grudges. We had come a long way. Dallas drove, I sat shotgun and Landon hung in the back. The music streamed out of the speakers and it lulled me to sleep. I couldn't help it with the slow melodies of the music and the hum of the car on the road.

My slumber didn't last long. I awoke in a scream. Dallas almost drove the car off the road and Landon practically jumped into the front seat to see if I was okay. I was covered in sweat and I was freezing. Dallas pulled off the road and threw the truck into park. He reached over and held me asking over and over if I was okay. I just didn't know what to say. I didn't remember my dream or why I screamed. I wondered if I was okay too. Landon looked worried as well and I assured them both I was fine. I just wanted to be there already.

Once they both believed me we took off again. I knew the cabin wasn't too far away so we should be there soon. Landon started to talk to me idly about pretty much anything and everything to keep me from falling asleep. And as much as I didn't really care to hear about his stocks or his business deals I listened even though it didn't really help. I was still tired and frightened. It was safe to say that my day sucked.

I didn't want to drag them down too so I tried to smile and laugh at the appropriate remarks. We needed gas so Dallas pulled into a station and went to go pay. I jumped out of the truck to stretch my legs. Landon came around the truck and joined me in the stretching. He looked sort of adorable while he stretched.

"So what happened? Are you gonna tell me?" I was taken aback by his question. He wasn't normally so pushy or nosy. I didn't really even have an answer for him.

"If you're asking about the dream, which I am sure you are, I don't remember. But it must have scared me." He looked at me with a doubtful expression and then moved on to another topic.

"So, what's this cabin like?"

"It's beautiful. Right off the lake and it has its own dock. Oh, there's a boat too, but I doubt we will have time for boating," I laughed.

He laughed too but I saw worry in his blue eyes. He shook the hair out of his face and smiled at me. I remembered the first time I met him. I had deemed him the cutest guy ever. And he still was pretty cute. There were times when I felt guilty about eyeing him up and down, and right now was one of those times. So I stopped and decided to tell him all about the cabin and its surroundings. He listened intently until Dallas was done pumping gas and came over. Just as I was walking towards the truck Landon's hand brushed up against mine.

Henry stood at the altar in a dark black suit. I peeked through the door of the church at the awaiting guests and my soon to be groom. I giggled as I saw the whole town, and many more, were assembled there just for us. I closed the door and walked back to the side room where my bridesmaids waited for me. I took another glance down at my dress, admiring the lace detail. I was the first one to wear this design. I felt so proud and I blushed at the thought of everyone seeing me in it. "Its time," my mother said ushering me to my father. I took a deep breath and tried to chase away the butterflies that now rested in my belly.

I pulled my hand away quickly and shot him a warning glance. I didn't want to see anymore of that vision. It was my wedding to Henry. I was so selfish in that life and I had seen enough.

"Well according to the guy in the store we have about another sixty miles until we are there. So you both ready?" Dallas asked.

"Yep!" I answered for the both of us and we got back into the truck. I was ready to go there and to make our plans. I worried that this would be dangerous. I didn't even know the plan for sure. All I knew for now was that we were all going to be together. No matter what would happen I would be ready to go up against Dedrick and whoever else stood in our way.

What happened to me at that store with Benjamin would never happen to me again. That was a promise I made to myself.

Chapter 24
The Cabin

We pulled onto the gravel road that lead up to the cabin and I remembered the last time Kerri and I were here. It had been a very hot summer and we decided to come here for the weekend. It was a total blast. We stayed up late talking and drinking. The next morning she and I went down to the dock and swam. She, of course, looked terrific in a bathing suit but I was really shy even though she kept telling me how cute I looked in my new white bikini. She always kept my spirits up. I really missed her. I knew as soon as this stuff was over she and I would hang out more often. I really hoped we would be able to be together again and that things would go back to normal. Normal was before Lucy died. Before all the bizarre happened. Landon interrupted my thoughts by asking which cabin it was.

"Oh, sorry. The last one on the street." I pointed to the last cabin on the road. Dallas pulled the truck into the newly paved driveway. The cabin was so peaceful looking. The sun was just now going down over the lake and it had cast a glow around the cabin.

"Wow, this is more like a mansion than a cabin," Dallas remarked. I laughed loudly. It was very true. When you think cabin you do not picture this place. This cabin was more glass than cabin. The whole front was wood but the sides and back was pretty much all windows. It was three story's high and the yard was huge compared to all the other lots. The front of the yard had the best landscaping on the street.

Kerri's parents had money, and it was easy to tell when you

looked at this place. They had definitely wanted their daughter to do more than manage a retirement home. They would have preferred her to be a doctor or lawyer but according to Kerri she felt Sunrise Estate's was where she wanted to be. All I knew was she was supremely happy.

I, on the other hand, well that remains to be seen. If you would have told me I would be an aide for Sunrise Estates I would have laughed, but I do love my job. I felt sort of sad, like I missed it. It had been forever since I was there.

We went inside and dropped our bags at the foot of the stairs. It smelled heavily of lavender and I knew that the maid service had just been here to clean. Mrs. Louse loves lavender and she requested that the house always smell of it. I had no idea how they did it, but they did.

Landon went straight into the living room area and stared out towards the lake. Dallas took my hand and led me upstairs, shushing me on the way up. I giggled like a little girl, totally forgetting why we were here in the first place. The second floor consisted of three bedrooms spaced evenly throughout the floor. Each had their own bathroom and huge walk in closet. It was more like there was three master bedrooms.

We continued to the third floor which had an office to the far left and a huge room that was considered the entertainment room. The massive windows surrounding the rooms came with room darkening shutters that covered the windows with a push of a button. There was a drop down movie screen with another push of a button.

We didn't stop to enjoy any of this, today we just went out to the deck through the sliding glass doors. The air hit me as soon as we walked out and I breathed deeply, clearing my nostrils of that horrid lavender scent. The lake was quiet and we watched the sun continue to settle while he wrapped me in his strong arms. I had never felt safer in all these few months. I did not want to leave his arms. He began kissing my neck and it sent shivers throughout my body. I had really wanted to spend the first night here alone with him, but plans had changed. I guessed we would have to play catch up another time.

“This place is amazing isn’t it?” Dallas asked sounding like a kid in a candy store.

“Yeah it’s one of my favorite places. It’s magical here.”

“Right here in your arms, this is magic. I love you Avery and I am so scared that I will lose you.” His voice choked.

I turned to face him. His head was down, his dark hair almost red with the glow of the setting sun. He would not look at me. I didn’t know what I could say to assure him that things would be okay. Heck, I didn’t even know if they would be okay. I was just as scared. We were going up against something very dark and very unreal. I tried my best to sound reassuring.

“Everything will be okay as long as we stay together, remember?”

He nodded, still not looking at me, and I grabbed onto him as he scooped me up into his arms. We stood that way for a while. When I opened my eyes I peered over Dallas’ shoulder and saw Landon looking at us from inside the room. He just stood there watching us.

The rest of the evening was pretty quiet. Landon went to bed early, presumably because of his unhappiness. I tried to ignore it, he had to get over it. Dallas and I watched old movies on the TV downstairs deciding that the movie theatre would be too weird. We opted for quaint and romantic. There was popcorn in the cupboards along with tons of other food that we could use for the remaining time spent here. I knew Kerri had something to do with that.

We sat snuggled up on the couch, no talking, just being with each other. It was about an hour later when I heard a thump upstairs. I jumped up, scaring the daylights out of Dallas, he had been asleep and I didn’t know it. The thump noise was very loud like something big fell. I took off running up the stairs as fast as I could. I felt the burning in my very out-of-shape legs as I decided to take two stairs at a time. Dallas was right behind me and trying to push past me. I suppose it was a protective boyfriend thing so I let him pass me. He went for the door to Landon’s room, but it was locked.

"Landon, you alright in there?" He yelled. There was no response on the other side. I stared to get worried. What the hell was he doing in there? And why did he lock the door? It seemed so strange to me. Dallas banged on the door but still no response.

"Okay babe, stand back I am gonna have to break the door down." He was pushing me out of the way.

"Go ahead..." I did what he said and got out of the way, nervous as to what was behind the door. Dallas took three big steps back, turned to his side and rammed the door with his body. It broke open and he rushed inside with me following. Landon was on the floor of the room, lying in his stomach. I ran over to him and we both tried to wake him. He just lay there, motionless. I put my hand in front of his open mouth and I felt air. Dallas checked his pulse, something I didn't think to do.

"He's alive, but unresponsive," he concluded. He ran for the phone and once he picked it up I saw a feather. It was ebony black. I jumped away from it, crawling on hands and knees to Dallas. I thought if I was quiet about showing it to him we could somehow protect ourselves better. I stood up slowly and grabbed the phone out of his hand.

"Avery what the hell are you doing? I have to call the..." He stopped short as he noticed what I was pointing to. His face went pure white. He grabbed me and we walked toward the window. He looked outside onto the balcony and so did I. We saw nothing so we checked the closet and bathroom. Still nothing. Landon remained motionless but breathing heavily now. It instantly came to me I knew what was happening.

"He's dreaming. Dallas he is dreaming and the feather means that Dedrick is there with him."

"Then why is the feather here? And how the hell did he get on the floor?" He pretty much shouted. I took a step toward Landon eyeing up the feather.

"Oh my God! I know why. Lillith did it as a sign to show us what is happening to him. Spirit Guides can't get involved or help their souls against the Dark Guides." I was proud that I had figured it out. "She knew if she put the feather here we would know who it involved. And she pushed him off the bed so that we would hear him fall. Maybe she couldn't talk to us to warn us. They did say they had a meeting with the council today."

Dallas picked up the feather and observed it, flipping it over in his fingers.

"Yeah that makes sense. Maybe the council said no more interfering or maybe no more talking with us. I think we are on our own." He looked up at me and I knew it was a big possibility that he was right.

Plan

We sat there for a few more dumbfounding minutes trying to think of what the hell to do. Then it dawned on me what I needed to do. The answer was there all along. I needed my Watcher, a twin soul and a Spirit Guide willing to break the rules. Only the last part confused me. Obviously they weren't interested in breaking the rules since they were not here now. Lillith did volunteer for the job, but I didn't see her.

I ran down the stairs almost as fast as I had ran up them and I grabbed my phone on the landing. I dialed Justin and he answered on the first ring. He sounded weary and I felt sorry for that. I spoke as fast as I could and told him what was going on.

"Okay so you need me there right?" He was obviously still half asleep. Of course I needed him, he was moral support in a way. The next number I called was my father. Unfortunately he didn't answer his phone so I had to leave a very awkward message. I hoped that he understood what it was I needed from him. It was imperative that he be here and help. After that was all over I started to pace back and forth. It was all I could do now since I couldn't do anything without them being here. And they lived far away, my father living the farthest.

So it was about two hours later when I heard a knock on the front door. I was in the living room by myself reading trash magazines to kill time. Dallas had not left Landon's side. I didn't speak my plan to him but I think he trusted what I came up with. I opened the door and shockingly saw Ianni standing with Justin and my father. I almost cried at the sight of them all standing there. I reached out and grabbed Ianni into a very strange but needed hug. She hugged me back and although it was comforting it felt somewhat different.

"How did you get them here? I thought you didn't come to help because you were in trouble or something." I ushered them into the house and I saw three more figures walking up the driveway. I stood there peering into the darkness straining my already tired eyes.

"Don't do that with your eyes Av, it will cause wrinkles." It was Kerri followed by Aunt Paul and Lillith. I screamed and ran towards them. I blame my tiredness for my weird behavior. I grabbed Kerri and my aunt into a huge giant group hug. They giggled and hugged back. I smiled at Lillith and voiced a quiet, 'Thank You' to her. She smiled back and bowed her head.

Once we were all assembled into the house they all spread out in the living room. Kerri made sure everyone was comfy and didn't need anything. Then she sat down next to Justin and listened in.

"Okay, so I think you all know what you're doing here right?" I asked as I got a nod and yes from them all. Dallas was the only silent one. "Well I have a plan to help Landon and it's going to be crazy but I will need all of your help and support. I don't want to hear anyone try to talk me out of it. Got it?" They nodded again.

Now came the hard part. I had to tell them what my crazy tired brain had come up with. I also wondered, at this point, how filled in everyone was on the situation but knowing they all rode over here in one car I knew either Lillith or Ianni took care of that.

"Well if I enter a dream state I can definitely get to Landon. But that won't help him any. Even though Mr. Grey will most likely be there and Lillith can be, I can't get my father there. So my idea is a little more intense and it involves bringing Dedrick to me." I took a heavy breathe before continuing and I was interrupted by Ianni who stood up.

"I have to tell you first about what happened today at the council before you think of doing anything Avery." She said it so quietly I almost asked her to speak up. "The council will not allow us to interfere in anything that involves the Dark Guide's no matter the situation."

"But wait! I thought Lillith was willing to volunteer as the Guide who breaks the rules." I exclaimed.

"Yes. Please listen Avery. If she does she will be cast out. We are not talking about small ramifications like the changing of wing colors."

I wanted to cry when she said this. I couldn't see that happen to Lillith. She loved her souls too much to leave them and live on Earth. I looked at her and she stared at me with a burning fire in her eyes. I knew that her unhappiness had nothing to do with me, but for the situation. She loved Landon and she was mad she couldn't help him. I also knew she wanted to take a chance to get to Dedrick and end him.

"So anyhow with that said we have devised a plan of our own." She faced Lillith who now stood. "I have been feeling this certain way for a long time. And it only happens to a handful of Guides. I mean not every Guide wants to become human."

"What?! No, not you. You can't," I yelled fighting back tears. I couldn't see Ianni lose her home and be stuck here on Earth. She would never return Home. She would be stuck here forever.

"I have thought about this a long time Avery. Way before this situation presented itself. I actually think this is a sign that I should do it. I have always longed to be human. So it will be I who breaks the rules." My head spun I was so upset. I looked around and everyone looked at me like they all agreed with her decision.

"Someone help me talk her out of this." I was hoping for backup but never received it.

"Ianni spoke to everyone in the car and they are all on board. She wants this Avery, let her do it. We can't take down Dedrick without her." Lillith's voice made me sick but I listened and sat down. Dallas rubbed my back. I looked up at him but his eyes didn't meet mine.

"So what now? You're going to go a rogue and come to Earth after you are cast out? What will you do with your life, work in fast food?" I knew it sounded stupid but I had to know what she planned on doing with her new life.

"Well I was sort of hoping you could help me until I got myself situated here. Maybe we could be roommates or something like that," she replied very seriously. "After our meeting today we convinced Gunther to only shave one of your memories instead of all three of you." She smiled so hard I recognized that she was proud of her accomplishment. But I wasn't, I didn't want any of us to forget. But did we have a choice?

"Of course I will help you Ianni, but I have to ask who Gunther is and why is he so eager for us to forget?" I asked her but it was Lillith who answered me.

"Gunther is the head of the ReLife Council. Let's just say he is a big deal there okay? He wants us to be able to return unharmed and for your souls to return unknowing of what you know. With a little help we changed his mind. He feels now that maybe two of you should remember. That this will bring you peace in your lives. But one must not remember."

"It will be Landon right?" Dallas interrupted. He stopped rubbing my back. I knew he would be against my plan and especially now hearing that Landon could forget everything that was too hard for him to swallow.

"Dallas it's the right thing to do. He won't forget everything about his life just the supernatural part of it. That's all," Ianni said encouragingly. I could not argue with Ianni on this part. It made me think that maybe it was right. Maybe it would end up being a blessing in disguise. He would be able to live without the pain of knowing who he really was and who I was. Dallas looked down at me, meeting my eyes for the first time in hours and said

"Do you think this is right? Are you okay with this?" I nodded just to appease him and then he sat back in his chair and gave up. He just wanted what was best and I guess me being okay with it made it okay in his mind.

"Okay now for my plan," I spoke. "I need you all to leave the house. I will call him here and I will stage a fight with Dallas. I will be very distraught and upset and I will tell him I want to make a deal with him. He will come. He always comes where pain is."

"Why would we leave the house?" Kerri asked.

"Because Kerri he will know you are all here. The Dark Guides won't come where an audience is," Ianni responded. "He won't come if you simply call him Avery. He has what he wants right now. He has Landon, why would he give that up to come here?" This part I did think about. I thought about it as I paced back and forth waiting for all of them to arrive.

"I am going to call Benjamin, not Dedrick. Benjamin wants me and Dedrick wants Landon. And when he comes I will make a deal with him. My soul for Landon's."

They all screamed at me. I heard some 'no ways' and some 'are you out of your minds' I knew they would respond like this so I sat there patiently waiting for it to sink into them. It was a good enough plan and it was all we had right now. Landon was upstairs lying on the floor still. We had no clue as to what was going on with him. I just prayed he would be strong. After a few minutes they all calmed down and I got to finish my statement.

"I am not going to really give it to him guys. I will offer it and ask that Dedrick be the one to take my soul, so then he will have to rip Dedrick from Landon's dream. I will make up some elaborate story as to why. And when this happens, Lillith I need you to go get Landon out of this house." She gave me a reassuring nod. She would do it and I knew she would.

"Then what? We rush in and take them down?" Justin asked. It was then that I realized he had been so quiet all night.

"No, that won't work, they don't go down like that. They are not easily killed. They are pretty much indestructible. You will be needed Justin. In order for this to work we will need your abilities to read them. To read the situation going on in the house," Ianni said. "Once Landon is out of the house I will come in and assist Avery. I will help with my Light to kill one of them. You see, they are bonded by the Darkness and we the Light. So if I interfere I will be killing one of them. Something forbidden. You don't use the Light to cause harm."

"That is why you will be cast out?" Aunt Paul asked. She sat with her hands carefully folded onto her lap.

"Yes Paulina, that is correct. The Dark Guides will not be expecting this. They would never think we would give up our lives as Guides to save a human." It hurt me to hear that Ianni would be using her God given abilities to cause harm. I knew it was my fault and I felt very guilty. If not for me she would not be in this situation. Unfortunately I didn't really know any other Spirit Guide willing to do it.

"Well who will kill the other one? The one you don't kill?" Kerri asked.

"The Watcher will take care of him," Lillith answered. Mr. Grey, I couldn't have him being punished as well. I knew we needed him to help but I just didn't know how to put all the puzzle pieces together. I knew what my job was, a diversion. That left me wondering why my father was needed.

"Don't worry it is a Watcher's job to cause harm if their soul is in harm's way. He can make a choice to either help or not but I am pretty sure he will help. Avery, you are his soul to watch and he will do anything to protect you. That is how a Watcher works," Ianni said.

Pretty sure? That was not 100% sure. This was looking like one big test. I wasn't even sure that Benjamin would come to me. I knew he wanted me, especially after what had just happened in the shop. Speaking of which, my head hurt a lot due to his lovely handiwork. I would enjoy seeing him disappear.

We talked more about our plan, which didn't include what my father was to do, but that was okay. I really wanted him to stay safe and out of it. Dallas decided that they would all go to the neighbor's boathouse to wait. He didn't want to leave Landon or I but he was willing to do whatever it took to help save us. Kerri came up to me and hugged me before she and Justin left. Then it was like a procession line, everyone coming up to say their goodbyes. It was rather depressing. Aunt Paul just mumbled, "Be careful," before she left the house with her head down. I felt bad that she was dragged into this. For some reason Ianni and Lillith thought she needed to be here.

Justin promised he would be, "Listening in from the boathouse." Which I knew was his psychic way of listening. Lillith gave me a hug and that threw me off, because I know she didn't like me, but I hugged her back.

Dallas was next, his eyes looking the saddest I have ever seen. I didn't realize until now that this had to scare the crap out of him. He lost his parents and now he could lose his cousin and his girlfriend. I kissed him passionately hoping that it would send him good vibes. It must not have worked, because when our kiss broke he still looked sad. He said nothing and walked away. His face caused me more pain then my head did. My heart broke for him. I was just as scared as he was but I tried not to show it. My father grabbed me and held me in a hug. It had been so long since I was wrapped in his arms. It felt like a lifetime.

He whispered in my ear, "The Angels are on our side. Once this is all over we will have nothing but time to help us heal from the past." I fought back the tears.

"Okay father," was all I could reply. Then he left too. Ianni stood before me now. A beautiful Angel before me. It was like my father had said, the Angels were on our side and I knew it was true.

"I will not fail you Avery. I promise you. I will give all my Light to protect you. I know you don't understand what I am willing to do. This is all I have wanted and instead of being shunned out like Dedrick I will be cast out for saving a human and taking down a Dark Guide." She was really proud of her decision. I had to rethink the whole guilt thing. If this is what she wanted for her self then who was I to stop her? She was sacrificing a lot to help us, but ever since our short discussion about pillows I had an idea Ianni wanted to be human.

"You really want to be human don't you? Why?" I had to know reason.

"Avery I can't really explain it to you. All I can say is for centuries of watching and standing by to guide humans, it has done nothing but make me long to have the things you have. To have emotions like you do. Like love." She practically squealed. "I just never acted on my wants, I stood by and waited. I would never cast myself out and become like Dedrick. This is like a door opened and I want to take it."

"Yeah, an exit door. Exit right out of Heaven." She laughed and so did I.

“I want to be able to return a hug from you with real feelings. I don’t feel anything when we hug. It’s just empty.”

I thought that sounded very sad and I couldn’t imagine hugging someone and not feeling anything. It sounded very lonely to guide someone for centuries and not be able to talk to them. That was like being invisible to everyone. It made me feel better to think that since she had shown herself to me she seemed to have gotten what she needed emotionally.

Chapter 26

Facing the Dark

They were all gone, even Ianni. I stood in the entertainment room shaking badly and all alone. I was letting my nerves get to me. I did some breathing exercises to calm myself down but it hardly did any good so I gave up. I was supposed to be upset right? I was faking a fight with Dallas, so maybe shaking would be okay. I had to really try to get myself so upset that Benjamin would come. The Dark Guides come to those who are in their worst hours. I had yet to have Dedrick come to me awake but I had seen Benjamin in the shop and I was awake then. So maybe he had the power to come to me while I was awake. I would face him no matter what. I needed to help Landon so I had to put my best actress face on. I tried pretending to cry but it didn't really work out. So I just faked it. I put my head in my hands and focused on the worst thing that has ever happened to me. I thought of losing my mom and the tears started to fall. Just the thought of her being gone took over my emotions and the tears flowed. I thought of the day she died, right in front of me, and a vision came to my mind;

"Avery, we need chocolate chips to put in the batter," she said as she added the egg to the batter. I ran to the counter and grabbed the bag of chocolate chips. They were my absolute favorite cookies. I handed them to her and she tore into the bag and put them into the mix. I looked at her, admiring how she mixed it all together. Her apron that we had sewn together hung from her neck.

"All done, do you want to lick the spoon?" She asked me as I

practically grabbed it out of her hands. What a silly thing to ask, of course I did. I loved licking the spoon. I sat at the table enjoying the batter when my mother started putting the cookie batter onto a baking sheet.

As she started putting them into the oven I turned my head and looked out the window. I saw the kids from across the street playing hide and go seek. Something I loved to play with them.

"Mom can I go outside?" There was no answer. I turned to face her and that is when I saw her falling. It was like slow motion. The cookie sheet fell to the ground first. Then my mother fell next with a large thud. I ran over to her and I screamed. At first I thought she was joking with me.

"Mom!" I yelled shaking her lifeless body. But this time she was not joking. My mother lay dead on the cold kitchen floor. I ran outside yelling for someone to help us.

When the vision ended I was in the state of sadness that was needed to have a Dark Guide come. I wondered how the vision had come to me. It was the first vision of my mom that had ever come to me. The only visions I had ever had was of Landon and I. This was new.

Then I did it. I called him. I screamed his name as loud as I could, "Benjamin!" I hated the way even saying his name made me feel. Like insects crawling around in my mouth. I wanted to puke, but maybe it was good to feel so upset and grossed out. I waited a while and nothing happened. I thought about what Ianni had said you can't simply call them. So I did the most drastic thing I could think of doing.

He wanted my soul right? Well he would come if I would do something he wouldn't want me to do. End my own life or at least threaten to. I opened the door to the balcony and stepped outside. The night was pitch black and freezing cold. I looked out over the lake and then looked down. It was definitely high enough to do some real damage.

I walked to the hand railing and swung my leg up over the side of it. Now balancing on the railing I tried again.

"Benjamin. I will do it, I will kill myself." The night air became colder, if that was even possible. I didn't think it could in a matter of just seconds. That is how I knew that he was here. A chill ran up my spine. I was too afraid to turn around but I felt his presence there with me.

"What in the name of all things demon are you doing?" He asked me, his hot breath steaming up my back. I shook at the feeling of the cold air from outside mixing with the heat from him. It was a very odd feeling. "You better bring your skinny ass down from there. I don't feel like fooling around with you tonight. I have better things to do." So he didn't take me seriously did he? Well that would be no problem I would just have to do better.

"The only way I am coming down is well, down," I said, motioning to the ground beneath me. His breath on my back got hotter so I knew he was coming closer. "Don't come any closer freak! I will do it. After what I saw you do to Katherine I don't trust you."

"Okay so you want me to just stand here and let you take your own life?" It actually sounded like he felt bad or worried. What did he care? That wasn't possible. He didn't care about me any more than he cared about Katherine. "So what do you want from me? Why did you call me here, huh?" He was becoming impatient. Good.

"Well, I don't want my soul to go to waste. I want to take Dedrick up on his deal. I want to give him my soul. I called you here because I haven't been able to reach Dedrick except for in my dreams, and since I can't sleep that's not possible is it?" I tried to hide my trembling voice.

"Well I guess not. I can bring him here, but I have to ask, why him and not me? I can promise the same things he can," he said in a sexy voice. Ugh he was so disgusting. But he had a good question. Why Dedrick? I raced through my mind to think of a good answer. It had to make complete sense if he was to make Dedrick leave Landon.

"Because, he was the first to confront me about it and, and I..." I stumbled across my own words. "I like him. I don't like or trust you, I trust him. I know he won't screw with me," I lied.

"Fair enough. I can understand your feelings for Dedrick, he is enticing isn't he?" Double ugh! I turned to face him so that I could look him in the eyes. I had to make sure he knew I wasn't fooling around. So I carefully turned the upper half of my body and when I faced him, he looked entirely different than before. This time he was a tall handsome man. With blue eyes, jet black hair, and a pair of lips very thick and full. I didn't let his good looks faze me or change my mind. These guys thought they could trick people with their good looks. No way, not me. Maybe the weak or depressed, like Katherine, but I was becoming stronger and almost bad assed. No more weak Avery, not after these past few months. I had cried enough tears.

"I want Dedrick now or I go off this balcony and I mean it, I will. There is nothing left for me here." Just saying these words to him made me feel so terrible because they were so far from true. I had a lot to live for and I was ready to be the Avery that Dallas deserved and the friend that Landon, Kerri and Ianni needed.

"Fine, let me beckon him, he will come." He turned and walked away. I heard him whispering something unintelligible. I looked away and tried to say in my head; *"Everything will be okay, he is calling Dedrick."* I said it to Justin hoping he was reading my thoughts. I didn't know if he was telepathic for sure but he had read them before.

I looked out across the lake and watched the swans circling each other in the moonlight. They had a romantic quality about them. As soon as I lost myself in my thoughts about the swans I was quickly brought back to reality when I heard shouting behind me. I turned to look and there stood Dedrick. His black wings were pulled up tight against his body, but he was naked. No clothes, just wings covering his butt. I turned my head and swallowed hard. Yuck, what the hell was he doing naked? This was certainly sick. I just prayed Lillith was upstairs getting Landon out of there like she promised.

"Oh, so you want to talk do you? Do you know what you just pulled me from? I had him in my grasp, only moments away from agreeing. And here you demand I give up what has been promised to me for how many years, for this?" He yelled. I tried not to make it seem as though I was listening in.

"You will do this Dedrick, I demand it. This is mine and has been mine for just as long. If she happens to request you, well then so be it," Benjamin shouted back.

I was so confused. I was his? How? If I was truly promised to Benjamin this was news to me. God I hoped not. They stopped shouting and Dedrick came out to the balcony. I tried not to look at him in all his naked nastiness. I didn't want to see all of that and be imagining it in the future.

"So you want me, huh? I find this all too strange Avery. You didn't want me around at our last meeting. Why now sweetheart? Do you want what I promised you?"

He was beyond gross, he was revolting. I nodded and tried to fight back the bile rising to my throat. He smelled awful, like death and decay, but that's what they were right? They ate people's souls, they brought death and caused decay, so it made sense.

"Yes I want what you promised me. I want to be happy and not sad anymore." Just as I said these words he grabbed me from the balcony and pulled me into the house. Benjamin helped by holding me down. Dedrick stood over me and expanded his wings. His dark eyes turned a shade of gray, it was the scariest moment of my life. If Ianni didn't come now I was as good as dead.

"You are going to give me your soul!" Dedrick yelled. He raised his hand above his head and his fingernails turned into claws. I screamed as loud as I could. So loud, in fact, I think I injured my own eardrums. He only laughed, my fear was like pleasure to him. Benjamin raised my head and then slammed it down into the hardwood floor. I felt a rush of something wet and warm run down my neck. Blood. He had split my head open. I was starting to get woozy and dizzy. Dedrick swung his hand down and thrashed through my chest with his claws. My white shirt was now bright red with blood.

He raised his hand again saying, "Tu affero vita, tu affero vita. You give life." He swung his hand back down and I closed my eyes. I was giving up all hope that anyone would save me. How could they? There were two very strong Dark beings in this house. I thought of everyone out there. I thought of Ianni and how I would miss seeing her turn human. I would miss so much, but I also wondered if I could go Home? I knew once you made a deal with them, you went somewhere else and not to Heaven.

I braced for the impact of his claws but it never came. I waited and still nothing came. I felt Benjamin let my arms go but for some reason I heard nothing. It was silent. Then there was a bright light that I could see and feel on my face. I was too scared to open my eyes so instead I closed them and rolled to my side. My head pounded and I reached back to feel the blood. There was a lot of blood and a huge cut in my skull. I laid in a fetal position still not hearing anything. Was I dying? Did he actually kill me and that is why I am deaf? Maybe I am passing on.

"Avery open your eyes! It's okay, open them," a voice invaded my head. I knew this voice, it was mom!

"Mom?"

"Yes honey. Open your eyes and fight back. Don't let them win. You are stronger than they are. Although you don't believe it, you are."

"Mom, are you still in between, or did you go Home?"

"Darling, I will go Home, the promise I have made with Dedrick is now over. Once you and Landon pass on and come Home, well then so will I."

"Wait, so we have to die first? I don't understand."

"I told you before Avery, your souls must return Home in order for me to return. But that is okay. Time here is different than on Earth. I will be Home soon. Until then I will continue to watch over you. I love you and can't wait to see you live your life. Now open your eyes!"

Her voice left my head and I knew she was gone.

I did as I was told and opened them slowly. The bright light took over the whole room and I could see that I was still in the house. I strained my eyes and tried to see what was happening. I saw a figure on the ground lying next to me. Benjamin. He was dead. His eyes were glassy and hazed over. His wings were no longer black like once before, they were turning to ash. I tried to stand but I just fell back down. My equilibrium was totally off. As my eyes focused I saw Ianni basked in a glowing light. Her light. That was what was so bright. It was beautiful.

"Ianni," I moaned, my voice catching in my throat.

"Stay down Avery!" She shouted. I watched her sway and move holding some sort of sword in her hand. The sword was glowing with a white fire, that was the only way I could describe it. She swung it and Dedrick jumped out of her way, his clawed hands thrashing wildly at her. They were fighting over me.

I rolled myself over to the couch in the corner and tried to prop myself up, completely ignoring Ianni's request to stay down. That is when I saw another bright light enter the room. He stood there in a cloak of white, holding a sword as well, his burning with white fire also. Mr. Grey.

"No stay away!" Dedrick shouted. He was actually afraid. Mr. Grey did not stay away, instead he joined in the fight holding his sword in front of him and chopping into Dedrick's body. He sliced him several times and each time he opened him up a black liquid poured from his body. They continued to attack him, now two on one. Dedrick's body turning ashen, like Benjamin's.

I felt hands grab me from behind the couch and I screamed in terror. I stopped when I realized that they were my father's hands. He lifted me into his arms, like a baby, and carried me through the bright room and out of the house. Once we were outside it dawned on me that that was why he was needed in this fight. He had to be the one to save me. Two Affinity's were stronger than just two normal souls.

"You had to be the one to carry me out right?" I asked.

"Yes. No one else could enter the house while the fight went on. Any other soul could not enter, let alone see, in the light of the Angel. Only Affinity's can see through the light, due to how pure our souls are." He checked me over and once he saw my head he took off his sweatshirt and placed in gently on the gash. My chest burned, but he didn't have anything to place on those cuts.

"Mom, she spoke to me," I told him.

"Me too. She is the one who told me all that. How the hell else was I to know?” He laughed. I laughed, or tried to, but my head started spinning and I could see the blackness coming over my vision. And then I passed out.

Chapter 27

Only the Light Remains

When I awoke I was in my own bed at home. I looked over the room and didn't see anything alarming. I slowly raised my head off the pillow, bracing against the pain, but it didn't come. Well at least it was not what I expected. I mean, it hurt but not like before. My chest didn't hurt too badly either but I didn't want to look. I noticed a glass of water on my bedside table and drank it. I was insanely thirsty. It tasted stale, maybe a day old, but it did the job.

I slid my legs from the bed noticing I was in my favorite cotton pajamas and I wondered who dressed me. It really didn't matter, more than anything I wanted to see everyone, mostly to see if Landon was okay. So I walked across the room and opened the door. I saw several people in my living room but the only one to notice I was standing there was Kerri. She flew off the armchair and ran towards me. I met her halfway and we hugged.

"I am so happy you are okay. How do you feel?" She asked looking me over like a concerned parent.

"I feel okay. My head only hurts a little. Shouldn't it hurt worse? I mean it was split open just last night." She laughed and so did everyone else.

"What's so funny?" I asked.

"Av, you have been asleep for three days. I guess you really needed to catch up huh?"

Three days? Holy crap! That was the longest I had slept in months. I felt good, but also very guilty. I had lost three days of my life. What had I missed?

"Landon and Ianni? How are they?" I asked ignoring everyone's laughter.

"He is home and he is fine." A beautiful red head rose from the couch. She was slender but busty. Her red hair was glossy and wavy. Her face was the picture of perfection, like a super model, like an Angel. Ianni walked over to me, dressed in a beautiful pure white blouse and white skinny jeans with red stiletto heels. She turned around to show off her new ensemble and I couldn't help but notice there were no more wings. It sort of saddened me. My Guide was gone and before me stood another beautiful human.

"Well we did it. We took care of the problem! You and Landon are safe. And I am a human," she boasted. "Thank you Avery."

"For what?" She was the one who had saved us. I did nothing but drag the evil in.

"You brought them into the house and you almost died doing it. Don't doubt your significance in the matter. Without you they would have taken Landon." I looked away. I didn't even want to think about Benjamin or Dedrick ever again. I caught my father's stare. He smiled at me, looking very happy to see me in one piece,

"Where is Dallas?" I asked Kerri.

"I just texted him to come over when we heard you waking up in there. Sorry you had to wake up alone but Ianni thought it was best." So Dallas wasn't even here? I tried not to worry about that. He had a life to live, didn't he? I couldn't shake the feeling that something bad had happened. So I just plain out asked.

"Okay, so is everything all well and good? Dedrick and Benjamin are gone but there is something you are not telling me. So go ahead say it." They all looked at each other. It was Lillith who stood. I didn't even know she was there. I thought it was only Kerri, Justin, my father and the new Ianni. Lillith looked tired and less beautiful, if that was even possible for her to look. She came over and stood next to Ianni.

"Well here's the deal. You knew it was going to happen. There was absolutely no way of avoiding it." She paused. "They shaved his memories, Landon's. He doesn't remember anything."

I fought the urge to scream and hit Lillith right in the face. Even though I knew it was what we had all agreed to. We knew it was the deal they had made with the council and that there was no way of avoiding it. But I was so pissed. He didn't know me, he didn't remember us. I didn't know why I was so mad. I had thought this would be a good idea. For him to be free of our memories together.

"Avery, you knew this was going to happen," Ianni told me. Her very human hand reaching for mine as I pulled away.

"No. I knew this, but I am still not happy. What did you think? That I would be okay?" I stormed through the living room. They parted, letting me through. I went outside and downstairs. When I came to his door I pounded loudly. It took a minute but he answered, his blonde hair hanging in his eyes. It took my breath away to see a smile form on his lips.

"Hi, can I help you?" Oh god he didn't remember. It was true.

"Yeah I'm Avery," I said. Hoping he would remember my name but knowing it was a shot in the dark. He still smiled, confused.

"Sorry I don't know you, Avery. Wait... your name. I know you." He laughed shaking the hair from his eyes. He was remembering I hoped. "You're Dallas' girl aren't you?" I was wrong. "He did tell me you lived in this building. Nice to finally meet you." He held his hand out for me to shake. I wondered if our hands touched if a vision would come so I grabbed it.

Landon stood outside the house in a dank and dark boathouse. Looking above to see anything happening up there. Lillith had told him to stay here, but the love of his all his lives was up there in trouble. That was when the bright piercing light flew out of all the windows. Ianni had made it; he knew the light was hers. He at least hoped it was hers.

"Is it?"

"Yes Landon. That is the light of the Angel," she answered him.

He noticed Dallas trying to fight his way to the house, Avery's dad holding him back. He would assist him he couldn't let Dallas go into that house. And Richard was not strong enough to hold Dallas off for long. He grabbed Dallas with one hand and pulled him back.

"Do you want to die? You will if you enter that house. I know how you feel but you have to stay here. They will do their jobs. They will protect her, cousin. Please don't be a fool." No matter how jealous he felt he would not let anything happen to his cousin. Although the thought of seeing them embrace again like earlier today pained him, he held him down. Dallas agreed and calmed down. He looked around for Richard and didn't see him.

The light stayed on for awhile, too long. He felt the urge to go up there himself, but instead tried to think of her. He focused his thoughts on her smile, her eyes, her hair, her unknowing beauty and her soul. He took a deep breath.

Several minutes later the light went out and they were surrounded by darkness. He heard the sound of talking in the front of the house. He didn't think, he just ran towards the noise. There she lay on the ground, blood rushing from her head and her shirt slashed open. Her dad was placing his shirt on her head and he saw her go limp.

"No Avery, please don't die," he called to her. When he reached her he noticed she had only blacked out but still she had lost a lot of blood. Her father lifted her, but he struggled. Landon reached for her and Richard agreed passing her limp body into his arms. Landon carried her to Dallas' truck. He laid her in the back seat and softy kissed her lips. Would this be the last time he would get to do that? He knew the council had said his memories would be taken. Lillith had filled him in on all the details. While he was fighting off Dedrick they all planned on saving him.

No, this will not be the last time he would kiss her. He had to believe he would remember again. He would not anything take her away from him.

"I love you, we will be together again. I can only hope for that and I will hold on to that." She mumbled something. Was she waking up? He leaned closer to hear her better.

"I love you too."

Hope! He had hope. She did love him too.

When he took his hand away I looked into his eyes for any sign that he saw it, but nothing changed. It was like looking at a stranger.

"Nice to meet you too." And I walked away. It was weak, I knew this, but it was all I could say. I couldn't say, *"Oh no, I am more than your cousin's girlfriend. I am your twin soul."* Not now. He didn't remember me and he had known that he would forget. I had told him I loved him too. I didn't remember that, but I said it and I felt it. But now it was worth nothing. Now I was in his shoes for once. Loving someone who doesn't even know who you are.

Several months passed by and the winter came full force. Snow dusted the ground everywhere you looked. It was beautiful and reminded me of how pure the white light had been that night. We didn't really speak of those times. We just moved on like nothing happened. Ianni did move in with me, although she didn't actually have things to move in with. She took the spare bedroom that I had just used as storage. She and Kerri had gone shopping and she got herself a big beautiful bed with lots of pillows.

She says one can never have enough. Her closet is also filled with tons of beautiful clothes, all designer. Who knew she would have such expensive taste? She gave herself a last name, Maxwell. We were sitting together drinking coffee and trying for hours to come up with a name, when she picked up the jar of Maxwell's House coffee. That is what she stuck with, she says it flows.

We talk like girlfriends her, Kerri and I. We shop together and drink coffee and stay up and watch romance movies. Kerri hired her at Sunrise Estates. She helps me with the residence for now. It's just until she can get used to being around the souls so close to moving on. She says it's a bit scary for her but we all know she will come around. Of course we haven't figured out how to get her a driver's license or a birth certificate yet. Justin says he can help us with that. For now Ianni is happy, and I am happy with her being here. We don't see Lillith anymore and for that I am a bit sad. But I don't miss all of the weird and I relish in the normal for now.

Dallas is getting ready to open his restaurant. Things are very busy for him but we still try to get in our dates as much as possible. Like tonight, I am going to his house for dinner and to sleep over. I figure Ianni needs to be alone sometimes. She doesn't need to be treated like a baby.

My father and I are talking regularly. He is still in Laguna, just until the house sells, then he will move up here. I can't wait. We are working on our relationship and so far it's going great. Aunt Pauline calls every Monday to chat. She is in a new relationship and I am beyond happy for her. She never brings up that night. So neither do I.

Landon is still living downstairs. He still doesn't remember me, or any of the paranormal things, that happened in his life. Our last vision still haunts my thoughts. We still do not know exactly what he went through that night while he was alone with Dedrick. It is Dallas and I who fight to get him to remember everything. We only try to think of ways to break through and nothing works or sounds like it will work. Ianni tells me nothing will work but Dallas and I won't take no for an answer.

I try to fight my feelings for him on a daily basis because I do love him and Dallas. I am in love with them both. I can't help it I am weak when it comes to them. Even if Landon remembered I am not sure I could choose between them. Landon pretty much stays to himself, hanging with Dallas, when I am not around. For all I know he thinks I am Dallas' strange girlfriend. I see him sometimes walking in the snow looking around at the kids playing and couples walking. Just like tonight, I am watching him from my window. He is walking around downstairs and he stops and looks up directly to me. He waves and my heart stops. I wave back. I want to run down there and play in the snow with him. But I don't, I just smile and wave back at my boyfriend's cousin, because that is all he is to me.

Where am I to go from here? Right now I can't answer that. So I am just living my life, it is all I can do and I know that he would want me to do that. I will not give up on him, because he didn't give up on me. As I wave to him he says something and I can't hear it. So I open the doors and step into the snowy night, my feet freeze as they touch the ground.

"What? I couldn't hear you," I call down to him.

"Do you like the snow?" He screams back.

"Yes I love the snow. It's my last name," I holler back to him with a smile.

"Then come down here and build a snow man with me."

"Really?" I think about it. It's a crazy idea, Dallas is coming to pick me up soon, but I have a few minutes to spare. "Okay I will be right down."

I am giddy now as I throw on my boots, jacket and my ultra-thick gloves. I look into the mirror and I am pleased with how I look. I even feel beautiful for once. When I make it down the stairs and outside he is already started building the body. So I jump in by collection things for his face. We laugh like kids and we build the perfect snowman.

"You are my sunshine, my only sunshine..." He sings.

"What are you singing?" I interrupt him. I know exactly what it is, it is our song. Well, was our song.

"I don't know why but I can't stop singing that song, sorry."

"No, don't be sorry. Keep singing," I say. He does and I hum along.

About the Author

Christy Sloat is a Southern California native who now lives in New Jersey with her husband and two daughters. She believes that reading is a passion and it should be embraced. If she is not reading or writing she is cooking or spending quality time with her children. She believes in past lives and love that can last lifetimes. She is huge Twilight and Harry Potter fan who watches the movies constantly. Some of her favorite vacation spots are Maine, Massachusetts and California.

Find her on her Blog http://christysloat.blogspot.com/,
Facebook: Christy Sloat Author
www.facebook.com/pastlivestrilogy.
Twitter: ChristySloat

Continue on with the Past Lives Series with this exciting novella!

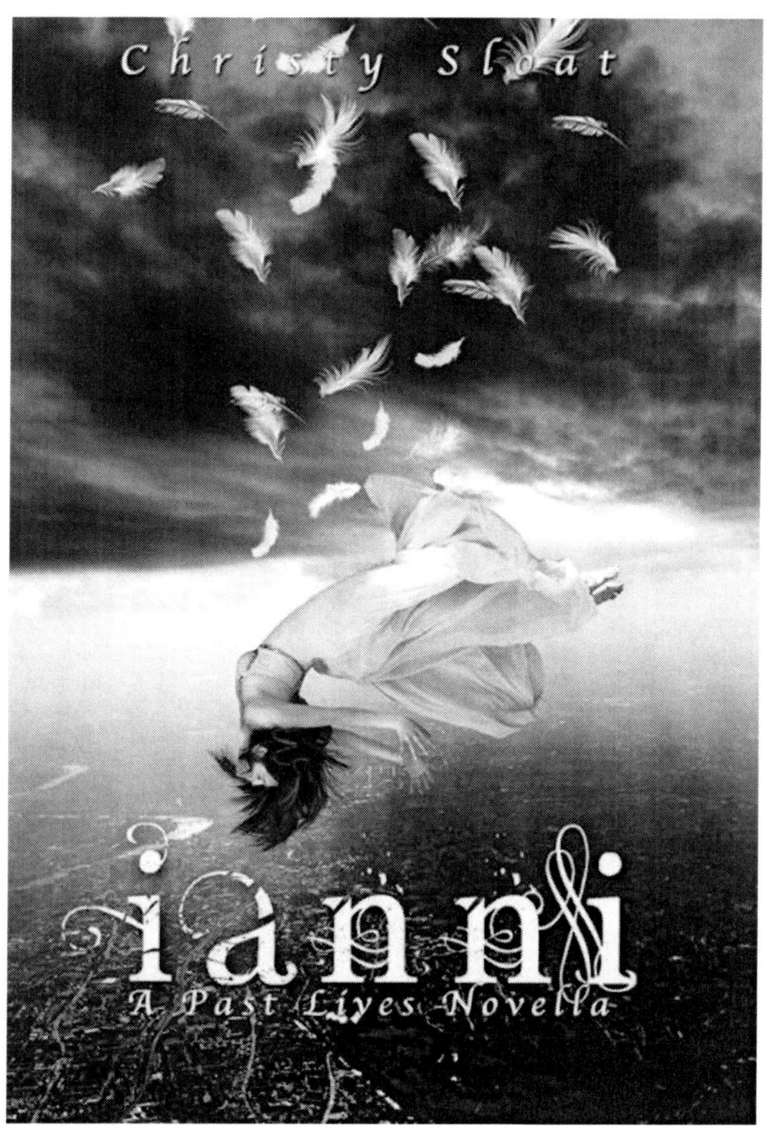

CPSIA information can be obtained at www.ICGtesting.com
Printed in the USA
LVOW102224160912
299044LV00007B/141/P